CRITICAL ACCLAIM FOR ED GORMAN

"The hard-boiled thriller boasts few better practitioners than Ed Gorman."
—*San Diego Union*

"Gorman is one of the masters of the detective genre."—***The Drood Review***

"Ed Gorman is the modern master of the lean and mean thriller."—***Rocky Mountain News***

"Ed Gorman's work is fresh, polished, excitingly paced, thoroughly entertaining—and has something to say."—***Dean Koontz***

"Gorman has a way of getting into his characters and they have a way of getting into you."
—**Robert Bloch**

"One of the world's great storytellers."—*Million*

MYSTERY AND SUSPENSE
published by ibooks, inc.:

THE LAWRENCE BLOCK COLLECTION
Deadly Honeymoon • After the First Death
You Could Call It Murder • Coward's Kiss

Samantha
A Maseo Masuto Mystery
by Howard Fast

Cry Me a River
by Patricia Hagan

KAYCEE MILLER MYSTERIES
by Jodie Larsen
At First Sight • The Darkest Night

RUNNER IN THE DARK

ED GORMAN

ibooks
new york
www.ibooks.net

DISTRIBUTED BY SIMON & SCHUSTER, INC.

A Publication of ibooks, inc.

Copyright © 1996 by Ed Gorman

This novel is a work of fiction. Names, characters, places, and incidents either are the product of the author's imagination or are used fictitiously. Any resemblance to actual persons living or dead, events, or locales is entirely coincidental.

All rights reserved, including the right to reproduce this book or portions thereof in any form whatsoever.
Distributed by Simon & Schuster, Inc.
1230 Avenue of the Americas, New York, NY 10020

ibooks, inc.
24 West 25th Street
New York, NY 10010

The ibooks World Wide Web Site Address is:
www.ibooks.net

ISBN 0-7434-9810-0
First ibooks, inc. printing December 2004
10 9 8 7 6 5 4 3 2 1

Printed in the U.S.A.

To Mike Bailey —
editor, writer
and very good man

I used a fine book, *Pure Cop*, by Connie Fletcher, as background for this novel.

THE BEGINNING

Channel 6 was the first to reach the air with a news bulletin. The newsman, the somewhat rumpled Charles Mannering, interrupted a network soap opera to read the following words: 'There has been a reported shooting at the courthouse within the last ten minutes. According to a Channel 6 reporter on the scene, several people have been shot, perhaps including a judge. Stay tuned to Channel 6 for more updates on this breaking story . . .'

In the end, the death toll would reach nine, there in the courtroom on the fourth floor, there on that gray, rainy morning.

The killers, who had murdered the guard standing next to the metal detector, entered the courtroom and opened fire. There was no warning whatsoever.

Now, the killers and the man they'd freed from police custody were arcing across the wide river in a helicopter that had swooped down to pick them up.

In pursuit were two helicopters belonging to the police department, the first of which contained two police sharpshooters, one named Mullins, one named Reed.

All three helicopters were having some trouble. On a rainy November morning like this, the pilots encountered strong headwinds, meaning that none of them could achieve a speed exceeding 100 knots, and even at this speed the machines got thrown around pretty hard.

Under ordinary circumstances, there was a strict prohibition against firing from police helicopters. That was a good way to get the people below killed. But they were over the river now, and these were hardly ordinary circumstances . . .

Mullins leaned out of the helicopter and opened fire . . .

★ ★ ★

'Is it true the Judge is dead?' the reporter asked Jessica Dennis, the beautiful young Assistant District Attorney who had just now come from the carnage inside the courtroom. The police had the entire floor taped off. This enterprising reporter had snuck up the side stairs.

At first, Jessica scarcely heard him. She was still numb from everything that had happened. One moment she had been questioning a witness in the most important criminal trial of her life, and the next moment she was throwing herself to the floor, to duck the bullets that had suddenly started spraying from the automatic weapons held by two ski-masked men standing just behind where Jessica's associates and assistants sat.

Ear-shattering explosions from the guns. Screams. People thrown into walls from the impact of the bullets. Jessica, from her position on the floor, seeing blood dripping off the edge of the Judge's bench. Even from here, she could see that two of her associates were dead. And Phil Stafford, the District Attorney, was slumped forward on the table, unmoving. She prayed he was not dead . . .

When she raised her elegant blonde head to look at the reporter, Jessica noticed her hands and the jacket of her tailored gray silk suit. Both were spattered with blood.

'I'm not sure,' she said. She spoke in a soft, trance-like voice. Shock. 'All I know is that they took him away in an ambulance.'

For the first time, Jessica recognized the reporter: Michael Shaw from Channel 8. She'd always thought of him as so crudely ugly that he was handsome. His book about Viet Nam had won him a Pulitzer; and he'd won a second Pulitzer a few years ago for his work on a hospital scandal. He was big to the point of being imposing, yet there was a melancholy about the man that kept him from being threatening.

Shaw said, 'You weren't shot, were you?' He nodded at her hands and jacket.

'I – I just got some of Phil's blood on me,' she said in that same trance-like voice.

She would never forget what she'd seen over the past twenty minutes. She'd been sitting next to Phil when the first bullets reached him, and bloody pieces of his head were ripped away.

She could still hear herself screaming.

'Wait a minute,' Shaw said.

'What?' Jessica said, having no idea what he was talking about.

'Let me look at your back.' Shaw walked up close to her, turned her gently around.

'I hate to tell you this, Jessica, but you've been shot.' He touched a spot just above her hip. 'It looks like a flesh wound. The bullet probably just went in and out without doing much damage. But I'm going to help you down to the ambulance right now.'

So many crazed and fearful images: the rear doors of the courtroom being flung open. Two gunmen wearing black ski-masks and carrying AK-47s. Killing the bailiff and a deputy instantly. Grabbing the jury foreman as hostage. Taking double-murder defendant Roy Gerard from the custody of the other deputies. And then opening fire on the courtroom. For no good reason at all . . .

They'd managed to circumvent security by landing on the roof in a helicopter. The courtroom was on the fourth floor. By killing one guard, the assassins were able to get into the courtroom . . .

'Lean on me for support,' Michael Shaw was saying.

'I'm fine,' Jessica said. 'I know I am.'

But after taking two more steps, she realized that she was starting to feel weak, faint...

Then she did more than simply lean on Shaw.

She collapsed into his arms.

The shots from the police helicopter had missed their target entirely, giving the four men escaping – brothers Roy and David Gerard, another gunman and the pilot – the opportunity to put even more distance between themselves and the pursuing police.

Below them, as they streaked down the sky, the river looked wide and dark and choppy. Dangerous. If they were shot down—

'Give Reed a try,' came the radio command in the helicopter with the two SWAT team-members.

The pilot said to the two sharpshooters behind him: 'You hear that?'

Both of them nodded.

Mullins had tried four times. With no luck.

Now the Commander wanted to give Reed a try.

It so happened Reed was a woman.

Reed took her position, leaning half-in and half-out of the helicopter. She was actually afraid of heights. She kept telling herself not to look down at those turbulent gray waters beneath her...

She took very careful aim and said a prayer, the way basketball players do right before they shoot a very important free-throw.

She squeezed off six shots.

Not a single round did the slightest damage to the fleeing helicopter.

'Where am I?'

'An ambulance.'

RUNNER IN THE DARK

'You're—'

'Michael Shaw.'

He smiled.

'I guess you don't remember. You were coming out of the courtroom. I'd snuck up to interview you and—'

'Oh God,' she said.

Because it was all coming back to her.

Everything that had happened in the courtroom.

And Michael Shaw telling her that she'd been wounded.

'Phil is—'

'Don't worry about that now.'

But she could tell by the tone of his voice that Phil was dead.

Only then did she realize that Michael Shaw was holding her hand as she lay on the stretcher in the back of the ambulance, gray city scenes running like a movie in the one window not covered with a curtain. She knew this, of course.

His hand felt strong, good.

He leaned forward, putting his face close to hers: 'You need to close your eyes and rest. Don't fight it anymore.'

Then she realized something else.

Michael Shaw's breath.

Whiskey.

While she'd lost track of time, she knew that it could be no later than mid-morning.

And he was drinking already.

Bleak memories of her father came back to her, unbidden. Memories of a million domestic arguments – her father cursing, smashing things; her mother sobbing; Jessica and her sister hiding, terrified in the closet – shrilled in her mind now . . . shrill as the ambulance siren above her.

She slowly eased her hand away from Michael Shaw's.

Took three different tries but Reed finally managed it.

The first two passes, she did what the other sharpshooter had tried – hitting the escaping killers themselves. But that was difficult if not impossible when the machines were moving this fast and bucking up and down in headwinds this strong.

So she decided to go for the tail-rotor and that was when she pulled it off.

She asked the pilot to get as close to the other machine as possible and then to bank to the right.

The pilot nodded and gave the machine as much power as he could.

Reed got herself ready.

One more prayer wouldn't hurt.

The pilot started to bank to the right.

She hit the tail-rotor with her second squeeze of the trigger.

The other machine flew on for a time then started abruptly pitching left and right. And then simply fell from the sky.

No other way to describe it.

Simply dropped straight down into the choppy gray waters below.

You could hear their screams.

See the pilot's frantic efforts to keep the machine under control.

Watch the cockpit vanish into the waters.

And the feathery fluttering of the tail-rotor vanish shortly thereafter.

A little prayer sure didn't hurt every once in a while, Reed thought.

Then she saw the large, dark boat racing towards the sinking helicopter. The killers had apparently covered every contingency, right down to being shot down and falling into the river . . .

Then Reed saw the two police boats, full throttle, approaching the dark craft that the killers were scrambling aboard—

He came to her hospital room that night, Shaw. Hadn't simply been a flesh wound after all. A bullet had torn into one of her ribs.

Brought an explosion of long-stemmed red roses, which he put in a vase on the table next to her bed.

Then sat in a chair and proceeded to fascinate her.

Even though she didn't want to be fascinated.

And proceeded to even make her laugh a few times.

Even though she didn't want to laugh.

And proceeded to make her like him very much indeed.

Even though she didn't want to like him at all.

He let her cry, let her drift in and out of sleep, let her just lie there and stare, let her use him to go downstairs and buy her some magazines, let her cry some more about Phil Stafford and how much she'd loved him, and how he'd been her *real* spiritual father on this earth.

And then he'd said, 'You need some sleep. I'll be back in the morning.'

And then she looked up at his ugly beautiful face and thought of how vital and bright and sorrowful he looked all at the same time.

And then he leaned down to give her a simple tender kiss.

And she smelled it again.

The way she used to smell it on her father.

The way she'd smelled it on Shaw this morning.

Whiskey.

FIVE YEARS LATER

Part One

Chapter One

1

Cancer.

When the old woman stood up from the Communion rail and turned around, tears shone in her sad ancient eyes, and on her pale drawn cheeks.

Cancer, Jessica thought.

She has cancer, or someone close to her does.

On a rainy Tuesday, just after the early-morning Mass, St Matthew's Church was empty except for the old woman now walking away from the Communion rail, and Jessica and her Aunt Ellen sitting in a pew in the center of the church.

Jessica thought of all the times her own mother had come to this church, to this same Communion rail, to pray for a relative or friend with cancer.

Old Monsignor Sullivan had once told Jessica that most people who lit the flickering red and green and yellow and blue votive candles were praying for God to cure someone of cancer.

'Poor old thing,' Aunt Ellen said, as the elderly woman moved down the center aisle of the church, past the Stations of the Cross on the wall, toward the ba.k, where the choir loft and baptism fountain lay.

The woman was dressed in a faded winter coat and a faded and frayed blue headscarf. Her croupy cough echoed in the empty church.

'I'd like to go light a candle, dear,' Aunt Ellen said.

Jessica nodded. 'Need any help?'

'I'll be fine, dear.'

Seven months ago, seventy-three-year-old Ellen Brody had fallen down and broken her hip. Only when Jessica was able to pick her up and drive her around was Ellen able to leave the house.

These days, her hip was better, and Ellen took every opportunity to demonstrate it.

As her aunt walked up to the statue of the Virgin, in front of which were displayed the votive candles, Jessica was struck as always by how much Ellen and Amy, Jessica's mother, resembled each other: small, pretty, delicate Irishwomen with sardonic brown eyes and smiles easy to ignite.

Aunt Ellen wore her pride and joy, a navy-blue cashmere coat bought at the most expensive store in the city. A lesson that both the Brody girls had been taught by their immigrant mother – always buy the best, it'll save you money in the long run. Jessica had learned the same lesson.

Aunt Ellen lit a green candle and then knelt at the Communion rail and bowed her head before the splendid altar in front of her.

Jessica knew what Aunt Ellen would be praying for, of course. That her sister Amy was with the Lord, and had been since that terrible night eight years ago when Amy and Michael Dennis had been killed at a railroad crossing. The Coroner's report had indicated that Michael Dennis, the driver, had been legally drunk.

All the old resentments and furies awakened in Jessica as she sat in the pew, her fingers playing idly with the black beads of her rosary.

How was it possible to both love and hate a man as much as she'd loved and hated her father, who had been a lost alcoholic all her life, and who finally took the life of her own beloved mother?

Aunt Ellen, wiser in the ways of the old country, and therefore more forgiving, had never once raised her voice against Michael Dennis. 'He wasn't a bad man, dear. He meant well and, God love him, he did the best he could.' How many times had Aunt Ellen tried to soothe her with such words when the resentments and furies seized Jessica once again?

Jessica leaned back in the pew and looked around the church.

Easy to remember Christmas and Easter Mass in this venerable old building, how handsome her parents had always managed to look on such special occasions, even though her father was likely half-drunk... the church smelling of flowers and incense... the choir voices resonant and powerful to hear.

How faithful and dutiful her mother had always been, even on those two occasions when she'd had to endure the humiliation of going down to the police station and bailing her husband out of the drunk tank, even when her friends had advised her to get a divorce and find somebody new.

But her mother had loved him too much for that. She was an old-fashioned woman, one raised in the ways of County Cork, and her love was eternal.

All Jessica could wonder was... did she feel the same kind of eternal love for Michael Shaw? Could she ever trust him again after what he'd done six months ago?

'I think I'm ready now, dear.'

Aunt Ellen was there, standing in the aisle outside the pew. She tired easily nowadays. She was tired now.

2

In Jessica's new black Volvo, handsome but sensible, a combination Jessica loved, Aunt Ellen said, 'How's Michael these days?'

'He's fine,' she replied, then realized she'd said it too quickly. She was still cold from outside, and pulled her camelhair coat collar closer to her neck. She was careful about her looks but not obsessive about them. Too many women spent too much time trying to look perfect. There were far more important things in life than trying to impress people with your looks. She would rather impress them with her brains and her dedication to her job.

'Then you're seeing him again?'

'Sometimes I am.' Jessica's azure eyes winced with the pain of her situation with Michael. And Aunt Ellen saw it.

'But the marriage plans are on hold?'

Jessica couldn't help but smile. 'You'd make a great cross-examiner, Aunt Ellen.'

The woman laughed her small, almost child-like laugh. She'd always had an impish sense of humor. 'In other words, your old aunt is pushing her nose in where it doesn't belong.'

Jessica looked out at the city on this gray, rainy day, recalling another rainy day, five years ago, when the courtroom she was in had suddenly been invaded by two masked men with automatic weapons...

'I'm just giving you my opinion, dear. That's what God wants little old ladies like me to do.'

Jessica laughed. 'You've talked to Him about that?'

'Oh yes, many times. He told me that He created little old ladies so they'll irritate beautiful young ladies into using good common sense.'

'And good common sense means marrying Michael?'

'You love him, don't you?'

He's an alcoholic, Jessica was about to say, *just like my father was an alcoholic*.

But then the cellular phone rang and instead, Jessica said, 'Excuse me . . . Hello?'

'Morning, Jessica.'

'Morning, Sam.' Samantha Davies was her lovely black assistant. When Jessica had won election to District Attorney two years ago, she'd taken Sam along with her.

'The TV studio called. They wanted to know if you could get there by six o'clock tonight.'

'I guess I don't see why not.' She sighed. 'I just wish I hadn't agreed to do it, at least not tonight. It's kind of ghoulish.'

Six hours before Roy Gerard was to be executed at the state prison tonight, there would be a TV debate between herself and a priest named Father Josek about capital punishment. The debate was to be conducted by William Cornell, a corpulent, pompous TV commentator whose vicious style had won him favor with a wide viewing public. Blood sport, as one TV critic had dubbed Cornell's show NEWS BEAT. And as if that wasn't pressure enough, CNN would be picking up the debate from the local station and broadcasting it nationally.

'May I tell them you'll be there early?'

'Sure. That's fine.'

'Michael called, too. Wanted to know about lunch.'

'Tell him I'll call him back.'

'Oops, there's the other line. See you in a while, Jessica.'

'She sure seems like a nice woman,' Aunt Ellen said, after Jessica hung up.

'She sure is. I'm very lucky.'

They rode in silence for a time, passing through the northern edge of the downtown area with all its Federal architecture from the previous century. In the seventies, the then-Mayor and his staff had been obsessed with tearing down the elegant old and replacing it with the hasty new. Fortunately, the next administration, and the one following that, had fought to keep as much of the 'old' city as possible.

Just now, on her right, Jessica saw a small park with a mounted Union soldier statue on it – a Civil War memorial that only looked nobler in the mist and rain.

'Can your old aunt put her nose into one more thing – now that I've convinced you to marry Michael?'

Jessica grinned, her dark eyes sparkling, her somewhat large mouth twisting wryly. 'So we've settled the Michael subject, eh?'

'We certainly have, dear,' Aunt Ellen said.

'So now what do you want to talk about?'

'Now I want to talk about why you aren't under an armed guard.'

Jessica anxiously touched the dark brown scarf that complemented the lustrous color of her hair. The scarf went well with the tan-colored business suit. She knew what Aunt Ellen was referring to. She'd tried to banish the subject from her mind.

'On the TV they said that they'd found his fingerprints in Los Angeles last week. During a murder investigation.'

'Yes, I guess they did.'

'Then two days ago, there was another killing in Chicago. His fingerprints again.'

Jessica smiled anxiously. 'If you mean to make me nervous, Aunt Ellen, you're doing a good job.'

'I just want to know why there aren't two armed police officers in the back seat. You're the District Attorney, dear. They owe you that protection.'

Los Angeles, Chicago.

On that day five years ago, when the police helicopters had

given chase to the Gerard brothers, the crash had allowed David Gerard to escape, while his brother went back to prison, and the pilot and the other gunman eventually died of injuries suffered in the accident.

Shortly after Jessica won the District Attorney's seat, she'd received a letter postmarked Paris, France.

The letter said:

> *You're dead, bitch.*
> *David Gerard.*

The FBI had checked the handwriting and found that it did indeed belong to David Gerard. His fingerprints were also found on the letter.

In Los Angeles a few days ago, one of the criminals who'd turned state's evidence against the Gerard brothers had been found with his throat cut. Then another man who'd testified had been found burned alive in his bed. He'd been soaked with gasoline then set afire.

'You're not afraid, dear?'

'A little, I suppose. But it should all be over tonight. With the execution, I mean.'

Aunt Ellen sighed. 'I hope so.'

Jessica pulled up in the parking lot of Aunt Ellen's apartment house. It was a three-story clapboard affair with a front porch and gables that recalled a long-vanished era.

'It was nice going to Mass with you,' Aunt Ellen said.

'It's a special day,' Jessica said. 'You know, Mom's birthday.'

Aunt Ellen took Jessica's hand and squeezed it tenderly. 'Do you know that I still talk to her? Right out loud, too, as if she's standing right next to me. I was doing the dishes last night and darned if we didn't get into a conversation about Terry Bolger. He was a ninth-grade boy we both had crushes on at the time. I think we were six.'

Jessica could no longer stop herself. She leaned over and hugged Aunt Ellen. She was hugging a whole history here, a history of a gentler and better time, when her mother and father had been young and healthy with their lives all ahead of them – a history of which Jessica was a part, too, the next generation.

'Would you like me to walk you upstairs?'

'Are you kidding? I want to show you how well I'm getting around.'

'You sure?'

'I'm sure.'

Aunt Ellen touched Jessica's hand. 'I know he fell off the wagon six months ago, Jessica, but I think you need to give him another chance. I really do.'

'I want to, Aunt Ellen. It's just that I'm—'

'—afraid. And I don't blame you. But at least think about it, will you?'

Michael had won Aunt Ellen over the first time they'd met. He'd played up his one-eighth Irishness to the maximum limit. As Jessica had said later, he'd done everything except dance a jig.

'And think about getting police protection, too. That David Gerard is a real animal.'

'Yes, he is,' Jessica said, trying not to think of all the people he'd butchered and slaughtered over the past eight years. 'Yes, he is.'

3

Max's restaurant, two blocks east of the courthouse, was a great place to argue while you had a little breakfast or lunch.

And because the clientèle mostly ran to journalists and lawyers, arguing was usually the chief endeavor. Max's had fifteen small tables that seated four each and a counter that seated eight. There was a joke that he only painted the place every time there was a total eclipse of the sun. This decade, the walls were a mustard yellow, and the floor was faded red linoleum. Max had three waiters, all of whom mysteriously looked like each other though none were related, and two waitresses who had heard even the most inventive come-on at least four thousand times. He had two cooks, one black, one white, who could turn omelets and hamburgers into food that would rival the best cuisine anywhere. As for Max himself, he constantly committed the most unpardonable of sins and got away with it: he always gave you advice whether you wanted it or not, and somehow he did so without making you mad.

Mornings like this, the place smelled wonderfully of fresh-brewed coffee and fresh-baked cinnamon rolls. Max insisted on baking his own.

'Now tonight, Jessica,' Max was saying, 'don't back off just because this guy's a priest. I mean, I'm a good Catholic myself – a name like Cardini, how could I miss, kiddo? – but just because he's got that Roman collar on, don't mean he's infallible. The Pope says *he's* infallible, all right, I'll take his word for it. But not just some priest. You got me?'

'Got you, Max.'

Jessica was trying to listen politely and finish her scrambled eggs at the same time. She'd decided on a fast stop at Max's because she knew that today would be a long one, probably not ending until late tonight.

But she had to hurry.

'You got that, kiddo?' Max said again, wiping wide, peasant hands on his starkly white apron. That was another thing that recommen_ _d Max's. Every inch of the place was spotless.

'I got that, Max.'

Jessica's attention strayed to one of the waiters who'd picked up the wall-phone behind the cash-register.

The waiter waggled the phone in Max's direction.

'For me?' Max said.

The waiter shook his head. Angled the phone a little more towards Jessica. 'Miss Dennis.'

Trouble.

That was Jessica's first reaction.

Nobody ever called her at Max's unless there was trouble. Big trouble.

She decided to pay her bill, so she swooped up purse, camelhair coat, and green ticket, and walked to the cash-register.

She gave the waiter a crisp ten, told him to leave the remainder as a tip, and then she walked around the cash-register and picked up the receiver he'd set down for her.

'Hello?'

'I'm sorry to bother you, Jessica. I'm sure you want to relax a little before you get here this morning.'

'It's all right, Sam. What's up?'

'A homicide detective named Ribicoff just called and said that you, Ward and Culligan are all to have police protection today. You'll each be assigned an officer.'

Jessica laughed. 'I wonder if my Aunt Ellen called him.'

'Pardon?'

'Private joke. Sorry.'

'Anyway, look out the window.'

'Out of Max's window, you mean?'

'Uh-huh.'

There was steamy moisture on the window but Jessica got a good sense of the street anyway.

'All right. I'm looking.'

'See a tall black man in a dark topcoat? He's got slightly graying hair.'

She didn't see him at first. Then she spotted him in the far-left corner of the window.

'Oh, right. There he is.'

'His name is Flynn. He's a Police Inspector, works for Detective Ribicoff. He's your protection. When you leave the restaurant, you're supposed to go up to him and ask for some ID. Then he'll be with you for the rest of the day.'

'But I've got to park my car and everything yet.'

'You'll have a passenger, now.' Sam paused. 'Detective Ribicoff told me that they think David Gerard will probably make some attempt on your life today.'

All around her was the noise of a day just beginning. The waitresses and waiters were moving faster than ever; the 'ready' bell in the kitchen *binged* more frequently; and Max himself was so busy now, he didn't have time to give anybody any advice.

'You there?' Sam said.

'Still here,' Jessica said. 'Just trying to sort it all out.'

'It's going to be a long day.'

'It sure is.'

'And remember it starts in fifteen minutes with Al DeWitt.'

'Oh God,' Jessica groaned. 'I forgot all about that little jerk.'

Al DeWitt was the star prosecution witness in a case of which one of Jessica's Assistant District Attorneys was in charge. The trouble was, the Assistant DA didn't believe Al DeWitt's story, and neither did Jessica.

Some people told lies to get lighter sentences for themselves. Other witnesses told lies to enhance their own importance. Al DeWitt belonged to the latter category.

'I guess I'd better go see Inspector Fl_nn,' Jessica said. 'See you in a little while.'

Chapter Two

1

Michael Shaw got out of his car, shrugged deep into his Burberry raincoat, and started to look around the parking lot.

The WhileAway Motel was one of those places that all the country and western songwriters loved to put their pens to – a whitewashed rundown one-story motel with twenty-four units you just drove right up to. Most of the numbers on the doors were askew and in need of screws and nails to set them right. Half the doorknobs hung loose. Many of the windows were cracked and covered with adhesive tape.

The WhileAway was a place well familiar with adultery, fist-fights, buggery between strangers, drug deals, sad little kids whose mammas and daddies had gone off to party at the nearest honky-tonk, fugitives, illegal aliens and wandering dangerous madmen of various and assorted types.

Every night in the WhileAway, hearts and heads alike were broken.

Shaw stuffed his hands deep into the pockets of his Burberry.

In the left pocket was a voice-activated tape recorder half the size of a paperback book.

In the right pocket was a .38 Policeman's Special. He'd carried it constantly back in his reporting days.

Shaw approached Room 24. A DO NOT DISTURB tag hung from the loose doorknob.

A cleaning woman, plump, pale, fatigued, was leaving the room on the far side of it, setting a plastic bottle of Mr Clean and a rag on the top of her cart.

There were no other rooms on this side of the motel. Shaw waited for her to go around the corner.

Her bottom was too big for the yellow polyester slacks she wore. He sensed her whole life in the cheap, ill-fitting slacks, and felt sorry for her. She would live and die with little more to show for it than a succession of minimum-wage jobs. She'd know little joy.

When she disappeared around the corner, Shaw hurried over to Room 24.

The curtains were drawn.

He put an ear to the door.

No sounds from inside, just the swishing of heavy semi tires on the rainy highway nearby.

He put his left hand on the doorknob.

The knob felt as if it would come loose in his hand.

He turned it to the right.

The door was unlocked.

He knew then:

Something was wrong here.

2

Five hours ago, a little after 4:00 A.M., the phone next to Shaw's bed had rung.

Shaw's first sleepy reaction was that he was caught up in some kind of time warp. In his reporting days, the phone had frequently rung at 4:00 A.M. But not anymore.

Must be part of a dream.

But the ringing persisted.

He picked it up. 'Michael Shaw.'

Silence. But Shaw sensed somebody on the other end of the line.

'Hello?' Shaw said.

Silence. Then: 'I need to see you.'

Female. Young. Drunk.

Shaw rolled over and punched on the tape recorder connected to the phone. Another left-over from his reporting days.

He also turned on the table lamp.

His bedroom was done in charcoal gray and white, with white drapes and charcoal-colored designer shutters. The carpeting was black and matched the varnished black five-drawer bureau. For him the room combined style with comfort. He wasn't afraid to drag a TV set in here and watch a ballgame while decked out in his BVDs.

He threw his legs over the side of the bed. He always slept in pajama bottoms. No tops. He had some major chest hair but not enough to qualify him as simian.

'All right?' he said, coming awake. 'What can I do for you?'

'I know something you should know.'

'You can't tell me over the phone?'

Sputtering anger. 'This is serious shit.'

'I didn't say it wasn't.'

Drunk.

'Ma'am, maybe we could talk in the morning.'

'It *is* the morning.'

He sighed. 'Would you like to meet now?'

'Not now.' A sense of fear in her voice. 'At nine-fifteen.'

'This morning?' he said.

'Right.'

'Where?'

'You know the WhileAway Motel?'
'Out by the Reeves Industrial Park?'
'Yes. Room 24.'
'I'll be there.'
'You better not let me down.'
'I won't let you down.'
'You promise?' She sounded like a child.
'I promise,' he said.
'You be here,' she said, angry again. Then she slammed down the phone.

Shaw turned off the light, the tape recorder, and then put himself back into bed and beneath the sleep-warm covers. He'd try and get another hour's sleep before the alarm went off.

But it didn't work.

He kept thinking about the woman who'd called, her voice a perfect amalgam of misery and terror.

Something you should know.

He took her seriously. No doubt about it.

Then he lay there in the darkness and allowed himself a brief smile.

It was fun to be a real reporter again, even if it did mean losing a good night's sleep.

3

The room was a small box.

The carpet smelled of mildew. The air was abrasive with lingering cigarette smoke. Shaw had once been a smoker. Now the least exposure to cigarette smoke played hell with his sinuses.

The motel owners had made the mistake of putting a brown

bedspread on the sagging double bed. The spread showed spills, cigarette burns, and a few stains that Shaw did not care to make any guesses about. Above the headboard was a bad painting of a Norman Rockwellian skating pond. All the heads were disproportionate to the bodies.

He got down on his knees and looked under the bed.

Dust, a few crumpled cigarette packs, a Trojan wrapper. No doubt about it. This place was a palace.

There was a writing desk of dark pressed wood. Both the desk and the TV set that sat next to it were chained to the floor.

He opened the accordion doors to the closet. Dead air, crypt-stale, rushed at him.

Three faded blouses hung on steel hangers. A skirt with its hem hanging down was hooked over a nail. The black flat-heeled shoes on the floor hadn't been polished recently. He slapped empty hangers together. They made tinny, bell-like music.

He came back to the foot of the bed and looked down the short walk to the bathroom, which was on his right with the door closed.

In there.

If she was here, she was in the bathroom.

He had to remind himself that in the old days there had been virtually nothing that had scared him, probably the result of having been a Special Services combat soldier in Viet Nam, a tour that segued nicely into the rough times he saw as an investigative reporter.

But he was older now.

Sober.

In love, and wanting a family very badly.

He was no longer the angry alcoholic who'd face any demons but his own.

He was a forty-seven-year-old anchorman who'd gotten

accustomed to at least a slice of the good life.

Thinking about the hallowed days of being a tough journalist was far different from confronting a dead body.

He took a deep breath and stalked to the bathroom door.

He pushed it open.

He couldn't really see much. Too dark.

He flipped on the light.

A small overhead exhaust fan roared into life.

Blood was splashed all over the white bathtub and the off-white tiles.

But there was no body.

He opened the narrow towel closet to his left and looked inside. It contained five shelves.

No way you could hide a body in there.

Then where the hell was she?

Shaw went back to the front room and started all over again, wondering if he'd possibly missed some place where a body *could* be hidden.

He even checked under the bed again, though he knew of course there was no body there.

Just to be safe. Certain.

A little anal-retentive, Shaw supposed, but he had it coming. After all, he hadn't gotten a whole hell of a lot of sleep last night.

He was just starting to double-check the closet again when he heard the woman's scream.

It was a masterpiece of a scream, one any self-respecting director of horror movies would pay to have on his soundtrack.

Out came the .38 from the right pocket of Shaw's Burberry.

He walked quickly to the door, opened it, then looked carefully to the left and right.

And saw nothing.

All the same cars seemed to be in the same place.

RUNNER IN THE DARK

There was no sign of anybody moving across the parking lot. Just the steady drizzle.

And then the scream came again.

This time, Shaw was able to track it.

Around the corner. Where the cleaning woman had gone with her cart.

Shaw took off running.

When he reached the other side, he saw three rusting dumpsters out in the back, sitting on the edge of the asphalt. Beyond this was the faded grass of an unused lot.

The cleaning woman stood in front of the middle dumpster.

Her hands covered her face.

She was screaming now, or sobbing.

She was apparently trying to compose herself.

Shaw stuck the .38 back into his pocket and walked over to her. When he reached the halfway point, the sickening-sweet reek of garbage hit him.

The company that leased the dumpsters – B & N HAULING – should think of hosing off their dumpsters once in a while, whether the dumpsters needed it or not.

The cleaning woman looked up from behind her hands just about the time Shaw spoke to her.

'What happened?'

She nodded at the center dumpster.

'In there,' she said, her voice sounding like somebody who'd just received a sedative. 'All cut up.'

Shaw kept himself composed then walked over to the dumpster and lifted the lid up.

The smell of rotting garbage was now just about intolerable. Not even the rain cut the odor.

But the young woman's naked body instantly made him forget about the smell.

Whoever had killed her had taken great pleasure in doing so.

Her body had been defiled and defaced in every way imaginable. Even three of her fingers had been hacked off.

She was buoyed up by the heaps of garbage but lay atop a dark, inexpensive dress coat. Probably hers. The killer had wrapped her in it to sneak her body out to the dumpster.

He'd obviously killed her back there in the bathtub.

Then Shaw saw the piece of newspaper that lay, bloody and balled up, just above her pubic hair, as if the killer had flung it there as he was hurrying away.

Even without looking closer, he recognized the woman in the newspaper article: Jessica.

It was the picture that two city papers had run yesterday in their front-page pieces on the pending execution of Roy Gerard.

The woman who'd called him had wanted to tell him something about Jessica.

He was sure of it.

He gently led the cleaning woman away from the dumpster then went up to the front desk to call the police.

David Gerard was a busy boy these days.

Last week, he'd killed two people in California.

Now he was back on his home turf.

Where Jessica lived.

Chapter Three

1

Jessica had always preferred the small conference room to the large one.

The décor of the District Attorney's office reflected the tastes of the past three or four DAs. The man who'd held the post two terms ago had had a wife who was an interior decorator. Unlike most cases of nepotism, this one turned out very well. There was enough budget for the woman to redo four areas of the huge, noisy office, and the small conference room was one of them.

Now, as she paced back and forth in front of the full-height glass panels that overlooked the city, Jessica took time to appreciate the parchment-finished table, the leather upholstered chairs and the off-blue wool fabric on the walls.

There was only one thing that looked out of place in this room and that was the man sitting at the conference table.

His name was Al DeWitt. He looked as if he'd just escaped from a road company version of *Grease*. He had long black oily hair; a black leather jacket that creaked whenever he moved; innumerable rings and tattoos on his fingers and hands; and an annoying little silver earring hanging from his left lobe. The earring was apparently DeWitt's one sop to the present day. Otherwise, he was ready to time travel back to 1958. Al was fifty-seven years old. The long black hair came from a bottle and the tattoos on the tops of his hands had to fight liver spots for dominance.

Jessica had spent the past half-hour trying to prove that Al, her star witness in an arson case, was lying about what he'd claimed to see. This was her third interview with him in the past week. She hoped it would be her last.

'I thought you said you left the theater right at 9:00 P.M.,' she said, continuing to pace.

'Well, you know, more or less.'

'More or less?'

He shrugged and gave her a cute little grin. That was the preposterous thing. Geeky as he was, he was cute.

'So which is it, Mr DeWitt? Nine o'clock or "more or less" nine o'clock?'

'You could always call me "Al." '

'I prefer the formality, if you don't mind.'

He looked at her, smirking. 'I kind of get to you a little bit, don't I?'

He was coming on to her.

Nine days before the trial was to start and he was still playing all his ridiculous caveman games.

'You don't "get to me," Mr DeWitt. You piss me off is what you do. I'm trying to prove that a very nice sixty-four-year-old cleaning woman was burned to death when Mr Raymond set his own dry-cleaning establishment on fire. God help me, you're the only witness I've got who claims to have seen Mr Raymond going into his business right before the fire started.'

He watched her with eyes that were just as black and greasy as his hair.

Breaking and entering; auto theft; possessing crack cocaine

with intent to deliver; and three charges (all dropped by the woman, of course) of severe spousal abuse. These had been the life and times of Allan Douglas DeWitt. He'd done time twice and would likely do time again. He was the only witness she had and he knew it and was taking advantage of it by goading her sexually.

'You think you're too good for me, don't you?'

She had a choice to make. She could be nice and diplomatic, or she could tell him the truth.

'You make me sick, Mr DeWitt. Very sick. You beat up women, you sell drugs to children, and you can't even do your civic duty by cooperating with the District Attorney on a very important case. I'm supposed to find you appealing?'

The smirk again. 'A lot of chicks have, babe, and don't think they haven't. I got certain talents, if you know what I mean.'

She sighed.

When she'd first started out in the DA's office seven years ago, a sage old counselor, Lars Philips – who had just turned up a star witness on an aggravated robbery case – had told her: 'Don't get too excited, Jessica. A lot of times, your best witness will turn out to be your worst enemy, at least by the time the defense team gets done with him.'

She glared down the table at Mr DeWitt.

He was still grinning at her, filling his eyes with the body she was concealing inside of her conservative suit and white high-collar blouse.

She could almost hear Lars whisper in her ear: *Jessica, meet Mr DeWitt.*

Your best witness.

And worst enemy.

'A lot of things a guy like me could teach a woman like you,' Mr Al DeWitt said modestly. 'A *whole* lot of things.'

2

'He patted me on the ass again today.'

'Who did?'

'DeWitt, who else?'

Jessica looked up from the new report she'd just gotten from the Fire Marshal's office. 'That jerk.'

'Told me he didn't have anything against black people, either.'

Samantha Davies was a slender, attractive black woman of thirty-three. She was Jessica's secretary and helpmate. Jessica was helping her find scholarships for her son, Daniel, who was a senior in high school. He had a 3.8 grade average, was an outstanding track star, and seemed to be pretty much an exemplary kid. Perfect material for a scholarship, usually anyway. But with massive federal cuts in aid to education, Daniel had gone wanting.

'You know what the terrible thing is?' Samantha said, laughing.

'What?'

'DeWitt really is kind of cute.'

'I know. Isn't that awful?'

'I think it's his teeth,' Samantha said. 'He has baby teeth and that's always kind of cute.'

'You're right. It's when he smiles.'

'Maybe,' Samantha said, 'we secretly have the hots for him.'

'Don't even say such a thing.'

Samantha leaned her head into Jessica's office to whisper: 'Is that Detective Flynn just going to sit out in the reception area all day?'

Jessica nodded. 'He goes where I go until the execution is over.'

'Did you happen to notice he was black?'

'Yes, I guess I noticed that.'

'Did you also happen to notice he was handsome?'

'I believe I noticed that, too.'

'Did you happen to notice if he was wearing a wedding ring?'

'I did happen to notice. He isn't.'

'Great,' Samantha laughed and then drifted back to her large desk in the reception area, leaving Jessica to her paperwork which, as District Attorney, was considerable.

Two things they didn't warn you about before you went to work for the DA's office: the cynicism and the paperwork.

The cynicism was easily enough explained. Much like police officers, people in the DA's office saw citizens at their absolute worst. Drugs. Violent robbery. Sexual and physical abuse. Murder. And lying. Not only did the people you were prosecuting lie, but so did many of your own witnesses. They had their own reasons for testifying – frequently so they could get charges against themselves lessened or dropped altogether – and consequently did not always tell the truth. The misty idealism of law school was long gone. Hard to remain idealistic around pimps, con artists, flashers, drug pushers and murderers.

And the paperwork: each case had its own mountain of memos and letters and petitions and forms. Just what you received from the arresting officer alone ... memo books, property vouchers, accident reports, rap sheets, on-line booking sheets, radio transmissions, ballistics reports, drug analyses, complaint reports, arrest reports ... all the paperwork required to keep both sides of the legal system – prosecution and defense – communicating on an equal basis.

This morning, as the county's leading lawyer, Jessica had a stack of seventeen file folders on her desk ... cases she had to review over the weekend.

Her phone rang. 'Yes?'

'Good morning, Jessica. This is William Cornell.'

He didn't really need to identify himself. William Cornell was the most important political columnist in the entire state. A dangerously overweight man given to dark three-piece suits and wearing his curly white hair in the almost ringleted fashion of a Roman senator, he had had five wives, destroyed two governors, one senator, at least five representatives, and innumerable mayors and judges. He didn't speak, he barked, his words coming out in harsh, theatrical bursts. Despite the fact that he owned three airplanes, two mansions, a condo in Vail, and spent at least a month each year in a Paris flat, he had managed to keep his common-man audience loyal for over thirty years, mainly because he fed their appetite for scandal. There was nothing that William Cornell loved more than having one of his three investigators turn up some dirt on a political figure. Then he'd start feeding little pieces of that political figure to the public bit by bloody bit.

'Yes, I recognized your voice.'

'I just wondered what you're doing for lunch.'

'Eating in, I'm afraid. I've got so much to do, I can't leave the office.'

'I see.' The voice was icy now.

William Cornell was a legendary lech. He wasn't as goofily obvious as Al DeWitt, and he knew enough to stay on this side of the sexual harassment line. Nonetheless, he hit on a good number of the women he encountered in a day's work. Now it was Jessica's turn. What was amazing was that so many women – smart, attractive women – took Cornell up on his offers. Henry Kissinger was right. Power *was* an aphrodisiac.

'I'm afraid I'll just have to see you in the studio tonight,' Jessica said. 'I'm buried in paperwork here.'

Still icy. 'Well, I was hoping I could give you a few pointers about TV over lunch. But I guess it'll have to wait until tonight.'

In addition to his column, Cornell had a half-hour talk show on the state educational channel. It got high ratings because Cornell loved to flay his guests.

'Thanks for the lunch offer,' Jessica said. 'I appreciate it.'

She hung up and got back to work.

3

Eight minutes later, her intercom buzzed.

'Jessica?'

He sounded harsh, angry.

'Hi, Tom.'

'Whose idea was the cop?'

Tom Culligan had started in the DA's office the same year as Jessica. Culligan and another Assistant DA had been the mainstays of the Gerard prosecution team.

'You mean the police protection?' Jessica said.

'Yeah. The guy sitting outside my office. The guy who just showed up at my house this morning and told me he was going to spend the rest of the day and night with me.'

His anger burned fiercely.

Why would he be so mad about having police protection?

'Tom, I don't understand what the problem is.'

'The problem is, Jess, that I've got things to do today and I don't want some guy trailing around after me.'

She sighed. 'Tom, we talked about this yesterday.'

'Not about police protection.'

'No, but you and I and Dick did talk about David Gerard killing those two people in California and at least one in Chicago. And we agreed that he might try to kill us, too.'

'I still don't want police protection, Jess.'

'Why don't you come in and we'll talk about it?'

'I can't right now. I've got Bob Carpenter coming up. That judge we think may be taking bribes, remember?'

'Right.'

'He's due here in another ten minutes. Then I'll come in.'

'This is Detective Ribicoff's idea, by the way. If this is what he wants, Tom, I don't see how we can turn him down. He's done a lot for this office and this is what makes him comfortable. And anyway, I've got to say – and I'm obviously just speaking for myself here – I don't mind having police protection knowing that David Gerard is probably back in town. You agree with me that David is even more psychotic than his brother.'

'Like I said, Jess,' Culligan said, the anger waning but still there, 'I don't want police protection even if you do. But we'll talk about it in a while, all right?'

'Sure, Tom. Fine.'

He hung up, leaving Jessica to sit there and wonder what the call had really been about.

What was going on in Tom Culligan's life that he didn't want a detective to find out about?'

Chapter Four

1

Me.

Sometimes, as now, David Gerard was startled to see the face that stared back at him.

He'd forget about all that extensive plastic surgery he'd had in England, and about his brand-new face.

The face that stared back at him now in the rearview mirror was more handsome than the old one, and more aristocratic – with a long, elegant nose, a smaller mouth and a longer jaw. The bleached hair, coupled with the new face, gave him the look of an international playboy. Or so he imagined.

He knew that this was a handsomer face because these days he scored far better with women than he ever had. And in Europe a stage director, one who seemed unnaturally interested in David, coaxed him to be in several small theater productions.

David had loved acting ever since, as a young boy, he had seen Jack Nicholson in *The Shining*. He had the same kind of evil person inside that Nicholson had in that movie. The same diabolical spirit eager to be set free. The audiences had responded appropriately. One woman, who he never saw again, had gone down on him seconds after the curtain descended, right in David's cramped dressing room. Her husband had been waiting for her out in the theater.

A passing car splashed dirty water all over the side of David's rental Pontiac, distracting him from his image in the mirror.

1127 Richter Boulevard was an old, dirty gable-front clapboard of the sort that was built in the twenties. There was a spindlework porch and patterned shingles with a little Queen Anne detailing for spice.

This was the kind of place where you grew up without dreams or aspirations; or crawled back to after decades of being dashed against your dreams or aspirations. Cheap, grubby, lonely was how the whole block looked to David.

The Gerard brothers came from one of the wealthiest families in the state.

It was, in fact, the wealth that prompted them to murder their parents. The boys, then twenty-two and twenty-one respectively, had run up huge debts, including one sizeable tab with a Vegas casino-owner.

They murdered their parents with knives and guns, to make it look as if a small gang had invaded the family mansion, then spent the next three months trying to make the police believe that they had nothing to do with the killings.

They might have persuaded the police of their innocence if they hadn't kept right on killing.

The murder of their parents had awakened a profound need to take other lives. They worked a three-state area and in a period of less than ninety days, murdered four more people, including an eleven-year-old girl whom they raped both before and after killing her.

Roy Gerard was captured and imprisoned. David remained in hiding, not seen again by law-enforcement officials until he showed up at his brother's trial and killed the judge and the others.

Now David had to free his brother once again...

He got out of the car.

Checked his watch. 9:37 A.M.

The schedule was critical today.

Had to stay on it exactly.

The sidewalk was covered with a few broken children's toys.

He took the walk leading to the front porch of number 1127, preparing himself for the odors he was about to encounter. He'd always had a terribly sensitive olfactory system. A lot of old houses like this – with their mixed smells of aging wood, decades of cooking, and many other overripe scents – literally nauseated him.

He took a last look at the block, making sure there was no one peering out of a window, no one sitting in a parked car, observing him.

A man like the one he was about to see... ever since the bombing of the federal building in Oklahoma City... this kind of fringe-group revolutionary was under constant FBI scrutiny.

He knocked on the door.

2

'Still raining?' the man said.

'Uh-huh.'

'Had a lot of it lately.'

'Uh-huh.'

'Tired of it, myself.'

This time David didn't answer him.

He hated small talk and had just now exhausted his patience for it this particular go-around.

The business was conducted, inevitably, in the basement.

David followed the short fleshy man with the black eyepatch down the painted wooden stairs into one large room. The walls were finished in fake sheets of knotty pine and the floor was covered with crude and inexpensive indoor-outdoor carpeting. There were two large Confederate flags draped across two of the walls. A Nazi helmet, probably a reproduction, sat on a small table in the west corner.

The east wall was filled with framed black and white photographs of Viet Nam, many of them grisly. There were also ribbons and commendations. David doubted that the man, whose name was Everett Grimes, had fought in Nam, nor that his eyepatch was anything more than ornamental. A lot of the militia-types lived rich fantasy lives.

At the far end of the basement was a big work-table. Grimes walked behind it as if he were a merchant displaying his wares. He wiped his hands on his plaid shirt and leather vest then reached behind him and lowered the volume on a station playing a Hank Williams, Jr record.

Grimes said, 'Push that magazine aside and sit on that stool here. I want to show you what we're dealing with here.'

David glanced at the magazine before setting it on the floor. *American Truth* was the title. The cover showed several well-dressed men standing in front of a major bank. The headline was: WHAT ARE THE JEWS DOING WITH *YOUR* MONEY?

'Kikes,' Grimes said, gesturing at the magazine. He laughed. 'Next time, we get every one of them.'

Then Grimes pointed to the table. 'A beauty, huh?'

Grimes, for all his Soldier of Fortune bullshit, was an acknowledged master at creating bombs. A half-dozen people had recommended him to David.

Even though he had studied explosives, David knew he was no expert. To be a master, the way Grimes was, required a great working knowledge of chemistry, electronics and demolitions. More than a third of amateur bomb-makers injured or killed themselves.

The table was strewn with electric wire, alligator clips, blasting caps, battery hydrometers, batteries of various sizes, and two silver containers the size of beer cans.

One of the containers was attached to a 3 x 5-inch piece of leather. There were straps with buckles sewn into the leather, so that the container could be fastened to a wrist or ankle.

'C-4,' Grimes said, indicating the containers. 'Just the way you wanted them.' He did a bad black-African imitation. 'Big boom, Bwana. Very big boom.'

A derivative of plastique, C-4 was the most dangerous explosive available. One of the silver containers could reduce a large house to fiery rubble. The look and feel of C-4 was harmless. You felt as if you were looking at and touching Silly Putty. But there was nothing silly about it.

'Big boom,' Grimes said again. Then, disappointed that he didn't get a laugh: 'All ready to go, too.'

He used an alligator clip to point to one of the containers.

'I put some extra whammy in that one.'

'Giant economy size, huh?'

'Exactly.'

'You have the suitcase?'

'Now it's my turn to ask if you're ready,' Grimes said.

'The money?'

'Yes, Bwana, the money.'

David tapped the envelope inside his blue windbreaker. 'Ready,' he said.

Grimes walked over to the corner where a specially packed aluminium suitcase sat.

He picked it up and brought it back to the table and began the delicate process of loading the containers.

As David watched him, he thought of the political underground he'd become aware of in the past few months.

In the sixties, it was the hippies blowing up government buildings.

Now it was fringe right-wingers.

They lived mostly in small towns, on farms, and in low-end motels. Every weekend, all across the fifty states, as many as two million of them got together. Guys who'd never risen above the rank of corporal in the real Army found themselves generals in these new armies. Nothing like a little promotion, even if you did have to give it to yourself.

'You know, you can trace all the troubles of the western world back to how the Jews took over banking right after they killed Christ,' Grimes said. He didn't look up.

'There were banks back then?'

'Of a sort,' Grimes said. 'And the kikes already owned most of them.'

'You really hate them, huh?'

Grimes stopped his work. His blue eyes burned when he raised them to David's face.

'You a Christian?'

'Look, man. I just want the fucking stuff, all right? I don't have time for a sermon.'

'You got a Bible?'

David sighed.

'I suppose. Somewhere.'

'Well, you look up the crucifixion. You read what the Jews did to Our Saviour sometime. Then you'll hate them as much as I do.'

Fucking wacko, David thought.

He didn't get out of there for another fifteen minutes, during which time Grimes tried to give him two more sermons about the Jews.

3

There were three weapons on the dining-room table: an Ingram MAC-10 machine pistol; a Walther PPK 9 mm; and a Heckler & Koch Model 94 assault rifle.

Ralph Harrigan had spent the last twenty minutes checking them out. David Gerard had put him in charge of firearms. Harrigan had been a Green Beret in Viet Nam. He spent the next fifteen years hiring himself out as a mercenary around the world. Mostly, he trained soldiers rather than fought alongside them. He'd never taken less than $150,000 a year plus a large number of perks. This gig was earning him half a million dollars.

'Everything all right?' Tim Cates said.

'Seems like I'm the one who should be asking that question,' Harrigan said.

Harrigan was a tall well-muscled man in his early fifties. His baldness only enhanced his masculinity. His skin was leathery from the scorching sun of a dozen nations. In his dark slacks, white button-down shirt, and rimless glasses, he looked like a very formidable businessman.

'What're you, some kind of den mother?' Cates joked.

'We were supposed to be here at ten o'clock last night and walk through everything again.'

'Yeah, well, I got detained,' Cates said, sipping steaming coffee from a Ronald McDonald mug. Cates was the opposite of Harrigan. He was a cowboy. Those who knew about such things spotted him for a battler immediately. The shoulder-length blond hair, the knife scar high on the left cheekbone, the nose broken in exactly the right place and way, the harsh black eyes ... Cates wanted you to know that he considered himself one dangerous hombre. He couldn't have been older than twenty-five.

He dressed that way, too – chambray shirt, expensive blue suede jacket, tan fitted slacks, and a pair of rattlesnake-skin Texas boots that had cost him a grand on his last trip to Abilene. Of course back then, six months ago, he'd been flush, having just come off an assassination team in a Balkan state. A gun could buy you many a strange and wondrous thing, from fancy cowboy boots to eleven-year-old pussy, if you were so inclined that way.

'Uh-huh,' Harrigan said. 'Until six-fucking-thirty this morning you got detained? Gerard was really pissed.'

'I was with a woman.'

'You could've brought her back here.'

'I was afraid you'd try to watch.'

'This isn't funny, man. He's paying us each a half million dollars.'

'Chill out, Harrigan. Just chill out, all right?'

Their voices echoed off the cracking plaster walls of this tiny tract house on the northwestern edge of the city. A few miles north, the cornfields started. Two weeks, they'd been here. David Gerard had brought them together. Even though they were in the same line of work, they'd never met before. And even though they were both trained killers, they were very different people.

'You know the toilet's broken again? I tried to flush it. Handle's shot.'

'Maybe *you* could try to fix it this time, Cates,' Harrigan said.

'I ain't worth a damn at mechanical stuff, man. Sorry.' He peered into his coffee mug. 'Need a refill.'

Harrigan was glad he was gone.

He needed to make another quick phone call.

Three times he'd called this morning.

Three frigging times and no answer yet.

Linda was still in surgery.

One of the many failings of this little crackerbox – in addition to the furnace not working very well, the toilet not flushing half the time, and none of the cupboard doors closing properly – was the fact that the only phone was in the living room. It was tough to make any personal calls without being overheard.

By now, Harrigan knew the Denver hospital number by heart.

He punched in the digits. When the hospital operator came on, he asked for Extension 87.

'Good morning. Are you inquiring about the status of a patient?' said a relentlessly happy female voice.

'It's me again.'

She recognized his voice immediately. And then she didn't sound so happy.

'It's only been twenty minutes, sir.'

'I understand that. But I'm her father.'

A sigh. 'Let me call up to the surgery floor. Hold on, please.'

Twenty-one years old and she finds a lump on her left breast. Eight days later she's in surgery. Twenty-one years old.

The thing was, Harrigan hadn't even kept track of her until a year ago. He'd always known he'd had a daughter back there in Terre Haute and every Christmas he always sent her a substantial check (plus several thousand to her mother for child support) but with all the minor skirmishes and wars going on, he'd been busy training soldiers. And her mother had been busy marrying. Four husbands in the kid's twenty-one years. The mother had been a waitress Harrigan had met in a country and western bar. They'd gotten married but he'd walked out after nine months. Married life didn't suit the lifestyle of a mercenary. Then one day he received an envelope with the picture of six-week-old Linda in it. The kid was his, no doubt. He always joked that God had played a very dirty trick on her. She looked like her dad and not her mom.

He hadn't even seen her in the flesh until last year. He'd taken her on a two-week fishing trip along with her boyfriend Perry, whom Harrigan hadn't liked at all. Didn't think the kid was properly respectful to Linda.

Now she was in surgery.

'Sir?'

'Yes.'

'I'm afraid she's still in surgery.'

'What time did she go in?'

'Right on time, sir. Eight o'clock.'

'Isn't it taking a long time?'

'Not necessarily.'

'They told her this would be a fairly simple operation.'

A pause.

'Well, you never know how a surgery is going to go. But the duration of it doesn't necessarily mean anything one way or another.'

'Then she goes into recovery, right?'

'Right.'

'Will you have a condition report, then?'

'I don't know about a condition report, but I can at least speak directly to a doctor or the chief surgical nurse.'

'I'd rather you spoke to the doctor.'

'I'll do what I can, sir.' Pause. 'You need to relax, sir. I'm sure everything is going to be fine. Dr Stern is considered to be one of the best surgeons in Denver.'

'So he's done this sort of thing before?'

'Many times before. Now why don't you just try to relax. Call back in an hour or so. I'm sure I'll have some information for you by then.'

'Thanks for being so nice.'

'Just doing my job, sir.'

As he was hanging up, he thought he heard the floorboard creak. Turned to see if it was Cates, if he had been eavesdropping.

But it must have been the wind on this blustery day. Because nobody was there.

Relax.

Good advice.

If only he could follow it.

But there was no way he could relax and he knew it, not with these two things on his mind.

First, there was Linda and her operation.

Second, there was Kray, the helicopter pilot David Gerard had hired for tonight.

After it was all over, and after David had led them to where he and his brother kept their five million dollars in cash, Harrigan and Kray were going to doublecross the Gerard brothers.

They were going to kill them and keep every single one of those five million dollars for themselves. Then Harrigan was going to have the distinct pleasure of killing Cates, too.

With things like that on his mind, no wonder Harrigan couldn't relax.

4

Cates, pouring himself more coffee, wondered if they'd found that bitch in the dumpster yet.

Wow, had he been drunk last night.

They'd gone back to her motel room – she was some kind of cocktail-lounge singer who toured the Midwest and stayed in el-cheapo motels – and somehow the newspaper article that

Cates had about DA Jessica Dennis had come out. He'd torn it out of a newspaper and stuck it in his shirt pocket.

By then, both Cates and the girl were really hammered.

She wanted to know why he had the story about the DA in his pocket. And she said she wouldn't go down on him until he told her.

So at first he was real coy, giving off very broad but pretty meaningless hints.

But then she started asking questions and he realized through his fog that he was a lot drunker than she was.

In fact, she seemed pretty sober.

And pretty interested all of a sudden in just what he was doing in town, and just what he planned to do to the DA.

The funny thing was, he couldn't even remember for sure what he said to her.

But there they were on the bed, him sliding his hand up her mini-skirt, his fingers sensing the hot wet treasure between her legs, and then her expression changed all of a sudden . . . and he knew that he must have said something that really tipped her off to what was going on.

She started finding reasons that she needed to go for a walk. Alone. Just needed space.

He let her go. But then right away, he got suspicious. He raced out of his room, found her half a block away, talking to some reporter named Shaw on the phone.

And then he began to understand what had happened – that he'd drunkenly told her about the operation – and now she was going to spill the beans to this reporter.

He dragged her back to his room.

He hadn't used his switchblade on anybody in a long time.

The first thing he did was knock her out. Cutting her up would be a lot more fun if she was conscious but he couldn't take the chance on her screaming.

When he was done with her, and he really took his time, he wrapped her up in her coat and carried her out to the dumpster.

Dawn was just starting to streak the night sky.

The rain was already steady and sodden.

He got into his car, then, and drove.

He thought he might have seen somebody peeking out from behind one of the room curtains but he couldn't be sure.

And there wasn't time to investigate.

Now, he sipped coffee.

Harrigan, who thought he was pretty big stuff in the brains department, would be really pissed if he knew about the girl in the dumpster.

He'd say killing somebody like that could jeopardize the whole operation, get the police curious.

Screw Harrigan.

He thought because he'd been in Nam he was some kind of big war hero.

Cates sipped his coffee.

Screw Harrigan; and screw David Gerard, too, for that matter.

Cates would just be glad when this thing was done with and he could head back to Abilene for a little R and R.

Chapter Five

1

People came to crime scenes for different reasons.

The cops and the lab people and the staff from the DA's office came because it was their job. Some of them were used to crime scenes by now, all the gore and sorrow; some of them would never get used to it.

But civilians came for a variety of reasons.

Some just loved anything that broke up the monotony of their gray, predictable lives. Plus it made for good story material later on at the bar. *You shoulda seen this chick. Man, she looked like somebody used a Veg-a-Matic on her whole body.*

Some loved to be scared. You could get only so many kicks from watching horror movies on the cable. A crime scene, however, was real. It could be you being stuffed into that ambulance. And it was even better if the killer hadn't been caught yet. Who wanted some candy-ass who turned himself over to the cops right away? Better if he was still on the loose and eager to kill again. A good bogeyman was hard to find.

And others came to the crime scene to prepare for their own deaths. There was an old Irish saying that the person you really mourn at a funeral is yourself. You know that it will someday be you in that coffin amidst all the flowers and incense and people sobbing up there next to the altar. So you prepare, try to prepare your own pounding heart by gazing as calmly as possible on the corpses of others.

Michael Shaw was there today because he didn't have any choice.

He had been interviewed by one cop and was just about to be interviewed by another.

Three squad cars, an ambulance, and a black Dodge sedan from the crime lab were all parked at various angles to the dumpster.

By now, even given the steady rain, the crowd of onlookers had swelled to at least twenty or thirty. One old man had borrowed a transparent plastic rain scarf from his wife. The weird thing was, he looked cute in it.

'How's the cleaning woman doing?' Shaw asked Detective Riley, who had just flipped his notebook open to ask Shaw some questions.

'I think the manager gave her a couple belts of his Old Grandad.'

'Good,' Shaw said. 'She doesn't get paid enough to put up with stuff like this.'

Detective Riley said, 'You stand a few more questions?'

'I'll try. But I wonder if I could make a quick phone call?'

Riley, a redhead who wore heavy bi-focals, shrugged. 'Sure. I need to check some other things out, anyway. No reason I can't do that first. Ten minutes?'

'Great,' Shaw said. 'I appreciate it.'

He walked over to his car.

He needed to talk to Jessica.

Warn her.

2

'He doesn't have to stand next to me at the urinal, does he?' Dick Ward said.

'Very funny.'

'What about when Sandy and I are making love? It's all right if he's in the room but he has to be very quiet, okay?'

As Jessica's favorite Assistant District Attorney, Dick Ward was also the office cynic. Give him even the grimmest news and he'd be able to put some kind of sarcastic spin on it. Ward did what cops did, dealt with grief by spoofing it.

He was doing that now, about having a police officer with him all day and night for protection.

'You could at least have gotten me a nice-looking *female* detective,' Ward grinned.

'One in a string bikini, maybe?'

'Wow. Is it too late to get me one like that?'

If there was such a thing as being an average American man, Richard Ward was it. Brown hair, brown eyes, neither fat nor skinny, neither handsome nor ugly, dressed nicely but not expensively. Richard Ward was a loving husband, dutiful father of two, moderate Republican, reasonably devout Methodist, frustrated golfer, and hard but not obsessive worker. Unlike half the people in the DA's office, he had no political ambitions. And when his time came to leave public service, he would not angle for a niche in a big, prestigious firm. He'd probably go to a small situation where working nights and Saturdays would be only occasional. He would like it there, and prosper.

'You want me to give you her measurements?' Dick said.

Jessica smiled.

'No, thanks. I can probably figure those out for myself.'

Then Dick surprised her by turning suddenly serious: 'They

really think David Gerard's going to try and kill us, huh?'

'That's what Detective Ribicoff thinks. And he's the best there is.'

'It's just kind of weird, having him with me all the time. He sits out in front of my door.'

'Mine's in the reception area.'

'I guess I'll just order a sandwich up here for lunch.'

'Me, too.'

'But I do have a two o'clock. I'm supposed to speak to that paralegal class out at the community college.'

'Oh, that's right. Just be sure to tell them to bring a spelling guide to work with them because lawyers can't spell.'

Dick sat across from her desk. He leaned forward, spoke in a somewhat conspiratorial tone.

'Culligan's really mad.'

'I know. What's it all about?'

'I don't know. But for some reason, he really doesn't want to have any police protection.'

Dick sat back, more relaxed now, giving up the whisper.

'There's obviously something going on he doesn't want anybody to know about.'

'That's what I'm thinking, too,' Jessica said. 'But Tom's so—'

'So nice and decent.'

'Exactly.'

'So what could he have to hide?'

'Right,' Jessica said.

An image of Tom came to her. At one time he'd been the picture of the merry fat man whom everybody liked. Then he went on a protein diet six months ago and now he looked completely different. He'd lost nearly seventy pounds and he looked great. The dishwater-blond hair that had always been slightly mussed was now perfectly coiffed. The suits that had been baggy and rack-bought were now flattering and custom-made. There had been a similar change in his attitude about himself. Women had started paying attention to him for the first time in his life. A certain arrogance could be heard in some remarks now, especially about his cute but plump little wife. Several times he'd said to Jessica, always in the guise of joking, that maybe it was time 'to trade up on a new model.'

'He has changed, you know.'

'I know,' Jessica said. 'So maybe—'

'—he does have something to hide.'

Her intercom buzzed.

'Excuse me. Yes, Samantha?'

'Michael's on line two. Says it's very important.'

Ward was up and on his feet.

He gave her a little wave and walked out the door.

'Hi,' Michael said.

'Hi.'

'Believe it or not, I'm not calling about you-know-what.'

'Michael, I'm glad to hear from you. You know that.'

'As long as we don't talk about marriage.' Then: 'Sorry. I shouldn't have said that. But the offer still stands.'

'I know. And I appreciate that.'

Though they'd gone out together for nearly five years, they'd never seriously discussed marriage until a year ago. At first, she'd accepted. Michael's drinking problem was behind him. He went to AA meetings virtually every day and had been cold sober for over four years. But then, six months ago, his younger brother, also an alcoholic, had killed himself over a divorce and Michael had fallen off the wagon. He went on a four-day bender, one so violent to his system that he ended up in the hospital for three days. This brought back Jessica's worst memories of her father, not simply of his drinking, but of what the drinking did to family life – all the insecurity, the emotional violence, the gnawing fear, the embarrassment in front of neighbors, the feeling that somehow she herself was to blame for her father's drinking. If only she wasn't such a bad little girl, her father would be a sober and loving husband and father. All her fault.

She loved Michael more than ever but now marriage to him terrified her.

What if he started falling off the wagon again? With an alcoholic, there were no guarantees.

Unfortunately, things were no longer so simple as saying yes or no. She needed to talk to him but this wasn't the time.

'Tonight's my big night,' she said.

'I know. Soon as I'm done in my studio, I'm coming next door to see how you're doing.'

'Nervous is how I'll be doing.'

'You'll be fine.'

'I just hope Cornell is his usual egomaniacal self and hogs all the camera-time.'

'That, you can count on,' Shaw said.

She said, 'Michael, I love you.'

'God, you don't know how glad I am to hear you say that. You know how much I love you, too.'

'I know you do, Michael. But we really need to talk.'

'You name the time.'

'Tonight. After the debate. How's a pizza sound?'

'A pizza sounds great.'

'Palligari's?'

'You're on.' Then: 'But now we've got to talk about something else.'

His good mood changed abruptly.

'What's wrong?' she said.

He told her where he was, at the motel, and told her about the young woman in the dumpster. And the newspaper story about Jessica that had been torn out.

'I don't want to scare you, Jessica, but I really think you should have police protection.'

'Detective Ribicoff is way ahead of you,' she said. And then told him about the police officers who'd been assigned to all three of them.

'That makes me feel better,' Shaw said. Then: 'Oh, sorry, Jessica. Just a minute.'

She heard him cup the receiver then come back abruptly.

'I'd better go. One of the detectives just came up and said that they found a woman who saw a man leaving the motel early this morning. She says she can positively identify him.'

'I'll let you go, Michael. I just want you to know that I'm really looking forward to tonight.'

'I sure do love you,' he said. 'I sure do.'

3

Twenty minutes later, as Jessica worked at her desk on a brief for a pending stock-fraud case, a polite but urgent knock sounded on her door.

'Yes?'

Samantha came in, looking upset.

'I know you're busy but I thought I'd better tell you about Tom.'

'Culligan?'

Samantha nodded.

'He's disappeared.'

'Wasn't there a police officer right outside his door?'

'Uh-huh. But Tom told him he wanted to go to the john and that it was just outside in the hall and that he'd be right back. The officer followed him anyway. Stood guard outside. But

Tom never came out. When the officer went in, the john was empty.'

Not exactly what they needed today, Jessica thought sardonically: a locked room mystery, the room in this case being the bathroom.

She followed Samantha out the door and took up the search with the others.

Three years ago . . .

She got the idea for Confession as she was going down in the elevator.

She had to do something. She couldn't face what had just happened up on the thirty-eighth floor.

Just couldn't face it at all.

She got off on Floor Six and then walked out into the cold shadowy concrete coffin of the parking garage. She tried not to think of how many women had been mugged in this very same place. A few years back, a woman had even been beaten to death up here.

But there was no trouble tonight. She found her three-year-old BMW. Inserted the key. Heard the motor kick over smoothly and competently. And then drove out of the garage.

The Loop looked eerie tonight. The heavy snow had caused many workers to leave for home early, and the Loop had a deserted, ominous air to it now. Evacuated – that was the word she wanted. Like those drive-in movies she always used to see as a girl, cities deserted after a nuclear explosion, mutants roaming the empty streets . . .

Maybe she got pregnant tonight.

Or maybe she got a disease.

My God! She'd never thought about this before, but what if Don was bi-sexual? She really didn't know anything more about him than he was her new account supervisor at the ad agency. He was so handsome, so sleek.

AIDS!

As she pulled up to a stop light, city snow-plows coming at her in the other lane like giant yellow insects, she opened the glove compartment and took out her emergency pack of Winstons. Technically, she'd given up smoking more than a year ago. But every once in a while...

The cigarette calmed her.

And she had the thought about Confession again.

Yes, that would be nice. Hadn't been to Mass let alone Confession in years.

But now would be a good time.

Confession before going home and seeing Bob and her two little girls...

Maybe saying the ancient familiar words would cleanse her not only of guilt but of memory... of Don easing her skirt up as he pushed her hard against the wall and then parted her legs with his hot knowing hand, obviously amused and delighted to find that she had not worn panties on this day when they were to be alone in his private office for most of the late afternoon...

At first, she thought that the old stone church was closed for the evening, but then she saw the faint flickering of the votive candles play against the colors of the stained-glass windows.

She parked and went inside.

The place was huge, one of those mini-cathedrals built back in the twenties when Chicago was the Midwest bastion of

Catholicism. The vaulted ceiling rose into deep shadow, the votive candles, red and green and blue and yellow, offering the only illumination in the entire nave. The altar had been stripped bare. A very sorrowful Christ, head bloody with His crown of thorns, gazed down upon the empty altar as if it was the last indignity He could endure. The air was tart with the scent of incense.

Once again, she was struck by a feeling of desertion, as if all human life had fled . . . She seemed to be the only person in this entire vast church.

She looked first at the confessional to her right. The light above the priest's door, signifying that he was on hand to hear her Confession, was dark.

Then she looked across the pews to the door on her far left. A small amber light shone above the door. A priest was hearing Confessions after all.

High heels clacking against the bare floor, she hurried over to the confessional, opened her door and went inside.

Another moment of panic: what if she couldn't remember the words to Confession?

But it was too late to worry about that now.

She knelt down.

In the hushed gloom, the priest said, 'Good evening.'

'Good evening, Father.'

'I was just about to go back to the rectory. Nobody's been here for the last half-hour.'

'I'm the only one here, Father. Would you mind hearing my Confession?'

'Of course not, dear.'

She liked the 'dear.' Paternal. She thought of her favourite priest, Father Daniels, back in Catholic grade school. Merry blue eyes; soft white hair. She imagined that it was Father Daniels on the other side of the curtain tonight.

'Bless me Father, for I have sinned.'
'How long has it been since your last Confession, dear?'
'Uh, twelve years at least, Father.'
A displeased silence. Priests and nuns knew how to use silences better than anybody she'd ever known.
'You're not a practicing Catholic?'
'Not anymore, Father. But I want to be – again.'
'How old are you, dear?'
'Thirty-seven.'
'You have children?'
'Yes, Father.'
'I take it they're not being raised Catholic?'
'No they're not, Father. But I'm going to start taking them to Mass. I promise you that, Father. I promise you that.'
'You sound upset tonight, dear. I assume that's why you came here to see me.'
'Yes, Father. But – it's been so long I'm not sure I remember the words.'
'Don't worry about the words, dear. Just tell me what's troubling you so much.'
'I committed adultery tonight, Father.'
'I see. You know that adultery is a terrible sin?'
'Yes, Father, I do.'
'You say this happened tonight?'
'Yes, Father. At the ad agency where I work. With my new boss.'
'Was this against your will in any way?'
'No, Father. I wish it had been. But I – I wanted it to happen as badly as he did. And now – I just feel ashamed. I've been married ten years, Father, and I was never unfaithful until tonight.'
There was a long pause. She heard his breathing shift, become deeper, more pronounced. He leaned closer. The small

cloth separating them danced with his breath.
'Father?'
It sounded as if he were standing up—
She looked at the door.
Something was definitely wrong here. All those strange questions he asked. And now he was doing something on the other side of the confessional—
Then her door was thrown open and there stood a tall handsome man in a leather bombardier's jacket and jeans. He had a large butcher knife in his hand, the steel glinting with the glow of the votive candles at the rear of the church.
'You've been a very naughty little girl,' the man said, and laughed.
'Where's the real priest?' she whispered.
'I'm afraid he's had a little accident.'
She started to scream but it was too late.
The man reached inside, grabbed her, turned her around and then covered her mouth with his hand.
He was powerful beyond belief, capable of hiking up both her coat and her skirt, bending her forward against the wall, and ramming himself inside her.
'I'll bet he wasn't half as good as I am,' the man said to the woman as he continued to thrust up inside her.
He waited until he was reaching orgasm to kill her.
Just as his mind was starting to darken with the release and relief of coming, he yanked her head back and slashed her throat, her blood spraying all over the center door of the confessional.
Moments later, the man, zipping himself up, fled the church.
Christ looked down from His bloody eyrie above the dark and bare altar, more sorrowful than ever.

Chapter Six

1

Russ Atkinson figured he was probably the only warden in the entire federal prison system whose old man had been a lifer.

That was how Atkinson had first discovered his interest in prisons, in fact.

Twice a month his mother would pile her three boys into the elderly rusting Plymouth and drive upstate to see the old man.

Mother and the two eldest boys hated the prison and everyone connected with it. They especially hated the guards with their nightsticks and Sam Browne belts and sneers.

But young Russ liked the military efficiency of the prison, the way the prisoners were moved around in single file, and always working from a precise, preordained schedule. Russ liked the way the big gates opened electronically; and the way the mirror-sunglassed guards in the tower toted their sawn-off shotguns.

But most of all young Russ was taken with the authority of the Warden. He was God, a man who shaped order out of chaos and safety out of danger. He was respected by his staff and feared by the inmates. Just the way it should be.

Russ' mother and brothers never ceased mocking Warden Dell. To them he was all things evil, a reckless man who delighted in persecuting poor innocent inmates who were only here because life had not been fair to them.

But Russ knew that was all self-pitying bullshit.

The old man was in here because he couldn't stop robbing liquor stores and gas stations. He went in the first time when Russ was three months old, and got out on Russ' sixth birthday. He stayed out for eleven months. Then one weekend he hit two liquor stores and a gas station. The old man was not what you'd call a creative thief. The cops had him within two hours of the last robbery and he was soon back in the slammer.

The same went for the old man's friends. Russ' mother was a good-looking woman. The old man's ex-con friends were always sniffing around her under the guise of 'just checking up to see if everything's OK.' Right. Selfless saints, they were. They had no honor, no loyalty to the old man.

But then prisoners in general, and here he'd have to include the old man, didn't have much honor or loyalty under any circumstances. Most of them weren't too bright, many of them were complete predators, and around ten per cent were flat-out evil and needed to be destroyed for the sake of the species. That was Russ' task as he saw it, to incarcerate those who preyed on the innocent and helpless. It was a task he took very seriously.

Russ had seen a number of kids from the neighborhood go on to reform school and, later, prison. Russ had never been one of them. In fact, if his two brothers hadn't been such incorrigible bad-asses, the other kids would have beaten up on Russ every single day of the year. His brothers started getting into serious trouble when Ned was fourteen and robbed his first gas station. He'd worn a ski-mask and carried a BB pistol that looked frighteningly like the real thing. Then Mike stole his first car when he was twelve. Mike had a thing about stealing new cars and piling them up and walking away from them intact. A macho thing.

By the time they were in their late teens, both of his brothers were serving their first prison terms.

Now, as Russ Atkinson stood at the head of Cell Block D on this rainy Tuesday morning, he had three years behind him as Warden here.

After getting his BA in business administration – being a successful Warden required great administrative skills – Russ went to work as a prison guard and then as a probation officer and then as head of a halfway house for recently released convicts. He'd seen the incarceration system from every angle. Then he hired on as Assistant Warden here, and from there his rise had been swift and sure.

Now he was about to oversee his sixth execution and he was not happy about it. The executioner he usually used was down with some very bad flu. The only man available today was one of those cowboys who thought his job of killing people was a real kick. Atkinson believed profoundly in the necessity of taking Roy Gerard's life but even a man like Gerard deserved expertise in his passing.

He just hoped the cowboy was up to the job.

2

The executioner's name was McCann. He had one of those long fox-like prairie faces that you see a lot in photos of the Old West. He wore a fancy brown western leather jacket, with fringes on the shoulders and sleeves, and a white western shirt with blue piping. He wore slim dark trousers that slipped easily into the tops of his snakeskin cowboy boots.

He had a pompadour that lay in greasy dizzying tiers atop his narrow head. And he had the hard soulless eyes of a lizard. He sat in the chair across from Atkinson's desk. In his lap was a small black medical bag. He had been a paramedic with an ambulance company. In this state, you had to use paramedics. Doctors didn't want any part of executions. All they'd do for you was pronounce the person dead afterwards. And write up a death certificate.

Atkinson was talking.

'I don't mean to make you uncomfortable, Mr McCann, but you had some trouble downstate earlier this year, and the press is going to get all over my ass for using you.'

'You ask me, the press is a bunch of fags,' McCann said.

Atkinson sighed and glanced around his office, as if drawing solace from its orderliness. One wall was pretty much covered with framed photos of Myrna and their two girls. Another wall was pretty much filled with commendations. The furnishings were stained oak, the rug a sedate and proper brown, and the overhead lighting soft. Atkinson had a goose-necked lamp for when he was doing serious work at his desk.

McCann could see that Atkinson wanted more of a response than his fag remark.

'I had trouble with the guy's vein was all,' McCann said. He shrugged. 'That's all.'

'The problem was the sequence of the shots, Mr McCann. You didn't have any trouble giving him the first two shots, the ones that paralyzed him completely, and, made breathing very, very difficult. But when you came to the third shot, the one that would kill him and take him out of his misery, you couldn't find the right vein again. It took you forty-five minutes to find it, and he was in incredible pain the whole time. That's why the press said it was barbaric, Mr McCann.'

'Shit happens, Warden.'

Atkinson stared at him in disbelief.

'That's your answer? "Shit happens?"'

'Anybody can have trouble finding a vein.'

'But for forty-five minutes? What the hell were you doing all that time?'

'I guess I panicked a little. You know, there's a lot of heat when you're killing somebody. All those jerk-offs standing there watching you.'

'But the prisoner was suffocating slowly all that time and—'

McCann sighed. 'Look, I know you wanted Jennings. It's too bad he had to be sick today. But I can kill this asshole without any trouble, believe me. Without any trouble at all.'

Atkinson wished he knew how to use a lethal injection himself. The state was, after all, taking a life and the moment should be proper and dignified and efficient.

McCann said, 'I've put twenty-seven men to death in the past six years and I've only had trouble with two of 'em.' He touched his black medical bag, as if for luck.

'Twenty-seven men,' McCann said again. 'That puts me right behind Baxter out on the east coast. He's iced thirty-one of them. But I'm gonna catch up and then beat his ass. You just wait and see if I don't.'

Atkinson looked across the desk at the cowboy and his damp dead lizard eyes.

Sometimes you didn't have much choice who you worked with.

Sometimes you didn't have much choice at all.

3

Roy Gerard sat in the nice little room that was no more than a quarter of a city block from the building where they planned to execute him tonight.

He was reading an old copy of *Time*.

Couple of times this morning, the guard had come in and seen Roy sitting there all nice and relaxed and everything, and he obviously hadn't known what to make of it.

Roy knew this was what was going through the guard's mind and he thought it was great.

Guard would go back to the other guards and say, 'That bastard's got balls of steel, you know that? Balls of steel, I swear. You know what he did all morning? He sits there and reads magazines. The day he's gonna god-damned fry, and he sits there and reads magazines.'

Delicious.

Roy had always enjoyed screwing around with people's minds and this was perfect.

'Anything I can get ya?' the guard said his third trip down here.

This particular guard, O'Hanlon, had never even been pleasant to Roy before, let alone ask him can he get him anything.

'No, thanks.'

O'Hanlon watched him another thirty seconds or so. 'Must be some magazine.'

Roy nodded and kind of waggled the copy of *Time* in O'Hanlon's direction. 'You know anything about quantum physics?'

'Uh, I guess not.'

'Well, there's a very interesting article in here about some new quantum physics theories.'

'No shit, huh?'

Roy tried very hard not to smile.

'Yeah,' he said. 'No shit.'

The priest showed up about ten minutes later.

'My name is Father McGivern.'

RUNNER IN THE DARK

Roy Gerard looked at the man who had just knocked and entered the shabby little room where condemned prisoners spent their last days with their families. The lumpy couch with the flowered throwcover and the equally lumpy armchair were strictly Salvation Army modern. Loved ones could spent most of the day with the prisoner in this room. Lawyers ran in and out with news of last-minute appeals, or possible stays of execution from the governor. It was in this room, too, that the condemned man took his legendary last meal. They really did bring you what you asked for. You always heard wild tales about what various notorious convicts wanted for their last meals. They had some pretty strange requests, including the guy who'd wanted hot dogs with sauerkraut and cream cheese on them. Men got strange when they knew it was time to die.

The priest was in his sixties, white of hair, dressed in a traditional black suit and Roman collar. Wrapped around his left hand was a rosary.

'I didn't ask for any priest,' Roy Gerard said.

'I thought perhaps—'

Gerard smiled. 'You going to save my soul?'

The priest laughed. 'Something like that, I suppose.'

Gerard went over to the window and looked out at the exercise yard. Low fog still clung to the ground on this rainy morning. The sky was dirty and bleak.

Without turning around, Gerard said to the chubby bald priest, 'You think you can actually prove that there's life after death?'

'I don't need to prove it, Mr Gerard.'

'No?'

'No. Because I have faith.'

Gerard smiled again. 'Faith. That comes in handy, doesn't it?'

'Very handy.'

Father McGivern seemed to be under the impression that he was winning this little argument they were having.

Gerard turned back to him.

'You want to have sex with me, padre? I hear most of you priests are gay. Are you gay, padre?'

'No, I don't happen to be gay, Mr Gerard, and even if I were, I'd only be here to help you make your peace, not to have sex with you.'

The priest looked pale, sad.

Gerard felt exhilarated.

'Believe it or not, I'm trying to help you, Mr Gerard.'

'No, you're not, padre. You're trying to help yourself feel good about yourself. Come in here and be nice to a scumbag like me, isn't that the idea?'

'We need to talk about the state of your soul, Mr Gerard.'

'How about the state of *your* soul, you pompous old asshole? Now get out of here and leave me alone.'

The priest looked even sadder now, and many years older than his age.

'You're an evil man, Mr Gerard. I hate to say it but it's the truth.'

'You're breaking my heart, padre.'

The priest shook his head.

And left.

Gerard watched the door close slowly, and smiled.

It wasn't his soul he wanted saved.

It was his body.

He sure hoped his brother David was taking care of things.

Chapter Seven

1

'My name is Martin Steinberg and I'm an alcoholic. It's been six months and twelve days since I had a drink.'

This was an Alcoholics Anonymous meeting in the basement of a synagogue. By the time Shaw had finished up with the police at the motel, it was nearly eleven o'clock. He decided to grab a burger at McDonald's and then drive on over to the studio, hitting an AA meeting on the way.

As a recovering alcoholic, Michael Shaw tried to make five meetings a week. He usually went different places at different times. The one he thought of as 'the old reliable' was this basement over the noon hour.

He'd faced any number of personal crises in this basement. Even though he was a Catholic of the lapsed variety, he believed that this synagogue brought him good luck.

Only a few people were here today.

Three men in suits and ties; one woman in a faded housedress and even more faded face. She looked as if she might have had her last drink quite recently.

They went around the table in the small light-blue room.

Now it was Shaw's turn.

'My name is Michael Shaw and I'm an alcoholic.'

He said this despite the fact that he knew the other three men quite well. Regulars.

He looked at the woman. She met his eyes then glanced sadly away.

He explained about the murder this morning and how it had shaken him and how, in the old days, he might have taken a drink to deal with what he'd seen in the dumpster.

'How're you doing now?' said Martin Steinberg.

Shaw nodded. 'Fine.'

Bill Feldman said, 'I'm always recruiting viewers for you, Michael. Now I've got one of my old uncles tuning in to your news show.'

Shaw laughed. 'Thanks. Maybe I could send you out with a sound truck.'

Feldman, who was in advertising, and Steinberg, who was in city government, were both Shaw's age. But they were both long-married and long-settled men. Much as he liked them, he felt he had more in common with Milt Simon, who had a marriage with as many stress points as Shaw's relationship with Jessica.

'I think it's time we pay some attention to our new friend,' Milt Simon said somberly.

Milt was a tall solemn man whose two passions were poker and telling stories about the window-washing business. Milt's company washed skyscraper windows. He himself frequently worked outside on the seventy-fifth floor . . . and upwards.

Now Milt nodded to the woman who had her hands over her face.

The woman started sobbing, and everybody turned to look at her, Feldman even getting up and going over to her and sliding his arm around her.

'You'll be all right,' he said as the woman shook with her grief.

Shaw got up, too, and stood on the other side of her.

'Would you like some coffee?'

She nodded tearily.

He got her some coffee.

When he handed it to her, she looked up at him and said, 'I fell off the wagon last night. And I was completely dry for eight years.'

Her words brought a frozen silence to the little room.

She'd just expressed what they all feared profoundly – going back to alcohol after years and years of abstinence.

They sat down and listened to her story.

Fascinated.

And terrified.

2

'How's my ass look?'

'Great.'

'I bet that sounds kind've weird, doesn't it, me being a guy and all?'

'Don't kid yourself, Mr Culligan. Men worry just as much about how their asses look as women do.'

'Not just gay guys?'

'Not just gay guys at all. I mean, they don't like to come right out and admit it, but a guy in my business, he sees them sneaking looks at themselves all the time. Especially with a nice pair of slacks like this one.'

'Well, that makes me feel a little better,' Tom Culligan said. As soon as he'd mentioned his ass, he felt he'd said something really bad. You know, the kind of thing that could make other guys wonder about just how much of a guy you really were. But he couldn't help it. He'd even noticed

Jessica looking at him admiringly these days. He saw her eyes appraising him. She'd never sleep with him, of course, she was too hung up on Michael Shaw no matter *how* many times they broke up. But still, for the first time in their long relationship, she looked at him as a real guy instead of just a chubby brotherly type.

So, yeah, these days, he did notice his ass. He was *proud* of his ass, when you came right down to it. Losing all that weight was no fun. Neither was *keeping* it off, for that matter.

At the moment, Culligan was in especially great spirits. He'd really faked that detective out this morning. He went in the can and stayed there for so long that the detective had no choice but to come in and look for him. When the detective started searching through the stalls, Culligan tiptoed out of the closet where he'd been hiding up near the door. He'd moved fast and gotten out of the building before the detective had any idea what had happened.

Rick, the salesman at Chauncey's Men's Store, just about the most expensive shop in the city, smiled and said, 'Tell you what, Mr Culligan. *I* worry about how my ass looks.'

'You do?'

'Hell, yes, I do.'

'That makes me feel better.'

'You just want to wear these?'

'Yeah. Great.'

'I had that shirt pressed for you. The one you picked out a few minutes ago.'

'You're kidding me.'

'Nope.' Rick, swarthy, sleek of dark hair, trim of body, conspiratorial of eye, leaned toward Culligan and said, 'Between you and me, Mr Culligan, I sense you might have something going on today.'

'Well...'

'They used to be called "a nooner," I believe.'

Culligan laughed. 'By God, I haven't heard that expression in years.'

'So, anyway, I figured you'd want to look your best.'

'I really appreciate that, Rick.'

This guy was going to get himself one hell of a tip today. Right on the American Express Gold. God, Culligan liked this place. Tiers of only the very best clothing. An atmosphere as cultured as the Mozart presently on the stereo system. And the kind of relationship you could have with only the very best salesman – almost an intimate relationship. In the old days, Culligan used to come in here and Rick would choose clothes for him that cunningly hid Culligan's girth. But now Rick obviously knew that Culligan was a changed man and wanted to be *treated* like a changed man.

Rick winked at him lasciviously, and then turned toward the door leading to the fitting rooms and the tailor's shop.

'Be right back, Mr Culligan.'

Culligan was still smiling. Couldn't help it. All his life he'd wanted to be this kind of guy. Maybe not a stud exactly but a mover. Mover and shaker. He tried not to think of his chubby and rather homely wife because whenever he did, he got guilty. Busting her buns out there in suburbia with three kids. But she was emblematic of his whole life. Third string on every sport he went out for. Rejected by the two first-tier fraternities he'd tried to pledge. Never quite the Dean's list in college. And he'd had to *settle* for a woman like his wife.

The kind of woman he really deep-down wanted, he couldn't get, of course. He wanted the kind that the other guys would want, too.

Well, actually, he had one.

Not the wife, certainly.

But the mistress.

It still sounded slightly seedy to use that word *mistress* – it had the resonance of something he'd read about in trashy novels.

Thinking of her now, he walked over to the desk and quickly punched out a number on the telephone.

That was another thing he liked about Chauncey's. You could make yourself at home. No need to kiss anybody's ass when you wanted to use the phone.

This was the world of movers and shakers.

You wanted something, you *took* it.

'Hi.'

'God, where are you?' Kandi said.

'Chauncey's.' He glanced around to make sure nobody was eavesdropping.

'Sexy underwear?'

'Different store, babe.'

Then she teased him the way he liked to be teased: 'You bringing me a present?'

'Yeah. A big one.'

'A big *hard* one?'

He couldn't help it. He supposed it was juvenile but he loved it when she talked dirty.

The wife, the one time he'd asked her to talk dirty, she'd just given him a very strange look and said, 'Maybe you haven't noticed, Tom, but I'm a lady, not some slut.'

That's what he got for marrying the daughter of a Methodist minister.

'Yeah,' he said, dropping his voice. 'A *real* hard one.'

'I can't wait.'

'Neither can I.'

'How long?'

'Soon as I can get on the expressway, babe, I'll be there.'

RUNNER IN THE DARK

That was another thing about Kandi. She liked it when he called her 'babe.'

The one time he'd called Michelle 'babe,' she'd said, 'Isn't that what Sonny used to call Cher?'

No doubt about it, God had put him on this earth to be with Kandi.

The trouble was, God hadn't told him as yet how Culligan could ever get through a divorce with even a modest bank account left.

Kandi loved expensive things, and didn't pretend otherwise.

'Here you go, Mr Culligan,' Rick said, bringing the newly pressed white shirt over to him.

The shirt smelled of steam pressing.

It had a tall collar and looked real good on him with two buttons left undone at the top.

He just wished he had more chest hair was all.

Rick probably had chest hair up the wazoo.

Rick winked again and said, 'Don't do anything I wouldn't do, Mr Culligan.'

They both had a nice long laugh about that one.

When Culligan got out of the men's store and back into his car, he glanced in his rearview mirror and noticed a dark blue sedan behind him. There was a guy in it. Reading a newspaper.

Gerard?

Then Culligan grinned. You paranoid sonofabitch.

All the cops up at the DA's office must've really gotten to him this morning.

Now he worried about everybody he saw.

He put the car in gear and pulled away from the curb.

A minute and a half after Culligan pulled out, David Gerard, sitting in the dark blue sedan, lowered his newspaper, put the car in gear, and started following Culligan.

3

The weird thing was, Culligan knew that some of the neighbor ladies were peeking at him from behind their curtains and instead of being pissed, he was quite excited about it.

Kinda cool, actually, him looking in his new shirt and trousers, walking very casually up to the door of the nice new duplex, for which he paid a damned pretty price every month.

But women like Kandi Rawlings were expensive.

Kandi.

When he'd first met her, he'd thought the name was kind of cheap. A name his parents, his staid and *very* conservative parents, would never approve of.

But the more he got to know her, how she liked dirty jokes and naughty cartoons and how she liked to do him while they were watching really sexy porno movies . . . he saw that the name Kandi somehow fit her.

He hoped she was wearing those electric-blue bikini panties with the slit in the crotch.

He loved getting up inside her through that friendly little slit.

He knocked and waited for her to answer.

This was the only real neighborhood in this burgeoning new area of instant suburbia. Everything else was low-end condos, big semi-Colonial structures that went on for miles and miles, two to a structure. He'd grown up on a tree-shaded cul-de-sac, and he could never get used to the raw and unfinished look of most housing developments.

So he'd picked out a street that most resembled the upper-middle-class streets of his boyhood.

Kandi opened the door.

She wore a T-shirt that said STILL A VIRGIN, the words stretched across the gigantic breasts he'd bought for her on a trip to the West Coast last year. The plastic surgeon had been among the best.

Her designer jeans were, as always, sprayed on.

In the background, he could hear the audience on one of those day-time confession talk shows oohing and aahing and laughing about something.

Guy had probably just admitted that he was screwing the family dog or something like that. Or eating it. A lot of these shows dealt with cannibalism and stuff like that, at least according to Kandi.

'What's the password?' she said on the other side of the screen, in her best giggly voice.

'Hard-on.'

Giggle. 'That was *last* week's password.'

'Pussy?'

'That was *two* weeks ago.'

'Oh.'

'I'll give you a hint.'

He loved this kind of thing; and she was so good at it.

'I'll spell it for you.'

'Great.'

'B-a-z-h-o-m.'

B-a-z-o-o-m was what she was trying to spell, of course.

He'd corrected her spelling once and it had devastated her.

She'd sat in the leather lounger that he was still paying for and cried her cute little ass off.

You think I'm stupid.

I do not.

You think just because I didn't finish high school and just because I hung out with that biker gang that I'm real low rent.

Kandi, listen, honest to God I don't. I really don't.

Then she's looked at him through teary eyes and said: *Then prove it to me. Buy me something.*

Sure, honey. Anything in particular?
Something really nice. Really *nice.*

Oh shit, he'd thought. Oh shit. This duplex and all its furnishings and what she called her 'walk-around money' was already setting him back so frigging much...

Like what?
Like a car.
A car? What's wrong with your Impala?

So she'd told him what was wrong with her Impala.

And the very next day he'd bought her that cute little Olds she liked so much...

'Bazoom.'

'Bazoom, right! You can come in now.'

So he came in, and closed the door behind him, and then threw his arms around her, and got down to serious business...

In the basement of Kandi's duplex, David Gerard took out a pocket wrench and began adjusting the water valves.

He spent a long time, getting it just right, with the hot-water valve.

Kandi was indeed wearing the electric-blue panties with the friendly slit in them... and her soft warm furry little friend was waiting wetly for Culligan to make his way homeward.

One thing about Kandi, she loved to scream.

A few times, her screaming had even scared Culligan a bit.

Good thing the woman in the other half of the duplex had a job and was gone during the day.

Otherwise she'd probably think they were into some really kinky sex on this side of the house.

Then they were done, sated and soaked, and lay atop the unmade bed letting their breathing find normal rhythm, and letting the cool air dry their sweat-slick bodies.

Then she said what she always said: 'I could really use a shower.'

And he said what *he* always said: 'I could, too.'

The purpose of the shower was two-fold. They really did want to be clean and dry when they got into their clothes again.

But Culligan liked a shower for another reason, too: it usually got him hard again.

Round two.

They walked hand-in-hand out of the bedroom, naked and content as Adam and Eve before the snake had gone and ruined their lives.

'It was great,' she said.

That was another thing he liked so much about Kandi.

She'd *tell* you what a stud you were.

His wife, he practically had to *pry* even a mild compliment from her.

'You were fabulous, babe,' he said.

Just before they reached the bathroom, she stopped abruptly and said: 'You hear something?'

'Huh-uh.'

She cocked her head. Listened.

'Hmm,' she said. 'I thought for sure I heard something.'

Then they went on into the bathroom.

The basement door opened into the kitchen.

He picked the lock and then went into the kitchen. He carried Browning Hi-Power automatic pistols.

He walked on tiptoes.

When he reached the living room, he paused a moment and listened.

He heard a moaning from the area of the bathroom.

★ ★ ★

Culligan hadn't needed a shower to be resuscitated today.

They were leaning against the sink and he was already way up in her and she was making those throaty noises that really excited him.

She heard something again, and opened one eye and looked over Culligan's shoulder.

A man with a fierce-looking weapon stood there.

She pulled her tongue unceremoniously out of Culligan's mouth.

'Oh shit,' she said.

'What's wrong?' Culligan said.

Then he glanced over *her* shoulder into the mirror above the sink.

And saw the man standing there.

One second later, he recognized the man.

The guy in the blue sedan.

Waiting there when Culligan came out of Chauncey's.

David said, 'Get in the shower.'

'What?' Culligan said.

David stepped into the bathroom. It was nice and big, all pink tiles and a double sink and huge closet packed with nubby towels.

'The shower,' David said. 'Get in.'

'But why?' Culligan said. He was shaking so bad he could barely speak. He'd slipped out of Kandi a couple minutes ago.

David waved his pistol at them.

Kandi started crying. 'He's going to kill us, isn't he?'

David herded them into the shower stall and kicked the door shut behind them.

The bathroom smelled sweetly of Dove soap and baby powder.

You could see them all pink on the other side of the glass door.

'Turn the water on,' Gerard said.

'But why?' Culligan said again.

'Turn it on,' Gerard said.

Their screams were immediate.

The water was scalding hot already. That's what David had done in the basement.

Fixed the isolation valve so that all that would come out of either hot or cold was steaming water.

It was fun watching the two of them jump around so pinkly and helplessly in there.

All the time screaming.

Culligan started to turn the tap off but David said, 'You turn that off, I'll shoot you right on the spot.'

The girl tried to get out of the door but David put his weapon in her face and she shrank back inside.

They kept jumping around crazily, the water scalding.

The screams were pleas now: 'Oh, please, please!' they cried.

David could imagine their skin all boiled and red. Third-degree burns, water got that hot.

Then Culligan couldn't take it anymore and he flung himself against the glass door and it smashed apart in two, three big pieces, an edge of it slicing off Culligan's nose.

His face erupted into blood, spraying all over the shower.

That was when David opened fire.

He would have liked to linger but he couldn't take the chance.

He pumped twenty bullets into them with his silenced weapon.

The bodies hung half-in, half-out of the shower.

Gerard turned off the water.

He could see where their skin had been burned horribly.

He bent down, and with his knife, quickly took a souvenir from Culligan. A finger. Cut clean off at the joint.

David took a long last look at them bloody and broken there in the shower, and then he walked over to Culligan and spat on him.

Then he left.

Part Two

Chapter One

1

Harrigan was calling the hospital again when the sketch of the murder suspect came on the tube.

Harrigan had been a good boy. Hadn't called the hospital in over an hour. Had sat and watched most of *The Glass Key* with Alan Ladd and William Bendix, two actors he'd always liked. Cates had been out in the kitchen for some time. Harrigan was glad. He didn't much like being around the kid.

When his hour wait was over, Harrigan got up and turned the TV way low, then walked over to the phone on the glass-topped end table and dialed the hospital.

Then the police sketch of the murder suspect came on TV and Harrigan couldn't believe it.

For one thing, Harrigan had never been able to identify anybody from police sketches. He'd always see the guy they later captured and wouldn't be able to spot any similarity between the guy and the sketch.

Usually.

But this time Harrigan saw right away who the suspect was.

No doubt about it.

Harrigan quietly replaced the phone – the general operator

had just said, 'Hello,' once – then crossed over the threadbare carpeting to the TV set.

He turned the volume up.

'Metropolitan police urge viewers to take no action if you see this man. He is considered armed and very dangerous. But do call metropolitan police at once.'

Harrigan turned off the TV and stood there taking deep breaths.

Back in Nam, he had a sergeant who always said that professional soldiers like Harrigan were like runners in the dark. They couldn't see, they didn't even know exactly where they were going sometimes, but through their strength, wisdom and determination they could get there. The pros always could. The amateurs would always lose their way, do something to damage or destroy the mission.

Harrigan kept on taking clear breaths. Yoga. He needed to relax. Keep his mind clear.

Deep, deep breaths.

Times like this, self-control was everything. Only amateurs acted on their emotions.

Deep breaths.

His eyes came open.

His hands formed into fists.

He marched straight through the small house to the kitchen.

Cates leaned against the sink, tipping a beer back to his mouth.

He didn't read Harrigan's expression until it was too late.

Harrigan slapped the beer from Cates' hand, causing a plume of foam to arc through the air.

The beer can smashed against the wall, then fell, crashing, to the floor.

Harrigan grabbed Cates by his long yellow hair. He brought his own knee up and Cates' face down to meet it. He didn't want to break the nose but he did want to inflict great pain.

Cates cried out.

Harrigan then picked him up by the front of his jacket and threw him across the room, into the wobbly table with the old-fashioned oilcloth cover.

'What the fuck is this all about?' Cates said, once he was able to stand up straight again. He wiped blood from his mouth with the back of his hand.

'You stupid bastard,' Harrigan said. 'You killed a woman last night, didn't you?'

Harrigan's rage was commensurate with the risk Cates had taken. If the cops had arrested him, Cates would have done a little trading. *You guys go easy on me – make it second-degree instead of first – and I'll tell you where you can find David Gerard. And what his plans are.*

Cates looked like an insolent little boy who'd been caught doing something nasty by his old man.

'She was calling some reporter,' Cates said. 'She was gonna tell him about everything.'

'How the hell did she find out about everything in the first place?'

Cates rubbed a hand across his face. He was sleek with sweat. 'I must've said something when I was drunk, I guess.'

Harrigan felt a brief flicker of rage again but then a curious weariness overtook him.

This was Harrigan's usual response to a job gone wrong. He got tired suddenly. Then he needed to summon all his strength just to get through, just to do what he'd agreed to do. When this one was over, he was going to take all of that good green money that had once belonged to the Gerard brothers, and he was going to enjoy himself. He'd even have Linda come and stay with him for a while. God, he wanted to see her.

'Your face is all over the tube, Cates.'

'What the hell do you mean by that?'

'What the hell do you *think* I mean? It's all over the tube. Somebody saw you last night. And identified you. We need to be out and about this afternoon, remember? Now somebody may recognize you.'

Cates looked scared and confused.

'I can disguise myself. When we go out, I mean.'

'Yeah, I suppose.'

The smallness of the house, the shabbiness of the rooms, the uncertainty about Linda . . . and now some dumb psycho move by Cates. Harrigan was starting to suffocate from it all.

He wanted to be out in the sunshine, walking in the countryside. There would be animals – dogs, cats, cows, deer – he didn't much care which. Harrigan was one of those guys who drew far more solace and serenity from animals than he ever had from people.

But on a drab rainy day like this one, being outside would be no comfort, either.

He walked over to the refrigerator and opened the door.

The refrigerator was at least thirty years old, like everything else in the house. The interior smelled moldy.

He took out a beer, closed the door.

He walked the beer over to Cates and put it in his hand.

'I fucked up, man,' Cates said.

'Yeah,' Harrigan said. 'You did.'

Then he walked out of the kitchen.

2

Samantha said, 'Jessica, I've got Governor Standish on line three.'

'Thank you.'

She took a moment to make sure that she sounded all right, not too worried, even though there had been no word from Tom Culligan yet.

The man had simply disappeared from the men's room with an armed police officer standing outside the door.

Impossible.

Where was Tom, and was he all right?

The police had put out an APB for him but as yet, no word had turned up.

'Good afternoon, Governor.'

'I know it's a busy day for you, Jessica, so I won't take up much of your time. I just wanted to call and wish you luck tonight. In the debate.'

Jessica liked Bob Standish. He was bright, honest, hard-working, and completely reliable. But—

He was a wimp.

He was the kind of moderate who had no real strong beliefs himself. He was frequently compared, and not in a flattering way, to former President George Bush.

And like Bush, he almost always did what his handler – in this case, a rather dashing and ambitious young man named Dylan Ames – told him to.

There was an oft-repeated joke about Governor Bob Standish.

The Governor is standing in his office window and his wife comes up behind him and slides her hand around to his groin.

'You horny?' she says.

'I'm not sure,' Bob replies, 'I'll have Dylan take a poll and we'll find out.'

Ames was a political consultant who dreamed of someday putting a man in the White House. Like his own candidates, Ames had no core beliefs. Politics, to him, was appeasement. Appease enough special-interest groups and you'd not only get elected to office, you'd *stay* in office.

Two years ago, Standish had managed to get elected as a moderate who did not particularly want to see the death penalty reintroduced into this state.

For a variety of reasons, his popularity began to wane. He was something of an environmentalist, which meant losing some jobs. He was also a believer in leaving the tax base alone. No higher taxes but no tampering with the present tax rates, either, not with the deficit he'd inherited. He also favored the moderate side on abortion, gay rights, and welfare.

Until Standish's wife heard about this daring young man named Dylan Ames, invited him to the Governor's mansion for lunch, and subsequently urged her husband to virtually hand his career over to Dylan.

The changes were immediate and startling.

Following the most exhaustive voter-polling the state had ever seen, Standish took a whole new series of stands on every important issue. They were the same stands that the majority of pollees took.

Dylan even started running some mid-term TV commercials with the theme line, 'The bad guys are scared of him 'cos he stands tall.' The echoes of John Wayne made many pundits smirk.

Jessica had actually liked Standish better when he was against capital punishment. Though she'd disagreed with him on the issue, she'd admired his willingness to take all the political hits.

Governor Standish said, 'We're lucky to have a spokesperson like you, Jessica. Bright and positive.'

'Thank you, Governor.'

'I was supposed to go to the execution – that was Dylan's suggestion anyway, but... Have you ever been to an execution, Jessica?'

RUNNER IN THE DARK

'Yes. One.'

'Was it – all right?'

'I didn't enjoy it, if that's what you mean. It stayed with me longer than I wanted it to. But he'd raped and murdered two little girls. I just kept thinking about mothers and fathers and how this man had destroyed all their lives. That's why I feel our society has the right to ask for vengeance.'

'You're going to do great tonight, Jessica. As I said, I just wanted to wish you well.'

'I appreciate it, Governor. I really do.'

'Talk to you soon.'

'Thanks again.'

For the next five minutes, Jessica ran her hands and eyes up and down the two stacks of case files set out in front of her.

Where did you even start on a pile like this?

Especially when you wanted to spend all of your time searching for Tom Culligan.

Detective Ribicoff was up here now, personally going through Culligan's desk, looking for anything that might explain his mysterious disappearance.

Jessica had told Ribicoff about Tom's strange reluctance to have police protection.

Ribicoff didn't know what to make of that, either.

Jessica decided to start on a high-profile case where more than thirty elderly people had been cheated out of their life savings by an extremely cunning con-artist . . . one who might, in fact, have figured out a way to beat the law.

Jessica wanted to nail him to the wall.

The way things were going in this country, children and the elderly were endangered species.

She had just opened the file and started to read the cover letter from the Assistant DA who'd been assigned to the case, when the phone rang.

'Jessica?'

'Yes.'

'This is Detective Ribicoff. I wonder if you would walk over to Culligan's office for a bit.'

'Of course. Did you find something?'

'Maybe,' Detective Ribicoff said mysteriously.

Jessica said goodbye, then got up from her desk and walked out of her office.

Maybe they'd finally be able to figure out where Tom had gone.

3

There was a gentle wisdom in the lined and creased face of Samuel Ribicoff, and merry as the blue eyes got, they were never quite merry enough to chase away all the sorrow they held. It was a long and elegant face, his – one that spoke of timeless truths, and timeless griefs. It was a face of great dignity. As a small child, Ribicoff had spent two years in one of Hitler's concentration camps. He had watched his mother, his father, his sister and his brother all go to grisly deaths. Ribicoff came to America in the year 1946. He stayed with his cousin, a policeman, for two months before setting about becoming a citizen, and figuring out how he would become a policeman, too. He made homicide detective in a very short time. As his Captain said, 'Sam Ribicoff uses the most powerful weapon of all. Those god-damned sad eyes of his.'

It was those same god-damned sad eyes that made little children feel safe, innocent people feel comfortable, and guilty people want to break down and tell him the truth.

When Jessica came into Tom Culligan's office, Sam Ribicoff was standing at the window looking out on the rain-washed city.

RUNNER IN THE DARK

He appeared so lost in thought that she was reluctant to interrupt him. She had worked closely with Sam on several dozen cases over the past seven years. He was her favorite cop, and one of her favorite people.

As she approached him, she saw the photo on the desk, and wondered who it was, and where it had come from.

The photo showed a somewhat overripe bottle blonde in the skimpiest of lime-green string bikinis. She sat on her haunches, with her legs parted slightly. The outline of her sex could clearly be seen against the bikini crotch. The background showed what appeared to be a motel swimming pool.

Ribicoff, not turning from the window, said, 'My best friend did the same thing.'

'What same thing.'

Now Ribicoff turned to see her.

'I should've at least said hello.'

She smiled. 'That's all right, Sam. But I still don't understand what you meant about your best friend.'

Ribicoff shook his head sadly.

'He turned fifty and he got scared. "My life's over and I haven't done any of the things I consider important." He's a successful surgeon and the father of three beautiful children, and he doesn't think he's accomplished anything important. So what does he do? He has an affair with one of his nurses. He moves out on his wife, one of the most honorable women I've ever known, and buys into one of those singles condos, with the nurse staying with him, of course. I kept warning him what he was doing to his wife and his children but he wouldn't listen. So what happens? A year later, the nurse dumps him for a younger surgeon, and my friend decides to go back home with his tail between his legs. But it's too late. His wife tells him that she's met a very nice widower at a synagogue dance. And that she's in love with him. And that the kids all like him very much. And so my friend's life is ruined. You know what he does today? I mean, after his surgeries are over? He pops Prozac, he goes and sees his shrink three times a week, and he drives over to his old house and begs his wife to take him back, even though they've now been divorced for two years.' Ribicoff shook his white-maned head. 'He threw away everything of value in his life.'

Jessica followed his eye to the photograph on the desk. 'You think that's what Tom Culligan is doing?'

Ribicoff didn't answer her directly.

'A man who is very angry about police protection? A man who manages to *elude* his police protection? And a man with a photo like this in his drawer?'

Ribicoff picked up the photo and turned it over.

Written in green ink on the other side was:

> *Can't wait till we're together always.*
> *Love,*
> *Kandi.*

'Has he ever mentioned anybody named Kandi?' Ribicoff said.

'Not to me.'

'That you know, is he a womanizer?'

She thought a moment.

'Six months ago I would've smiled at that thought. He was very overweight and very self-conscious about it. He told fat jokes about himself so nobody else would do it first. But then he decided to lose weight.'

'Medical reasons?'

'I don't think so. I think he just got tired of being overweight.'

Jessica walked over to the window where Detective Ribicoff had been standing.

'He's lost a lot of weight the last six months.'

'That can do it.'

'Womanizing, you mean?'

'Unfortunately, yes,' Ribicoff said. 'Like my friend, you forget what's really valuable in life. You think it's being popular or being thin or being clever. You forget that all that matters is your loved ones. When you lose them, it's too late to do anything about it.'

Jessica glanced at the photograph on the desk, recalling the times her father, coming off a bender, had smelled of perfume and lipstick. If her mother had noticed, she'd never said anything. Maybe the only way she could survive in the marriage was to deny the existence of certain facts.

As a little girl, Jessica had often sat on her mother's lap and worried aloud about her father. Sometimes, drunk, he'd fallen down and hurt himself. Jessica was terrified that he would die. She had not learned to hate him yet. Until she was ten years old, she had always believed that her father would magically change, that he would give up drinking and become like other fathers. Fathers who did not yell or fall down or spend all their paycheck on booze.

By the time she was thirteen, Jessica knew better. Her father would never change. Then, ironically, it became she who had to comfort her mother. And just as Amy Dennis had told her marvelous reassuring lies about her father changing . . . now it was Jessica telling her mother the lies. Her frail weary mother. She could have hated her father completely if only she hadn't sensed that he was suffering just as much as they were . . . that he, too, wanted to quit.

In and out of various treatment programs came her father. A month dry here; two months dry there. But always, always he went back to the bottle. And each time he went back, her mother became a little more frail, a little more silent. And partly to reassure herself that her mother would not simply die of heartbreak, Jessica's lies became more extravagant, until even she began to believe them again.

And then twelve years after graduating from college, Jessica came home to her drab flat to see her answering machine blinking.

The hospital had called.

Her parents – her father driving – had been struck by a train at a railroad crossing . . .

'Does he hang out with anybody in the office?' Detective Ribicoff said, pulling Jessica back to reality.

'Ken Sawyer.'

'An attorney?'

'Yes.'

'Is he here now?'

'Should be.'

'Would you ask him to come in here, please?'

'Of course.' Then: 'May I ask you a question?'

'My pleasure.'

'Do you – think something's happened to Tom?'

'I'm not sure. I know that's not what you want to hear, Jessica, but the circumstances are hard to read. If I had to bet on it, I'd say probably something has. You said earlier that he's very punctual. He's been gone over an hour and a half. He hasn't called in. He's not at home. It could all be innocent. But if I had to bet—'

The grave blue eyes were as somber as she'd ever seen them.

'We never have had that dinner,' she said, smiling sadly at him.

'I know. There was so much to do after Lucy—'

His wife had died of a stroke last year.

Jessica had promised many times to make him dinner some

evening but somehow it had never happened.

He was such a wise and gentle yet powerful man.

'I'm going to call you next week, Sam. We'll set a date, and then I shall go to the best market in town and buy everything I need for a roast beef dinner. And then we're going to have a nice, relaxed evening.' She leaned over and touched his elbow. 'I'll go find Ken Sawyer.'

Ribicoff smiled.

'I'm tasting that roast beef already.'

Two years ago . . .

Not until late in the day, when she was typing her last legal document for the week, did she decide to actually do it.

She was going to drive over to Pete's and confront him. She knew that his mistress would be there. She wanted his mistress to be there.

Get it over with once and for all.

The autumn night was brisk but the smoky smell was irresistible, so she kept her window down and the radio up. Loud rock and roll. Made her feel like a teenager again, even though she would soon turn forty-three.

That's what Pete was doing, of course – trading her in for a new model. Just the way he'd trade in an old car for a newer one. Pete was an English professor at a community college. He liked to play the romantic poet, pretend to be sensitive to everything in the universe. But when you came right down to it, he wasn't any more sensitive – or kinder – than the lawyers she worked for.

At least they were up-front about it.

We're assholes and proud to admit it.

She was just sweeping up the next hill – Sam's mistress lived in one of those new developments far out in the boonies – when she heard the siren behind her.

Glanced in the rearview mirror. Frowned. Said, 'Shit. That's all I need. A fucking ticket.'

The F word.

She'd been saying that a lot lately.

Unlike her, really.

But her husband and his mistress were undoing her.

She drove on without thinking but then the squad car swung even closer to her back bumper and started blinking its brights.

Frowning again, she pulled over.

No need to irritate him, get herself an even more expensive ticket. Just accept his little sermon, take the ticket and drive on over to Sam's mistress and have it out with both of them.

He didn't come forward for what seemed a long time.

She watched him climb out of the red-flashing patrol car. Tall. Slender. The way he was silhouetted in the emergency lights, he looked like a cowboy star. Clint Eastwood, maybe.

Whenever she got a ticket like this, she tried to hunch down in the seat so passing cars, filled with curious people, couldn't get a look at her.

But there was no sweat on this lonely back road.

There were no passing cars.

He came up and bent over and peered inside.

'You know how fast you were going?'

'Guess I don't.'

'Nearly seventy. The speed limit here's forty-five.'

'I'm sorry, officer. I've just got things on my mind, I guess.'

His eyes searched the interior of the car. She wondered if he was looking for drugs or something.

She got a good look at his face. Handsome, but a little

spooky, too. A certain vacant expression in the eyes. His crisply starched uniform appeared a little small for him, which she found odd.

'I'd like you to step out of the car.'

'But why?'

'Sobriety test.'

'You're kidding.'

'Afraid I'm not, ma'am.'

'I don't even drink. A little wine maybe on a special occasion.'

'Then you won't have any trouble with the test I'm going to give you.'

'I can refuse.'

'Yes, ma'am, you have that right.'

'But if I refuse, you'll think I'm drunk for sure, won't you?'

'I'm only trying to do my job, ma'am. You see a couple of drunk-driving accidents the way I have – accidents where a lot of innocent people get killed – you'd do all you could to keep drunks off the road.'

'But I'm in a hurry.'

'It won't take long.'

'God, this is really an inconvenience.'

He smiled. 'I'll tell you what.'

He had a great smile. Made up for the vacant spooky eyes.

She laughed. 'You're going to make me a deal?'

'That's exactly what I'm going to do, ma'am. You pass the sobriety test, and I won't even give you a speeding ticket. How's that?'

'Great,' she said.

And got out of the car.

And that was when he grabbed her.

Right there. Right on the edge of the roadway.

As if he could no longer control himself.

He grabbed her wrist and dragged her to the rear of the patrol car. He turned a key and the trunk popped open.

Inside was a bald man wearing a sleeveless T-shirt, red boxer shorts, black socks and black oxfords.

He was bound and gagged.

This was the real policeman.

'I'll try to go nice and easy on the bumps,' the man wearing the uniform said.

Then he raised his nightstick and brought it down hard against the side of her skull.

There was pain, terrible pain, but not for long.

And then there was nothing.

Nothing at all.

Cold.

Shivering.

Goosebumps.

Had to urinate.

'Have to make water, Mommy,' she recalled saying to her Mom so long long ago.

Make water, Mommy.

She was naked.

She managed to get her eyes open, though a strange gauzy film covered them momentarily, so that everything had a faintly cloudy aspect, as if in a cheap movie's nightmare sequence.

Then she was able to focus, see clearly.

Deep woods. Moonlight spilling down through the fiery-colored trees.

A narrow path winding between deep undergrowth.

The smoky smell of autumn.

Then her eyes looked directly at a tree standing no more than ten feet in front of her.

RUNNER IN THE DARK

The real cop, the one in the red boxer shorts was there, lashed arms and legs to the tree.

But his head was gone.

The man had cut the cop's head off, and all that remained was a large dark hole in the center of his shoulders, with ragged blood-soaked pieces of flesh hanging down from it.

Then the man in the policeman's uniform was there, stepping from the dark undergrowth into the silver-tinted circle of moonlight. He was holding something behind his back.

'Had to take a pee,' he said. 'Didn't feel right doing it in front of you.'

Then he brought the axe up. It glistened redly, still dripping heavy droplets of blood.

He said, 'You've got a very nice set of tits, you know that?'

'Please, don't do this,' she said.

'In fact, for a woman your age, you've got a spectacular set of tits.'

'Please, oh God. No, please, listen—'

'I don't want you to think I'm one of those men who hates women. On the contrary, I love women. In my very own special way.'

Every few moments, her eyes would wander to the headless corpse lashed to the tree.

She was going to look like that in just a few more moments.

She started to beg him again but he was quick about it now, swinging the axe up in a perfect, practiced arc.

Her last thought was of Sam's mistress.

Now the little bitch was going to be free to marry him.

The little—

He took her head right off her shoulders in one faultless pass through the flesh and bone of her neck.

One utterly faultless pass.

He had to wait a long time before the blood stopped geysering.

But finally, after he'd smoked three or four cigarettes — finally he was able to approach her, and unzip himself, and make love to her.

Chapter Two

1

'She's back in her room now.'

'Is there a phone there?' Harrigan asked.

'Yes, there is, sir.' She gave him the number.

'You couldn't tell me how the operation went?'

'Sir, all I know is that she's out of recovery and back in her own room. Maybe you could try that a little later.'

'Thank you. I appreciate it.'

Harrigan hung up.

Twenty-one years old and she gets breast cancer.

The kind of life she's had, no father around at all, her mother marrying everybody with testicles, and then she gets breast cancer on top of it.

Runner in the dark.

His daughter's life was turning out just as his had.

In the kitchen, Cates had the radio up loud.

Right at this moment, the thought of anybody having a good time, when the exact condition of Harrigan's daughter was still unknown, really irritated Harrigan.

He wanted to go out there and smash up the radio and then smash up Cates, too.

David Gerard had certainly bought into the theatrics Cates had been selling.

Lonesome hombre. Seen all those Eastwood westerns and fashioned my life after them. *Yessir, Mr Gerard, I'm the tough hombre you're looking for. No doubt about it.*

There was a knock on the front door.

Harrigan's Ruger .22 came out of the belt at his back and filled his hand. The cowboys were always telling him to get a more powerful weapon than the Ruger. But it had served him well.

All he could think of was the woman Cates had killed.

Somebody in this forlorn neighborhood might have spotted Cates and reported him to the police.

Had to be careful. Very careful.

Another knock.

Harrigan edged toward the drapes. He pulled the dusty grape-coloured cloth back a quarter-inch at a time, his Ruger ready for use.

His heart was a wild thing in his chest.

Stupid kid, anyway, killing a woman the night before everything was supposed to go down.

Harrigan got a good look at the man knocking on the door. In his flight jacket, dark slacks, expensive haircut, and with his handsome face and dark knowing eyes, Mitch Kray looked like a sleek stockbroker who flew airplanes on weekends. All he needed was the white scarf and Snoopy helmet. But Kray was anything but an amateur. He'd flown the getaway helicopter in two major bank robberies over the past sixteen months. He was the same age as Cates but he was a true professional. In fact, if anything, he was a little icy even for Harrigan's tastes.

Harrigan let him in.

Kray looked over the living room and laughed. 'Boy, the lap of luxury.'

David Gerard had brought all three of them together for a planning session eight weeks ago at a nice resort up at one of the lakes. They'd spent four days planning everything out. Harrigan had been impressed. When it was all over, they would end up in Cuba. Gerard had paid one of Castro's brothers-in-law a million dollars to guarantee them safe-haven for three years. Once they landed, Castro would get a million for himself. Gerard had worked out the rest of the plan as well as the Castro angle. They'd stayed in a cabin together and the only thing that had tainted their time there was Gerard's obsession with *The Shining* videotape. He played it over and over and then walked around doing all of Jack Nicholson's acting bits. For Harrigan, this was unsettling. It proved that Gerard really was a fruitcake. After the time at the lake, Gerard and Kray took separate hotels to stay in and Harrigan and Cates rented the ticky-tacky house in the working-class neighborhood. They did most of their conversing on the phone. They didn't want to be seen together unless it was absolutely necessary.

'You have indoor plumbing and everything?' Kray said, moving around the living room.

'Yeah, but it only works on even-numbered days,' Harrigan said.

'I believe it.' Then: 'Where's Cates?'

'Hear the rock music?'

'Uh-huh.'

'That's Cates.'

Harrigan told him about what Cates had done, the woman and all.

'Why the hell did Gerard ever hire him?' Kray said. He'd never liked Cates any better than Harrigan had.

Harrigan shrugged. 'Gerard probably bought into all his macho bullshit.'

'Macho,' sleek Mitch Kray said. 'I could kick his ass blindfolded.'

Then Kray said: 'Hey, how's your daughter?'

'Well, she's out of surgery, anyway.'

'I asked this nurse I met the other night about breast cancer. She said a girl your daughter's age, if they get it soon enough, she should be all right.'

'That's what they say about everything. If they get it soon enough.'

'Not pancreatic,' Kray said. 'That stuff gets you, you can kiss your ass goodbye.'

'Yeah, I had an uncle once who had that.'

'Didn't make it, I'll bet.'

Harrigan shook his head. 'Poor bastard.'

'Now somebody like Cates,' Kray said, 'he could use a little pancreatic cancer.'

'He sure could.'

'Killing some bimbo the night before. Stupid asshole.'

If anything, the radio was louder than it had been before. No need to worry about Cates overhearing them.

'I just came over to touch base,' Kray said.

'Glad you did.'

They went through their plan.

This was the plan that went into effect once they were up and away and Gerard's job was behind them.

This was the plan that was going to make them millionaires many times over.

Mitch Kray was something of a computer hacker. One day at the resort, just for the hell of it really, he'd hacked into Gerard's computer and learned that Gerard was draining several secret bank accounts. He was taking the entire Gerard fortune with him to Cuba. In cash. In two suitcases. Nine million dollars in big bills. He'd had to pay a broker more than a half a million just to help him set it up.

Kray told Harrigan about this and they started blue-skying and pretty soon they had their plan.

'The way I got it figured,' Mitch Kray said one night to Harrigan, 'he owes it to us for making us watch *The Shining* all those times.'

When they were done talking, Harrigan saw that he'd left the drapes parted. He went over to close them and looked out.

'Oh shit,' he said.

'What?' Kray said.

'There's a cop across the street with the woman who lives in the blue house.'

'Yeah?'

'And she's pointing over here.'

'You think she recognized Cates?'

'I don't know what else it could be,' Harrigan said.

The stupid amateur, Harrigan thought.

Now he'd gone and done it.

Now he'd gone and done it good.

Harrigan watched a few seconds longer as the cop went to his patrol car and talked with his partner.

And then they both started across the street.

Walking directly to the house where Harrigan and Cates were staying.

2

While Michael Shaw had a word processor, like everybody else in the newsroom, he preferred to write his news copy on his old IBM Selectric. He didn't go as far as Dan Rather – all the way back to an old upright manual Smith Corona – but a good sturdy reconditioned 1976 machine was fine by him.

He'd bought it for himself years ago.

Shaw was going through the stories, deciding which should get the most prominent positions in tonight's show. When he finished his pass at story order, he'd phone the news director and they'd compare notes. Most of the time he agreed with Beverly Perez. Only on occasion did they have any real disagreements.

He was just finishing up when his phone rang.

He picked up on the second ring.

'This is probably a bad time, isn't it?'

Although he was one of the most powerful men in the news business – some insisted *the* most powerful – William K. Wingate was a curiously self-effacing man. He had earned enough credits and kudos to let his history as a newsman – and now as news czar of the nation's most prominent network – speak for itself. He didn't have to impose himself on you.

'Always time to talk to you, William,' Shaw said. Then, laughing, he added, 'Well, most of the time, anyway.'

'How're things there?'

'We've got that big capital punishment debate tonight. That's got everybody here pretty nervous.'

'I see by the wire that David Gerard has been busy again.'

'The sonofabitch.'

'Indeed.' Then: 'I just came from a meeting with General Montrose.'

Montrose was the CEO of the network, a bona fide decorated general who had retired early from the Army to take the reins of the network when it seemed to lose its way for a few seasons. Industry cynics made a lot of jokes about Montrose, and predicted he'd be fired within six months. Instead, he put the network right back on top and, along with Wingate's work, made the network dominant in the evening news business again.

'He sends his best.'

'I appreciate that. You know how much I respect the General.'

A laugh. 'You know what's coming, don't you?'

'I think so.'

'Before you turn me down as usual, I want you to listen to a new scenario the General has come up with.'

'All right.'

'But I want you to listen *seriously*.'

'I promise.'

'With Sam Gifford's sixty-second birthday coming up, the General feels we should put a new person in place – but gradually, over the period of a year. We love Sam too much to just push him out the door.'

'Plus he's your biggest ratings draw. But I'm sure that doesn't enter into it at all.'

The laugh again. 'Not at all.' Then: 'The General's plan is to keep Sam on the air four nights a week. Every Friday, we'll put on our anchor-to-be. Four nights of Sam, one night of the new person. Great idea?'

'Great idea.'

'The General has spent the last three weeks looking at tapes of prospective new anchormen and anchorwomen that our consultants have sent us. And guess what? He still wants you. He's looked at all the heavy hitters around the country – men and women just drooling to get this gig – and he still wants you. "Good, strong, middle-American face. Good, strong, middle-American values." That's how he describes you. What do you say to that?'

'I say that I'm very flattered. I'm very flattered *every* time you call.'

'You're turning us down again?' Wingate couldn't keep the disappointment out of his voice.

'I'm afraid I am.'

'Jessica?'

'Mainly. And also the fact that I wouldn't get to be a reporter anymore. Here, I still get to cover at least a dozen big stories a year *and* be an anchorman. There, I'd just be an anchorman.'

'We could work it out. The General wanted me to make sure you understood how flexible we'll be about this.'

Shaw rarely mentioned Wingate's calls to anybody except Jessica. It would sound too vain, how America's network news czar was constantly pursuing him to take over America's number-one anchor slot. So Shaw kept it to himself, though secretly he couldn't help feeling proud. Not so many years ago, alcohol had led him down a long dark road, and he'd nearly gotten lost. But now he was back and better than ever. Wingate's calls were proof of that. He'd been offering Shaw senior positions for the past year and a half. Now he was offering him the most senior position of all.

'I wish I didn't like it here so much. Then I'd probably take you up on your offer.'

'Why don't we give you a week?'

Shaw smiled. 'I don't need a week, I'm afraid. I'm trying to concentrate on Jessica and I getting married, for one thing. She has her own career here; I can't ask her to move now. And for another, the station is starting to put a lot more money into our news operation, and it's becoming very exciting around here. I'd hate to leave at a time like this.'

'You know how many people would *kill* to have this job?'

'I know.'

'And the money would start at the two-million-dollar level – with an unbreakable three-year contract.'

'I wish I could say yes.'

'Take a week. Please.'

Shaw knew he'd never get Wingate off the phone if he didn't agree.

'I'll take a week.'

'Good. I'll tell the General that at least you didn't say no.'

'I really am flattered by this. I hope you understand that.'

'I'll be even more flattered when you call me back and say yes.'

Less than a minute later, after an exchange of more pleasantries, the conversation ended.

Ryan Ludlow was a former policeman who hired on as a security consultant after an armed burglar successfully sued the city because Ludlow shot him in the right leg and caused permanent paralysis in that limb. This was after the burglar had shot Ludlow in the arm and then threatened to do far worse. Ludlow, who liked to fish, took an early retirement, bought himself a rickety little fishing cabin way out on the river, and now spent his work days trying to keep the Trealor building safe from nuts of both left and right wings who were determined to blow up the three floors housing the TV station because said station was part of the A) Liberal-Jewish-Gay conspiracy to take over the world or part of the B) NRA-Militia-Biker conspiracy to take over the same world.

Ludlow was a Viet Nam vet. In fact, he'd been in Nam the same year as Michael Shaw, but they'd never met before coming to work here in the Trealor building. This was back when LBJ's troop commitment had exceeded 150,000 and Westmoreland and McNamara were declaring that the war would be won soon, very soon.

'Hey,' Ludlow said when Shaw knocked on his door. 'Good to see you.'

Ludlow, who was a big rumpled man in a brown suit, leaned back in his chair.

Shaw came into Ludlow's office and sat down.

Ludlow's walls were covered with schematic charts of every floor in this thirty-nine-story building.

The air was sweet with tobacco. Ludlow puffed on a battered old pipe a couple of times a day.

'I just wanted to ask you a favor,' Shaw said.

'You look worried.'

'I am. About Jessica.'

'How's she doing? I haven't seen her up here for a while.'

'She'd be doing better if David Gerard hadn't killed those two people in California and the one in Chicago last week. The police are pretty sure he's back here.'

But Ludlow was ahead of him on this one.

'The debate tonight, right? That's what you're worried about.'

'I just want to make sure that everything's going to be nice and tight.'

'I've put six extra people on tonight. They'll be here starting at five this afternoon.'

Shaw felt relieved to know that Ludlow was taking this as seriously as he was.

'Fantastic,' Shaw said. 'I should've known I could count on you, Ryan.' He reached across the desk to shake his hand.

After they shook, Ludlow walked him out of the office and over to the elevators.

'Well, one down, anyway,' Ludlow said when Shaw was on the elevator car and facing him.

'One down?' Shaw said.

'Yeah,' Ludlow smiled as the doors closed. 'Tonight, at least one of the Gerard brothers'll be dead.'

As the elevator car started moving upward, Shaw heard Ludlow's last remark: 'And good riddance.'

Chapter Three

Cates.

That was the only reason the two cops would be standing on the sidewalk across from this house.

Be cool. Professional.

A couple deep breaths.

Everything could go to hell right here – all the planning, the big payoff, the sweet life in Cuba, if Harrigan wasn't careful.

'They're coming over here,' Kray said from the other window.

From behind them, a voice said: 'Well, let 'em in and kill 'em.'

Harrigan turned to see Cates standing there with a Walther in his hand.

'Sure,' Harrigan said. 'They walk in here and we kill them and that old lady across the street nails our ass for sure.'

'We'll be gone by then,' Cates said.

'You must've taken a couple extra stupid pills this morning, you dumb asshole,' Kray said. 'Kill a cop?' He shook his head in disgust.

'She's seen at least two of us,' Harrigan said, trying to

reason with Cates. 'She may even have seen Kray come in this morning.'

He let the drape fall back into place.

Harrigan said, 'My car's out in the garage. Here's the keys.'

He dug in his pocket and tossed the keys to Cates.

'You go out there and get in the trunk. Leave the keys on the back bumper.'

'Good idea,' Kray said.

'What if the cops check the car?' Cates objected.

'Why would they do that?' Harrigan said, tired of arguing. 'If they check out the house and you're gone, then they'll just think you took off.'

Kray was still at the window.

'They're coming up the walk now,' he said.

'Hurry up,' Harrigan said to Cates.

'I still say we should kill 'em. That way we could buy ourselves some time.'

'Right,' Kray said. 'And every cop in the city wanting to find us and kill us.'

The doorbell rang, a startlingly sweet and clear sound in this dusty old tract house.

Cates turned away, walked out of the living room.

Harrigan felt a momentary panic: what if the asshole decided not to go to the car?

But then Harrigan stopped worrying. So far anyway, Cates had gone along with everything Harrigan had told him to do. Harrigan was older and more experienced and, however reluctantly, Cates seemed to acknowledge this.

From the window, Kray said, 'The old lady went back inside.'

Harrigan nodded and went to the door. There was only one cop there.

The cop was a kid, no older than twenty-five, twenty-six at

most. He had a scrubbed face and pug nose. His attempt at a mustache was almost comic – a wispy pathetic little thing. But he had a gun and a badge and just because he looked like a rube didn't mean anything. A rube could kill you as fast as anybody else. He was probably a kid from one of the surrounding farm towns. Back there among the cornfields, he'd rented a lot of Dirty Harry movies and probably figured he'd give it a whirl himself.

But what really concerned Harrigan was the second cop. He was most likely walking around the house, checking things out. Would he check out the garage?

Kray hid behind the door.

Harrigan opened up and said, 'Afternoon, officer.' He spoke in a TV announcer voice, open and hearty and affable.

'Afternoon. I wondered if you'd seen a blond guy around here this morning.'

'Blond guy?'

The officer gave Harrigan a very good description of Cates.

'Boy, I haven't seen anybody like that, officer. I'm sorry.'

He could see that the kid didn't believe him.

'Do you live alone here, sir?'

'Yes, I do. Friend of mine's over here right now. But usually I'm alone.'

'You say the friend is here now?'

'Uh-huh.'

'Mind if I speak to him a minute?'

'Not at all. Would you like to come in?'

'Thanks. I'd appreciate that.'

He noticed how the kid's right hand was now resting on the handle of his .357 Magnum. His uniform smelled of rain.

The kid was scared. Harrigan didn't blame him. Harrigan thought about the second cop. Would he be reaching the garage just about now?

As the cop was entering the house, Kray went over and sat down in the worn crushed-velour recliner.

Kray didn't look anything like the description of Cates.

Kray said, 'Afternoon.'

'Afternoon,' the cop said.

The kid's face showed disappointment. He'd been expecting Cates.

'You're visiting your friend here—'

'Amory,' Kray said. 'He's Bob Amory, I'm Ken Devlin.'

'You're the only two people in the house?'

'That's right,' Harrigan said.

'You have a wife, Mr Amory?'

Harrigan said, 'Yes, but she's visiting her mother in Seattle.'

'I see.'

The kid kept looking around the living room, as if he was afraid he'd missed something the first couple of times he'd looked around.

'Do you know anybody who fits that description I gave you?' the kid said to Harrigan.

'Afraid I don't, sir.'

Harrigan could see that the kid had bought the old lady's story. Some old ladies could be very convincing. Apparently, the one across the street was very convincing indeed.

The kid looked as if he was going to stand here until something broke his way.

'How about you, Mr Devlin? Do you know anybody who fits that description?'

'Yeah, I do,' Kray said, smiling. 'But it's a she not a he. I don't think I'd want to know any guy who had long blond hair down to his shoulders.'

The kid just nodded. Kept looking around.

Then he got an idea. And his rube face was so easy to read, Harrigan could actually see him *getting* the idea.

The kid probably figured he was really smart.

'Boy, I hate to ask you this, but do you think I could use your john?'

'The john?' Harrigan said.

The kid nodded. He wore a rube grin now to convince them that his intentions were perfectly innocent.

What the hell, Harrigan thought. The house was empty. All the weaponry had been put away. So what if he used the john?

'You go right through that doorway there and to your left,' Harrigan said.

'Thanks. I appreciate it.'

The kid nodded and walked out of the room.

His shoes squeaked and his Sam Browne belt squeaked. All the time he walked, he kept that right hand of his riding on the handle of his Magnum.

Kray gave Harrigan the thumbs up.

Everything was cool.

Harrigan gave him the thumbs up back.

That was when they heard the shots from outside.

The cop said, 'What the hell!' and ran into the dining room. Harrigan looked out the window. The second cop lay near the clothes-line pole. He wasn't moving. Cates stood over him with a gun.

The cop in the dining room was starting through the back door. His gun was out.

'Hey!' Harrigan shouted.

The kid was stupid enough to turn around.

Even with the gun in his hand, he wasn't so hot. Harrigan shot him twice in the face and twice in the chest. Harrigan and Kray stepped over his body and went outside.

Harrigan knelt down next to the cop near the clothes-line.

Kray came over and stood above Harrigan and the cop.

Harrigan looked up and shook his head.

The cop's bowels had just given way. The stench was awful.

The cop just lay there, sobbing.

He kept saying the name, 'Kathy, Kathy, Kathy,' over and over again.

Kathy was probably his wife.

The cop's eyes came open.

He stared up at Harrigan.

All Harrigan could think of was Linda.

She probably looked just as scared as this cop did when she was on the operating table.

'Kathy,' the cop said.

He put a trembling hand up, as if beseeching help.

Harrigan took it, slid the hand into his.

He'd done this a lot in Nam, let people cross over to the other side holding his hand, even that frigging second lieutenant he'd hated so much.

Harrigan said, 'You're going to be fine.'

The cop started crying again.

'I won't see Kathy again, will I?'

'Sure you will.'

The cop held his hand tighter. He needed his wife or his father. Harrigan was a piss-poor substitute.

'You promise I'll see her?' the cop said.

'I promise,' Harrigan said.

The hand in his went limp.

'The sonofabitch is dead, isn't he?' Cates said.

Harrigan lowered the cop's hand and put it over his stomach. The blood hadn't soaked all the way down there yet.

'We've got to get out of here,' Kray said. 'Fast.'

'Yeah,' Harrigan said.

He stood up and turned around and faced Cates.

He caught Cates in the groin with the tip of his boot and just as Cates was starting to fold in half, Harrigan grabbed his long pretty hair and started banging Cates' head against the clothesline pole.

Kray grabbed Harrigan's shoulder and said, 'We're supposed to be the pros, remember? You're letting all this shit get to you.'

'Yeah, I am,' Harrigan said.

He let Cates crumple to the ground.

Then he kicked him hard in the leg.

'Get your ass up, Cates. Right now.'

Cates, holding his crotch in an agony of lancing pain, knew better than to argue.

Chapter Four

1

As Wendy DeVries would later recount it to both the police and her friends, she was just riding her ten-speed, doing her job, when this car forced her off the street and up onto the sidewalk.

Wendy was properly pissed off about it, and not scared in the least.

At nineteen, Wendy DeVries was working hard to keep a good grade average at the university. And fourteen hours a week, she rode a ten-speed for the RELIABLE MESSENGER SERVICE, which delivered various kinds of packages in the downtown area – packages, that is, that could fit in the large basket mounted on the bicycle.

When the sun was out, Wendy wore T-shirts with RELIABLE MESSENGER SERVICE on the back.

But on days like this one, when it rained, she wore a yellow slicker with the company name across the back.

She was wearing the slicker when she went up over the curb and nearly slammed into the electrical pole that had been planted in the concrete a few feet away from the mailbox.

She managed to bring her bike under control, and then turned to display her middle finger to the passing car.

But the passing car was no longer passing.

It was parked a few feet ahead of her, and a guy was just now getting out and walking toward her.

He was blond, handsome, well-dressed, and he carried a small box that was about the size of a hefty paperback book. It was wrapped festively in pink, reminding Wendy of a birthday gift. A small but elegant white ribbon topped it.

The man carried it inside his coat like a small animal he was trying to keep dry.

'I'm sorry if I scared you,' the man said.

'You didn't scare me.'

'Oh, good.'

'You pissed me off.'

The man looked genuinely surprised.

'Well, I'm sorry about that, too.'

'You could've hurt me.'

'I said I was sorry. I misjudged.'

He reached into the pocket of his tweed sport coat – real Irish tweed from what Wendy could see – and pulled out a piece of American currency.

She couldn't see the denomination.

'I'd like you to deliver something for me.'

'God, that's why you ran me off the road?'

'As I said, I didn't *mean* to run you off the road.'

'Why didn't you just call the office?'

'I'm in a hurry. I need to catch a plane.'

'Oh.'

Between his good looks, his sincere manner, and the currency he had slipped under the bottom of the box, the stranger had managed to calm her down.

'You want me to deliver that?'

'If you would.'

'Downtown here? I only work downtown.'

'Right in the middle of downtown. The District Attorney's office.'

Angry drivers had to pull their cars around the man's vehicle. He was parked in a NO PARKING zone, right beneath a sign proclaiming it, in fact. But he wasn't in the least intimidated by the looks and honks the drivers shot him. It was almost as if he didn't notice.

'Oh, right. I take stuff over there all the time.'

'And you could keep all the money for yourself,' the man said. 'I mean, your boss wouldn't even have to know about it.'

If her father hadn't been laid off from his engineering job four months ago, Wendy might have been a little more suspicious, might have asked a few more questions. But with federal government cutbacks, the defense industry had gone in the tank, and taken her father with it. He now worked as a bag boy twenty-two hours a week at a supermarket. Wendy needed all the money she could get to make it through college, and this was *with* her student loans.

The man took the note out from beneath the bottom of the box and handed it to her.

It was a fifty-dollar bill. A nice crisp one.

Wendy almost said, 'Wow!' But that would have been kind of unprofessional, she supposed.

Instead, she just acted cool and professional.

'The District Attorney's office is on two floors. Is there an address on this?'

He handed her the box.

It was very light.

The address read:

JESSICA DENNIS
4th Floor
County Court Bldg.

Wendy allowed herself to say, 'How come you're not delivering this yourself?'

'She's my cousin.'

'Who's your cousin?'

'Jessica Dennis.'

'And that's why you're not delivering it yourself?'

The man smiled. He had a TV commercial smile.

'I know it sounds crazy but we've been giving each other gag gifts since we were little kids. If she saw me up in her office, she'd know it was a gag for sure.'

'Oh.'

'This way, if the RELIABLE MESSENGER SERVICE delivers it, I mean – well, she wouldn't suspect I was behind it.'

'So this is a gag gift?' Wendy said, hefting it a little in her hand.

'Uh-huh.'

'What *kind* of gag gift?'

'It's a very realistic-looking snake.'

'A snake?'

'A rubber snake. You open the box and it springs right out at you. It'll terrify her. She hates snakes.'

'I hate snakes, too.'

'That's the point,' the man said. 'That's what'll make this so funny. How much Jess hates snakes, I mean.'

Wendy noted how the man had just referred to her as Jess, the way a real cousin probably would.

She rubbed the crisp fifty-dollar bill between her thumb and forefinger. She felt an almost sexual pleasure. Maybe that's how hookers felt every time they took money.

'Well,' she said. 'I guess I'll do it.'

'Oh great. Thanks so much. I've really got to get out to the airport now.'

He touched her arm.

'I'm sorry about running you off the road.'

'Oh,' she said, smiling, 'I guess I'll probably survive.'

He nodded and walked back to his car.

Wendy couldn't stop thinking about the almost obscene tactile pleasure she'd received from holding the fifty-dollar bill.

Wow.

2

Samantha didn't leave.

Jessica went back to work, scanning page after page of depositions, until she became aware that Samantha hadn't left yet.

'Is everything all right?'

Samantha leaned against the closed door.

'That's what I was wondering, Jessica.'

Jessica set down the paper she'd been reading and said, 'The message from the doctor's office.'

'Right.'

'You're worried that something's terribly wrong.'

'Right.'

'With me.'

'Right. We've had so much bad news today it just kind of scared me.'

'And you want me to tell you if something *is* wrong.'

'Right.'

'Nothing's wrong.'

'That's what they called you to say?'

'That's what they called me to say.'

'Do you mind if I ask what they *suspected* was wrong?'

'They just wanted to make sure of something.'

Samantha grinned. 'You know I'm not going to leave here till you tell me.'

Jessica smiled. 'That's what I figured.'

'You have a lot to do, and I have a lot to do, so it would be a shame if we wasted all this time just staring at each other.'

'They thought I might have an ulcer.'

'Oh God, my uncle's got an ulcer!'

'But it wasn't an ulcer.'

'No? So what was it?'

'You really aren't going to leave till I tell you, are you?'

'No, ma'am.'

Jessica laughed.

'You know how much I hate that "Ma'am" crap.'

'Yes, ma'am. I'm trying to *irritate* you into telling me what's going on.'

Jessica laughed again, couldn't help it.

'All right. I'll tell you. But it's strictly between us.'

'Strictly.'

'Scout's honor?'

Samantha held her three fingers up in the Girl Scout pledge.

'Scout's honor.'

'Well, now I guess I have to tell you, don't I? With the Scouts' honor stuff, and all.'

'Yes, ma'am, you do.'

So Jessica finally broke down and told her.

3

Father McGivern had just left, the old priest for whom Warden Atkinson had a lot of respect and affection.

Atkinson knew he should just let it slide.

A few hours, more or less, and Roy Gerard would be dead anyway.

It was the principle of it that bugged Atkinson.

You take an old guy like the priest who'd devoted his life to helping people for no money, no prestige, not even very many creature comforts.

You take an old priest like that, one who drove up here of his own volition every time one of the inmates was being put to death... the least you could give the guy was a little respect.

And, hell, Atkinson wasn't even a Catholic. If he was anything at all, he was a Lutheran, same as his parents had been.

But Lutheran, Jewish, Catholic, Buddhist... you still should pay Father McGivern his due. All the condemned men had, too. Until today.

Today he goes down to talk to Roy Gerard about spiritual matters and what does Gerard do? Says vile and contemptible things to the old priest. Things nobody should *ever* say to anybody.

But that was the Gerard brothers for you.

They might come from the upper classes but they were thorough-going white trash as far as Atkinson was concerned.

His intercom buzzed. Call on line two, he was told by the inmate who ran the prison switchboard.

He took the call.

And then he made another call.

And then he glanced at the afternoon's stack of mail set there neatly by the inmate who ran the mailroom.

All this took maybe twenty minutes, and Atkinson still couldn't get it out of his head.

How Roy Gerard had treated Father McGivern.

And the vile, filthy things he'd said.

The old priest had been in tears when he'd left Atkinson's office.

In god-damned *tears*.

Now the sensible thing, the smart thing to do was just to let it slide.

Because Roy Gerard really would be dead in another few hours here.

So Atkinson would let go of it for a few moments, set his mind to dealing with some other dilemma, but then he would come right back to it.

Because there was a principle involved.

A serious principle.

The guard said, 'Would you like me to come inside with you?'

'No thanks, Earl.'

The guard nodded, then stepped forward, inserted the key and opened the door for Atkinson.

Atkinson walked inside.

Roy Gerard was gone.

That was Atkinson's first impression, anyway. No sign of the prisoner anywhere.

Then Gerard stood up from behind the couch.

He held a shiny coin up for the Warden to see.

'My lucky quarter. Fell out of my hand and rolled away.'

The death-house waiting room always reminded Russ Atkinson of those shabby furnished rooms he'd been forced to live in during his college years. They'd been a lot less expensive than dorms, that was for sure.

He supposed he should try to fix it up a little but somehow he couldn't quite bring himself to do it. The men and women who were put to death generally deserved it. With tax money so hard to come by, why squander his budget on fixing up a room like this?

Gerard's face broke into his familiar, insolent smile.

'I'll bet I can guess why you're here.'

'Oh?'

'You're mad because of the way I treated that old faggot priest you sent down here.'

'He's not a faggot.'

'All priests are faggots. Don't you read the papers?'

Atkinson kept himself calm.

'You shouldn't have spoken to him that way.'

Gerard flipped his lucky coin in the air.

Roy and David Gerard were starkly different people. Physically, anyway. Roy was short and dark; David tall and blond. He used to be blond, anyway. Atkinson wondered what he'd look like when they finally caught up with him.

'I want you to write him a note of apology.'

Gerard kept on flipping his lucky coin.

'Sure you don't want me to write something on the blackboard a hundred times?'

'I'm serious, Gerard. I want you to write him a note.'

Gerard stopped flipping the coin. He turned to Atkinson, and scowled.

'What're you going to do to me if I don't?' He laughed. 'Execute me or something like that?'

Gerard came out from behind the couch. He walked over to Atkinson and said, directly into his face, 'You decided to turn this place into a finishing school?'

'He deserved better treatment.'

'You're breaking my fucking heart, Warden. You really are.'

'I expect you to write him that note.'

That was when Gerard spat in his face. A nice big gob of spit put right on the bridge of Atkinson's nose.

'That's my answer, Warden. You didn't seem to understand me before. So maybe you'll understand me now. I'm not going to write that old fucking faggot a note, you got me?'

Over the past three years, Atkinson had been going to the

health club three nights a week. During the last ten months in particular, he'd been working out with weights, and even doing a little boxing with big gloves and headgear.

All his life he'd been bullied. He'd decided he wouldn't be having any of that anymore.

He'd been wanting to test his strength and speed and punching power, but no appropriate moment had come along. A warden just couldn't go around hitting people.

Then Roy Gerard went and spat in his face.

Atkinson calmly took out his handkerchief from his back pocket and carefully wiped the spittle from his face.

Gerard watched, amused.

When his face was dry, and the handkerchief had been put away, Atkinson said, 'There's a pad and pen over there. Why don't you go write him a note?'

Gerard gave him a funny look and Atkinson had the terrible feeling that he was actually going to do that, walk over there and sit down and write a note.

And then where would Atkinson be?

Much as he might not want to admit it to himself, he'd pushed the priest thing because he sensed that it would give him the opportunity to do to Roy Gerard what he'd always wanted to do, the Gerard brothers being among the most vicious killers Atkinson had ever worked with. Sure, there really was a principle involved, and a principle that Atkinson devoutly believed in, but there was also a pretext, one that would enable Atkinson to do what he'd been wanting to do all along.

'Fuck yourself, Warden,' Gerard said.

It was a darned good punch.

It was delivered underhanded, starting maybe six inches back of Atkinson's right ribcage.

It came up at about an 80-degree angle and it was aimed on

RUNNER IN THE DARK

a perfect trajectory for Gerard's solar plexus.

Gerard was mean but he wasn't savvy.

He got a glimpse of the punch just before it landed. He tried to sidestep it but it was too late.

The punch got him squarely in the solar plexus and landed strong enough that it slammed him back against the wall, where his head nicked the edge of a framed photograph of the Governor.

Gerard looked shocked.

Guards, you expected this kind of thing from. But wardens?

Atkinson wanted to keep on going, of course. He had all sorts of punches he wanted to try out. Fighting somebody in a gym with balloon gloves and headgear was one thing. But fighting somebody for real was another.

Atkinson hadn't felt this exhilarated since the snowy night when, at age twenty-two in the back seat of his ten-year-old Chevrolet, he'd lost his virginity.

Then Gerard pleased and delighted him in the most unexpected way.

He stood up straight and threw a right-handed haymaker at the Warden's head.

He missed.

But more importantly, he gave Atkinson the opportunity to deliver one more punch.

Atkinson coolly decided on trying another body shot, a rib shot this time, the sort of rib shot that 'Smokin' Joe Frazier' used to deliver, the kind that broke bones.

Atkinson threw his rib shot, an arcing left that landed hard and fast right in the middle of the cage.

Gerard pleased him by crying out.

Perfect, Atkinson thought, feeling fifteen years old.

Then he couldn't stop himself.

He had to throw one more punch.

Gerard was no longer Gerard. Now he was every bully Atkinson had ever had to face, every bully who had ever mocked ugly kids or fat kids or black kids or deformed kids or girly boys or boyish girls; every bully who had ever stolen lunch money or made kids pay protection money or torn up your homework just before you were due to hand it in.

He started to throw the punch.

It was a right hand aimed directly at Gerard's jaw.

Atkinson got his right arm cocked.

And was all ready to send Gerard the knockout blow—

When somebody grabbed his hand.

Stopped him from throwing it.

A moment of confusion.

Atkinson started to spin around and see who was behind him.

Earl the guard stood there.

'Probably not a real good idea, sir,' Earl said. 'This is the kind of thing the ACLU would have your job over.'

It was like *coitus interruptus*.

Here he'd been about to smash Gerard's jaw and—

Reality.

He was the Warden.

He was standing here breathing hard, his clothes disheveled.

Highly inappropriate. Highly.

'Thanks, Earl.'

'You're welcome, sir.'

People thought that just because Earl Sumner was as big as a mountain, and had a slight Kentucky drawl, he was an idiot. Not so. Earl had his BA in criminology and was taking night-school courses toward his MA.

'You sonofabitch,' Roy Gerard said, infuriated now that he'd been humiliated.

'Too bad we never got a chance to go a few rounds in the gym,' Atkinson said.

Then he preceded Earl out the door.

Atkinson was smiling. Right now, he was a very happy man. A very happy man.

4

The cops had gotten Kandi's address from an unnamed entry in Tom Culligan's address book under the letter 'K.'

By now, Ribicoff's throat was sore. He'd been fighting a cold for several days, he explained to Jessica as he sat on the other side of her desk.

'I sent a car over to her place,' he said hoarsely. 'There's no answer on the phone.'

'The diet.'

'Pardon?'

'The diet. That's what did it.'

'The woman, you mean?'

'Uh-huh. He's been heavy-set all his life and now that he's thin—' She shook her head. 'I just hope his wife doesn't find out.'

'You know her?'

'A little bit. She's a nice woman. And he's got two very nice kids.'

Thunder shook the sky.

Dark, dreary day.

Even the fiercest of office lighting seemed dim and inadequate on a day like this.

Jessica had to fight against feeling that way herself. First her dilemma with Michael – he really did love her; he really did want to marry her; she really was afraid of his alcoholism

– and now this with Tom Culligan.

Jessica had been married briefly right out of law school. He'd been one of those anachronisms who'd expected all his wife's plans to be secondary to his own.

He wanted a family, which meant he expected Jessica not to sign on with a law firm, but to stay home and have babies.

He wanted to impress his own clients, which meant he required Jessica to be a combination interior decorator and chef.

He wanted Jessica to remain incurious about his occasional late nights, his occasional lipstick stains.

She tried on two different occasions to forgive him his assignations. The third time, it was impossible. That, and his unrealistic preferences for her future, caused her to file for divorce.

She was heartbroken for nearly a year, not dating, not even seeing many of her old friends, simply burying herself in casework.

She wondered about Tom Culligan's wife, how she would handle Tom's being unfaithful.

'Kandi,' she said.

' "But liquor is quicker," ' Ribicoff smiled.

'What?'

'Dorothy Parker,' Ribicoff said. ' "Candy is dandy but liquor is quicker." I just read a biography of her.'

'I hope Tom comes to his senses before it's too late. He needs his wife much more than he realizes, I think. Right now he's strutting around in that brand-new body of his and forgetting about all the things he's got in his life.'

She'd noticed this in Tom's work, too.

Tom used to be the great compromiser.

He'd avoid confrontation by finding a middle ground that you could both accept. This was a vital role in a DA's office.

RUNNER IN THE DARK

You had a lot of bright, egotistical people running head-on into each other.

There had to be somebody who could step back and look at the whole process for the greater good.

Until recently, that had been Tom.

Until recently.

A knock.

Samantha put her pretty head between door and frame.

'Detective Ribicoff, there's a call for you. You can take it out here if you'd like.'

'Thank you.'

Jessica gestured at the stacks of case documents on her desk.

'Don't worry about me,' she said. 'I have a few little things to catch up on.'

Detective Ribicoff excused himself and followed Samantha out the door.

Jessica returned to work immediately. And intensively.

She didn't even notice Samantha come back in, a few minutes later.

Didn't notice her setting a small pink box on the corner of her desk.

Didn't notice her standing there expectantly, waiting for Jessica to look at the box and open it up.

'Ahem,' Samantha said.

Jessica looked up. 'Oh, hi.'

'Hi.'

'Didn't see you there.'

'I know.'

Jessica glanced at the gift-size box. 'What's this?'

'They brought this up from security downstairs,' Samantha said. 'It passed through the metal detector and everything, so they said to bring it up to you.'

'Thanks, Samantha,' Jessica said.

And promptly returned to studying her casework.

'Ahem.'

Jessica looked up. 'Yes?'

'I can't believe you're not going to open it.'

Jessica laughed. 'Like Christmas morning, huh?'

'Exactly. Gifts are meant to be opened.'

Jessica put her hand out. 'They've screened this?'

'Uh-huh.'

Jessica picked up the package and held it to her nose. 'I don't think it's perfume.'

Held it to her ear. 'Don't think it's a sea shell.'

Held it out in front of her. Stared at it. 'If only I had X-ray vision.'

'Of course, you could always just *open* it.'

'Maybe you're onto something there, Sam.'

But just as Jessica was starting to take the ribbon off the top of the package, Detective Ribicoff appeared.

'I told you I'd sent a car over to the woman's address?'

'Yes,' Jessica said.

'I just heard from the patrolman. He found two people dead in the shower. From his description, this sounds like your friend Culligan.'

'My God,' Jessica said.

'I'll leave you two alone,' Samantha said.

She hurried out of the office, looking as if she might cry at any time. She and Tom Culligan had been good friends.

'Gerard,' Detective Ribicoff said. 'David Gerard.'

Then he saw the package.

'What's this?'

'A gift. Probably from my friend Michael.'

'Went through the metal detector?'

'Uh-huh.'

Detective Ribicoff stared as Jessica picked it up to finish unwrapping it.

'Why don't you let me do that, Jessica?'

He didn't wait for an answer.

He leaned across her desk and took the small box gently from her fingers.

He sat down, set the package on the desk, took out a pocket knife, thumbed out the long blade, and then proceeded to do his work.

He took the ribbon off, set it politely on the desk, and then got busy on the wrapping and the box itself.

Inside, the box was plain white. Nothing remarkable at all.

Detective Ribicoff opened it up and looked inside.

'Did Culligan wear a ring?' he said softly.

'Yes. Why?'

'A Northwestern ring?'

'Yes, but I don't—'

'I'm afraid Tom Culligan is probably dead.'

'What?' said Jessica. 'Why?'

'Our friend David Gerard just sent us another message,' Detective Ribicoff said.

He put the lid back on the box before Jessica could see the contents. A bloody ring finger that had been violently severed at the joint lay on soft white wrapping paper.

A Northwestern class ring still sat on the finger.

Tom's ring.

Chapter Five

1

The interview was going pretty well. The reporter asked all the expected questions – how long have you been a journalist; how did you get to be an anchorman; do you miss working for a newspaper – and then he brought up the subject of Viet Nam.

'Your two best friends died over there with you, didn't they?' Frank Michener said from the other end of the phone.

Frank Michener was a senior at Andicott High School. He was also editor of the student newspaper. He was writing profiles of all four local news anchors. He'd called in advance to set the interview up.

Maybe it was the rainy day; maybe it was the uncertain turn his relationship with Jessica had taken; or maybe it was because, at the AA meeting this lunchtime, he'd flashed on the faces of his buddies in Nam. Whatever was bothering him, his mood had turned melancholy, even angry.

'Yeah,' Michael Shaw said. 'They did.'

'Would you care to talk about that?'

'You really think it's germane to the story?'

'I think for this kind of story, it is.'

Shaw was impressed with Michener's poise. He was polite but firm, the way a good reporter needed to be.

Shaw sighed.

'I'll try to make it fast for you.'

'I'm not in any hurry, sir.'

So Shaw told him how it had happened back there so long ago.

Shaw and his two friends had been fighting in the trenches for nearly two weeks. The VC kept up steady rocket attacks. American casualties had been high. Six of the men Shaw had gone through boot with were killed during that two-week period. It was the typical military situation, alternating between terror and boredom. The name of the place was Mole City, so nicknamed because of all the trenches the Americans had dug.

A new commander was installed. He started rotating the trench troops to Tay Ninh, a city with half a million population. It wasn't Saigon but it tried. Girls, booze and drugs were not exactly unheard of here.

There was a twelve-story hotel downtown where the best girls operated. Clark and Parker, his two best friends from college, men who believed in supporting their country in every situation, spent one steamy July night in the hotel. Shaw was supposed to go along but he'd been detained at the base.

By the time he reached downtown, he learned that Clark and Parker were being held hostage by three very angry VC who'd snuck into the room, killed the hookers and then announced to Tay Ninh police that the Americans would be killed if four VC prisoners weren't released immediately.

Shaw knew that the American Commander would never give in to this kind of blackmail.

He also knew that his friends were pretty much dead already. No way would the VC ever let them walk out of that tenth-story hotel room alive.

That's when Shaw got the idea about suspending a rope

RUNNER IN THE DARK

from the hotel roof and working his way down two floors to the four-foot ledge on the tenth floor. If he went the back way, maybe he could sneak onto the floor without being seen, then work over to the south end where Clark and Parker were being held. Worth a try, at any rate.

What he hadn't counted on – nor had anybody warned him about it – was the fanatical dispositions of these particular VCs. All religions have their zealots, and these men certainly qualified as that.

They had warned several times that if anybody attempted to rescue the hostages, the VC would blow up the entire floor.

Pretty much what hostage-takers always say to impress the police with their determination. Standard issue. Or so everybody thought.

The funny thing was, Shaw was usually afraid of heights, but that night he didn't seem to notice how far above the ground he swung on his rope.

Armed with a pistol in his holster, a rifle strapped to his back, and a knife jammed down the waistband of his trousers, he lowered himself to the tenth floor. The mosquitoes had a feast at his expense. The emergency lights below glittered like blood rubies.

He managed to reach the ledge without being spotted, then crawl inside an open window and start his way down the dark corridor. He could hear the VC shouting commands and curses to the Tay Ninh police below.

He eased his way toward the southernmost section of the hotel, moving slowly, carefully, at one with the deep shifting shadows.

He didn't see the VC until it was too late – a trim little man in a yellow shirt and blue trousers.

The VC had just turned the corner.

He had a pistol in his hand.

But he wasn't as fast as Shaw.

Shaw pumped off three quick shots but, quick as they were, the VC still had time to cry out.

Moments later, Shaw – who was walking over the dead VC and moving once again to where his friends were being held captive – realized the captors hadn't been bluffing.

An explosion more volcanic than Shaw had ever experienced turned his world into one of searing fire, gagging smoke, crashing ceilings, floors opening up earthquake-style.

They had made good on their threat to set off a bomb if anybody tried to save the captives.

Shaw was in surgery for eleven hours. It was two weeks before he could feed himself, two months before he could walk upright, four months before he could even begin to deal with his depression.

No matter who tried to comfort him, no matter who tried to persuade him that his feelings of guilt were misplaced, Shaw believed that if he hadn't been playing hero that night, his friends would be alive today.

Should have let the police handle it.

Should never have roped it down to the tenth floor and snuck in.

Should never ...

This was when he began to drink.

Stateside, his folks and his friends figured it was just a phase, the drinking.

Viet Nam had traumatized a lot of young American men and women.

But they'd get over it. In time.

Shaw became a print reporter. In five years, he worked on three newspapers, getting promoted at each of them. Then he heard the siren call of TV and signed on as an investigative reporter ...

Then he met Jessica Dennis and she helped him face up to his problem. But then his brother died six months ago – his only brother, older, a man with whom he'd had a troubled and turbulent relationship – and he'd made the mistake of slipping into a bar ... made the mistake of thinking that after a two-year stint on the wagon he could take just one little drink ... made the mistake of foolishly kidding himself.

He went on a short bender.

His relationship with Jessica hadn't been the same since.

Given her own background with alcoholism, he had managed to profoundly shake her faith in him and his ability to stay dry.

He didn't tell all this to the high-school reporter, of course.

He stuck to the story about Clark and Parker dying.

Frank Michener said, 'Were you scared when you were in Viet Nam?'

'All the time.'

'Really?'

'Really. Because you never knew when a VC was suddenly going to show up. You could be walking down the street or taking a nap or reading a newspaper from back home – and then some guy would walk in, some guy who looked just like everybody else, and lob a grenade into the middle of the room.'

'Wow. I really appreciate this – Michael.'

Shaw smiled. He'd told the boy to call him by his first name. Michener was still uncomfortable about it.

'If I have any follow-up questions, is it all right if I call you back?'

'Sure. And by the way, Frank, you did a great job.'

'I did?'

'You sure did.'

'Wow. Thanks.'

'And tell your journalism teacher I said so.'

Frank laughed. 'Don't worry. I will.'

Michael was just hanging up when a reporter stuck his head round the office door and said, 'You know Tom Culligan in Jessica's office?'

'What about him?' Shaw said.

'Found dead in some babe's apartment. In the shower. They were scalded with hot water and then shot to death.'

'Thanks for telling me,' Shaw said.

He picked up the receiver and called Jessica immediately.

2

Harrigan found an empty park by the river, and a pavilion up on a hill. He pulled in beside it.

There was a pay phone in the pavilion. Harrigan went straight to it. He wanted to leave the mobile phone-line free in case Gerard called in.

He was still shaking from the killing back at the house. Now he had crossed the line from being a mercenary to a criminal. There was no going back now.

Sirens could be heard in the distance by the time they were less than two blocks away.

Damn David Gerard anyway, hiring some cowboy like Cates.

He got the operator and asked for Linda's room number.

He didn't know what he'd say.

He was terrible at small talk.

The line was busy.

'Shit,' he said.

When he got back to the car, he saw that Cates was sitting on the edge of a picnic table, talking to Kray.

'I didn't have no choice,' Cates said.

'Sure you had a choice.'

'Harrigan shouldn't have let him in the house in the first place.'

'What was he supposed to do? Tell him he couldn't come in?'

Not only was Cates a screw-up, he was also a whiner, which was very hard to take.

Harrigan checked his watch.

'You'd better be heading out,' he said to Kray.

'Yeah. Gotta check out the chopper.'

'You got our mobile phone number?'

Kray nodded. Glanced at Cates. The younger man had his head down, sulking.

'Cates has some disguises for you,' Kray said. Then he gestured at Cates, unseen, and made a face. *Go easy on him*, he was saying. *We need him.*

Harrigan agreed. Cates, up to it or not, was a vital part of the whole operation.

'We'll be all right,' Harrigan said calmly. 'Cates and I know what we're doing.'

Cates looked up. He'd been almost pathetically taken with Harrigan's words.

Kray pointed to his car. He'd followed Harrigan out there.

'You get nervous right before it starts?'

'Yeah,' Harrigan said, 'but it's a good nervous.'

'I know what you mean.'

Cates said, 'I don't get nervous. I just don't let shit get to me.'

Kray smiled.

'You got more balls than we do, kid, that's for sure.' He raised his hand in goodbye. 'Well, be seeing you two later.'

Relieved that Harrigan wasn't going to rag on him anymore, Cates said, 'How's that daughter of yours doing?'

'I'm going to call again and find out.'

'Maybe I'll try on some of that disguise stuff. I've got a whole bag of it.'

'Great,' Harrigan said. 'I'll try mine on when I get back.'

Cates hopped down from the picnic table. The pavilion looked gray and lonely on a day like this. There should be watermelon and corn on the cob and beer and fiddle music and little kids running around.

'I'll be right back,' Harrigan said to Cates.

Harrigan dialed the number again. When the operator came on, he asked for his daughter's room.

After a moment, he said, 'Damn.'

The line was still busy.

Linda's mother was probably calling her relatives all over the country.

Harrigan went back to the car and tried on a couple of disguises.

He ended up with a short curly blond wig, a sandy-colored mustache, and a pair of wire-rimmed tinted glasses.

Cates at least knew what he was doing with disguises.

Harrigan looked like an overfed English teacher who wished that 1968 would come back real soon.

All he needed was a joint and some sitar music.

3

The man watched Dwiggins and Ward pull into the visitor's parking space where a tall man in a topcoat now stood. He wore a snap-brim fedora, like a thirties private eye. Every few minutes, the topcoated man reached into his pocket, took out a small walkie-talkie and talked to someone. He was a detective. He'd been sent on ahead to check out the auditorium and the

RUNNER IN THE DARK

parking facilities. The Police Commissioner wanted Ward's safety to be a guaranteed thing.

Dwiggins and Ward spoke to the policeman for a minute, and then went on into the redbrick auditorium that sat up on a grassy incline. A maintenance garage lay a hundred yards to the west. At this time of day, everybody was out working. The garage was empty.

The man waited until Dwiggins and Ward had been gone a few minutes before he went into action.

He emerged from the library, where he'd been watching the topcoat for the past twenty minutes.

He came down the three wide steps of the library and started walking briskly toward the parking lot.

He appeared to be a nice, normal person on his way to get his car from the lot.

He walked a ways past Topcoat, not paying him any obvious attention, but making certain that Topcoat had seen him.

When he got close to a gray Ford, he started to stumble, and then grabbed his chest.

Heart attack.

He fell to the ground.

Fewer than five seconds had passed before he heard the policeman's shoes slapping the concrete.

'Are you all right? Are you all right?' the policeman said as he neared the fallen man.

What an idiot, the man thought.

If I was all right, would I be lying on the concrete?

The policeman bent to check out the man more closely and that was when the man took a small can from his jacket pocket and sprayed the policeman's face.

David Gerard moved quickly.

He was up off his feet and grabbing Topcoat before he could fall to the ground.

Gerard put his arm through Topcoat's arm and started walking him quickly toward the maintenance garage, all the while scanning the surrounding area for any watching eyes.

But everybody was inside the auditorium.

After the seminar, Dick Ward, Jessica Dennis' favorite Assistant DA, called the office to see if there were any messages for him. There weren't. He said he'd be back in the office as soon as he and his police escort could get there.

Ward still felt kind of strange walking around with his robot-like police bodyguard.

The cop, whose name was Dwiggins, was not exactly good at small talk.

Driving over here from the DA's office to the meeting, Ward had tried a number of subjects on Dwiggins but had earned little more than a grunt or two.

Summer baseball didn't do it; the pending probe into police corruption didn't do it; the upcoming presidential election didn't do it.

Dwiggins of the rust-colored crew-cut and the ash-stained gray topcoat was your basic quiet guy.

But Ward was tireless.

He decided he'd give it one more try.

'Boy, some of those young college girls make you wish you were twenty again, don't they?'

Ward had spent the last hour talking to twenty-eight paralegals about what to concentrate on in their classes. There had been a high proportion of good-looking young women. Ward was a resolutely faithful husband but every now and then he daydreamed of being a stud, something he hadn't been even when young.

As soon as they got outside the building, Dwiggins lit up.

The light rain didn't deter him. He kept his big hand cupped over the Pall Mall.

'I suppose you've heard those are bad for you,' Ward said, smiling.

'Yeah, my eight-year-old daughter tells me every day.'

'You ever tried to quit?'

Dwiggins shrugged. 'I tried.'

'Didn't do any good, huh?'

'For a few months, it did. Then I woke up in the middle of one night, and I just *had* to have one. Had to. So then I was off to the races again.'

Ward had another flutter of nostalgia as he saw a group of laughing coeds come down the sidewalk. There were six of them and they were fighting for space under the two umbrellas. Their laughter was as precious as the finest silver, girlish and pure and free, and yet faintly imbued with eroticism all the same.

Oh, to be twenty years old again . . .

Every speaker who addressed the class got one of the fountain pens that all the paralegal classes chipped in to buy.

Pam Swanson was supposed to have given Richard Ward his fountain pen after he finished talking to the class.

But she hadn't yet worked up the nerve to approach him, she'd been so taken with him. Pam always figured that she had these mad crushes on older men because her father had walked out on her and her mother eighteen years ago. Pam was presently nineteen years old.

She wanted the approval of older men.

Cute older men.

And Richard Ward certainly qualified as that.

Now that she'd worked up enough courage, she had to give him his fountain pen.

And now she was running breathlessly after him.
Down the steps to the ground floor.
Across the lobby to the front doors.
Down the front steps.
Down the sidewalk.
Hurry. Hurry.
Hurry.

As they left the auditorium and neared the car, Detective Dwiggins looked around for sight of the topcoated detective who was guarding the vehicle.

There he was, several yards down the sidewalk, his back to them. He was hunched over, using his walkie-talkie.

Dwiggins figured everything was fine.

Inside the maintenance garage, behind three large oil drums, the detective squirmed and fought against the ropes that bound his wrists and ankles, against the gag that stopped him from calling for help.

He was cold, too.

The bastard had taken his topcoat and snap-brim fedora.

'Sometimes I think I enjoy cigarettes more than I enjoy sex,' Detective Dwiggins was saying to Richard Ward as they reached the visitor's section of the parking lot.

Ward had finally found a subject that made Dwiggins talkative. Cigarettes, for God's sake.

'I mean, if I let myself, I could smoke three packs a day.'

'Wow.'

'If I *let* myself. But I don't. I try to hold it down to one pack a day.'

'Well, that's better than three, anyway.'

They had reached Ward's red BMW sedan.

He knew that BMWs were sort of a cliché among people of his age and income bracket but he liked them. This was the fastest, smoothest, safest car he'd ever owned.

He climbed in and then reached over to open the passenger door for Dwiggins.

Dwiggins called out, 'Two more drags, then I'll get inside.'

'They're your lungs,' Ward said, feeling sorry for the guy because he was obviously so *addicted*.

Ward fixed himself behind the wheel and inserted the key.

As she ran towards Richard Ward's expensive new car, Pam Swanson wondered if she dared ask him if she could visit his office sometime.

Get a very personal tour from Ward himself.

Would she have nerve enough to ask?

He really *was* cute.

The passenger had just gotten into the car, and closed the door, when it happened.

Pam Swanson would never forget what she saw in the next few moments.

The car exploded.

There was no other way to say it.

The entire car disintegrated before her eyes.

Where there had been silence, there was now rumbling, terrifying thunder.

Where there had been metal and rubber and safety glass, there was now rolling yellow flames and curling, crawling gray smoke.

One or both of the men screamed and cried out for help.

Glass shattered.

The gas tank added a second explosion moments later.

Torn metal fell from the sky and clattered to the parking lot below.

Dozens of people came running from the nearest buildings, shocked, horrified.

Through the snapping flames, and the curling gray smoke, Pam could see that the BMW had been reduced to its frame and four wheels.

Nothing else was left standing.

She brought her hand up to her face and looked at the honorarium.

Poor Mr Ward.

He'd been so cute.

And nice.

And he hadn't even gotten his fountain pen.

Part Three

Chapter One

1

About fifteen minutes after Dick Ward's death had been confirmed, the press arrived at the District Attorney's office.

Samantha and her two assistants were enlisted to keep the over-eager journalists at bay. Samantha was a master at seeming to answer questions without actually imparting any information at all.

Word spread quickly through the office to take the back way down when going home tonight.

Early darkness filled the windows.

The rain, which had abated at various times today, was back now in full force, as if it had taken a nap and felt full of piss and vinegar.

Jessica gave up trying to get any work done.

Instead, she spent most of her time on the phone with various people she knew in the bomb squad, trying to determine if they'd discovered anything important yet.

No luck.

About all that was known for sure was that the bomb had been large enough to easily take out two cars.

There'd been little left of Dick Ward's BMW, and even less of Ward himself. Same for the policeman.

The only comforting thing, said her contact at the bomb squad, is that they'd probably died pretty quickly. The force of the explosion combined with the flames meant quick death.

Jessica doubted that the families of Ward or the policeman would be much comforted by this.

An All Points Bulletin had been announced again for David Gerard. They'd found the bicycle messenger, Wendy DeVries, and gotten a good description of him.

The most interesting bit of news came from the murder of a young police officer earlier this afternoon, over in a northwest-side neighborhood.

A neighbor had reported a murder suspect staying in a house across the street. The young police officer had gone over to check it out. He'd been killed along with his partner.

The house was empty by the time reinforcements arrived, but the homicide detective in charge of the investigation felt that there was a connection between this murder and David Gerard. The man may even have had a hand in it.

But nothing was definite, of course.

Right at 4:30, line one rang.

Knowing that Samantha was busy keeping the reporters at bay, Jessica picked up herself.

'District Attorney's office.'

'Hi. It's me.'

'Hi, Michael. It's a zoo here.'

'I just heard about Dick Ward.'

'I still haven't made it past Tom Culligan yet.'

'I hope the police are all over up there.'

'They are. Don't worry – we're very well protected.' Then: 'I'm looking forward to seeing you tonight. I – there's something we need to talk about. Something I haven't told you about yet.'

'Deep, dark and mysterious?'
She laughed.
'Well, something like that.'
'I don't even get a hint?'
'Not even a hint.'
'You're a cruel woman.'
'DAs have to be cruel. Don't you know that?'
'I'm worried about you.'

'I'll be fine, really. Once the execution's over – I think David Gerard will give up. I just can't believe what the Culligans and the Wards are going through. They had seven young children between them.'

'Well, at least David Gerard will save the state the expense of executing him.'

'I agree. He's going to die in a shoot-out of some kind.'

'I'd be sure and point out all these killings tonight at the debate.'

'The last thing I want to do right now is go to this debate. Tom's dead, Dick's dead... Michael, I've worked with these people for *years* and now they're gone... both brutally murdered in one day. I can't believe this is all happening. If the debate wasn't being picked up nationally by CNN I'd cancel the whole thing right now.'

'Yeah, I know how you must feel. But you're right, it's too late to get out of it. And I know you'll do a great job.'

'I hope so. And I'm told the priest is a real sweetheart.'

'Father Josek?' Shaw said. 'Yeah, he is. We've had him on other shows. He isn't a far-right nutcase. He's actually a very sensible and very decent guy. But you can't worry about him during the debate. You're there to argue your case.'

'I know. But that's why I hate things like this. You forget you're arguing with human beings. You start saying things to win no matter how they hurt the other person.'

He laughed.

'You keep on talking like that, the voters won't return you to office next time.'

'I know.'

'Are we still on for dinner?' Shaw said.

'Our friend Detective Ribicoff is bringing me something from the deli. After what happened to Dick Ward, Sam says he's going to be my personal bodyguard.'

'He's a good man.'

'He sure is.'

'I can't wait to see you, Jess.' Then: 'I sure hope we can work things out.'

'So do I, Michael. So do I.'

'God, you haven't said that in a long time.'

Pause.

'I love you, Michael. More than ever.'

'I love you, too, Jess. With all my heart.'

When she hung up, she was surprised to find she had tears in her eyes.

That was the sweetest conversation she'd had with Michael in weeks.

Maybe they really were going to get past this thing.

Maybe she really was going to learn to trust him again.

She hoped so.

She'd never loved anybody as much as she loved Michael.

And she doubted that she'd ever find anybody to replace him.

She got up from her desk and went to her door.

She wanted to peek out and listen to see if the press were still in the lobby.

Oh, they were there all right.

Samantha said, 'Now, you just sit down in your chairs and please be quiet. Please.'

She sounded like a teacher dealing with an unruly class of first-graders.

2

The big commercial airports didn't excite Kray much. Too many people, too much congestion, the whole idea of flying got lost in all the rush and noise of it all.

But now, as Kray drove his rental Pontiac into the small private airport on the western edge of the city, he felt as always the old thrill of flying.

His Uncle Ron had run just such an airport. Uncle Ron had basically raised him. Kray's parents were nightclub entertainers who were gone most of the time. Even when he saw them, they weren't particularly warm. They invariably doted on his good looks, his good grades, and his social skills. A perfect little gentleman, as they liked to say. But they never asked about him, what he liked, what he wanted to do with his life, did he ever get lonely, did he ever miss them . . . that they left to Uncle Ron and his endless string of girlfriends.

Uncle Ron's taste in ladies had been as good as his taste in airplanes. The women were not only physically attractive but they were bright, considerate and usually lots of fun. They also enjoyed flirting with Kray, especially as he got older. Kray had grown up hoping that Uncle Ron would marry at least one of them but he never did.

He was the same way with airplanes.

The *next* plane he bought, that was the one that was going to be the best plane he'd ever had.

And it always was.

For a month or two.

Then he'd start looking around again.

There was this new Cherokee.

Or he'd seen a brochure on the Aztec.

Or this guy had been telling him all about the new turbo-prop Merlin.

Planes and girlfriends.

Uncle Ron had had at least three new ones a year.

Six years ago, Uncle Ron had died of heart disease. Still been a relatively young guy, too. Fifty-nine.

Kray thought of him now as he pulled his car into an empty slot near one of the hangars.

In the darkening day, the rain silver and slanting and cold, the office looked snug and warm.

There'd be coffee brewing and music low on the radio and the voices of pilots upstairs talking about how nice it would be to get down out of this soup.

Well, for Kray, a long, long night lay ahead.

He pulled in, killed the headlights and engine, and then got out into the rain.

The hangar with the helicopter was open. A mechanic in overalls was giving a Bell Jet Ranger a going-over. Presumably this was the machine Kray was to have for tonight.

A charter service like this one was only as good as its mechanics.

The hangar smelled of oil and gasoline. There was an old Piper Cub in the far corner. A workbench was cluttered with tools of various kinds.

Kray watched the middle-aged guy. He had a little pot belly and his head shone from baldness and he liked country music – a radio bawling out some cornball lyrics – but all you had to do was watch his wrists and fingers to know that he was one of the brotherhood, one of the people who believed that flying was still a holy calling.

The guy was definitely doing it right.

Kray just stood there, impressed.

Guy greased the main rotor. Changed the oil. Walked around the machine three times checking and double-checking all the stress points.

With the money he and Harrigan were going to take from the Gerard brothers tonight, Kray was definitely going to get himself a machine like this when they ended up in Cuba.

Probably pick up a damned good one cheap from Mr Castro himself. Word was, Mr Castro was selling a lot of his excess military hardware for very reasonable prices.

A nice flying machine, an endless supply of lovely young Cuban women . . .

He smiled at himself.

God, he was turning out just like his Uncle Ron.

Probably trade the flying machine in for a different one every four, five months.

Probably trade the ladies in a little more often.

There was sure to be a nice supply of them down there.

'You really know what you're doing,' Kray said when the mechanic finally took note of his presence.

'Thanks. I like to think I do, anyway.'

'My name's Runyon,' Kray said. 'Is that my machine?'

'It sure is. We're a little worried about the weather, but given your experience, everything should be all right.'

'Right. Plus the latest word from the weather bureau is that this is all going to end in another hour or so.'

'Great,' the mechanic said.

Kray had called the weather bureau ten times so far today. Weather was a critical factor in the whole plan for tonight. Critical.

Rain wouldn't scrub the mission.

But rain sure wouldn't make it any easier.

'Guess I'll go in the office and get all the paperwork done.'
The mechanic shook his head.
'Mr Forbes already left for the evening. I'll have to do the paperwork. Tell you what, there's a pot of coffee in there. You go have yourself a cup and give me another ten minutes and I'll be along. All right?'
'Fine.'
Kray went back out into the rain. It was very cold now, the gathering night.

Since he had time to kill, he decided to stop by the car and pick up the maps he'd need tonight, and study them some more.

A good pilot always knew exactly where he was headed.

And tonight demanded precision.

Kray had flown some toughies before but none like this. At several points in the mission, there would be other people and planes eager to shoot him down. Kray had never faced guns before. Not up in the air, anyway.

His only concern was the kid, Cates.

David Gerard had sure chosen a bad one there, no doubt about it.

But if anybody could keep Cates in line it was somebody like Harrigan.

The longer Kray knew Harrigan, the spookier the other guy became.

Here was a man who was capable of *anything*.

That's why the thing about his daughter was so oddly touching.

Murderous sonofabitch like Harrigan . . . and then you see him almost in tears when he's on the phone talking to the hospital.

Yeah, if anybody could keep some punk like Cates in line, it was Harrigan all right.

Kray collected his maps and his coordinates, and then went inside the office and studied them.

3

The call came just before five.

On the intercom, Samantha said, 'Line one, Jessica. It's Michelle Culligan.'

Oh God, Jessica thought.

'All right. Thanks.'

She reached out for the receiver but then stopped herself. What was she going to say? Michelle would want comfort, reassurance. But what comfort and reassurance could Jessica possibly give?

It wasn't only that Tom Culligan had been murdered.

It was also *where* he'd been murdered.

Naked, and in the shower of the woman who was apparently his mistress.

She took a deep breath.

Lifted the receiver.

Punched line one.

'Hello, Michelle.'

'Hi, Jessica. I – I just wanted to talk to you.'

'You know how sorry I am.'

'They're really animals, aren't they – the Gerard brothers, I mean. Tom always said that, about them being animals. And he was right. I just don't know why they had to kill him.'

'During the trial, Roy Gerard always said that we had no right to try them. That because of the way their parents treated them – the sexual abuse and everything else the brothers alleged – we had no right to try them for what they'd done.'

Michelle started crying.

'They're animals.'

'Yes, they are. And they're going to pay for it. Roy Gerard will pay for it tonight.'

A pause.

'Jessica, I have to ask you something.'

The mistress, Jessica thought, and felt terribly sorry for Michelle and the children.

'All right.'

'Did you know her?'

'Kandi, you mean?'

'Uh-huh.'

'No, I didn't.'

'Did you ever see her?'

'No. Never even saw her, Michelle.'

'Did Tom – ever mention her?'

'No. Not to me, anyway.'

'I could've been a much better wife.'

'Don't say that, Michelle. You've been a very good wife. And a very good mother.'

'I'm fat.'

'Michelle, please—'

'I'm fat and I'm not any fun and I didn't even want him to go on that diet.'

'Michelle—'

'You know why – the diet, I mean? Because I knew this would happen. I knew he'd lose all that weight and then he'd look at me one morning and see how fat I was and all the stretchmarks and everything and—. And he wouldn't want me anymore. And that's just what happened.'

She started sobbing quietly.

'Michelle. You're a very good woman. I can't judge Tom, but seeing that woman – it wasn't a very honorable thing to do. It really wasn't. And you shouldn't blame yourself.'

'He wanted me to go on the diet with him. I tried, but I couldn't stick with it. I guess I just don't have any willpower.'

Then: 'I'll bet she had big breasts.'

'Michelle, you really shouldn't do this.'

'He asked me once if I wanted to get silicone implants but I was scared. You know, all the publicity and everything.'

Then: 'Maybe if I'd gotten the implants he wouldn't have taken up with her.'

'I'm sure he loved you, Michelle. I'm sure he did. He kept your photograph on his desk and a lot of times I'd go in there and he'd be staring at it.'

The saving lie, she thought. Henrik Ibsen. She'd taken a college term of Drama Studies and Ibsen had been her favorite playwright.

Michelle sounded like a grateful child.

'Are you making that up, Jessica? He really used to stare at my photograph?'

'All the time.'

'He really did?'

'He really did.'

'Oh God, Jessica, thanks for saying that. Thanks so much for saying that.'

Michelle began to weep, then, and all Jessica could do was listen and coo occasional meaningless words of comfort.

Chapter Two

1

The guard said, 'You don't want that stuff, I know a lot of guys who would.'

Roy Gerard looked up from the last meal they'd brought him and smiled.

'I guess I'm not being properly grateful, am I? The condemned man's supposed to send his compliments to the chef, right?'

Darkness pressed the windows of the Death Row waiting room and made it seem smaller. Ever since spitting on the Warden, a guard had stayed in the room with Gerard. Warden Atkinson wanted to deny him his last minutes of privacy.

Gerard looked down at the tray another guard had brought in five minutes ago.

Gerard had always wondered where the concept of the 'last meal' had come from. He supposed it was society's way of making itself feel noble and generous.

Even when it was about to kill somebody, society liked to pretend that it was full of largesse and compassion. It was the kind of hypocrisy that had always sickened Gerard. It sickened him now.

'How long you been a guard here, Mulligan?'

Mulligan shrugged.

'Eight years, I guess.'

'This what you really want to do with your life? Keep a bunch of men locked up in cages like animals?'

Mulligan pointed to the table where Gerard sat.

'You going to eat or not?'

'You didn't answer my question.'

'Got good benefits with this job, anyway,' Mulligan said. 'Good health insurance, and good dental.'

Gerard smirked.

'Good dental, huh?'

'Yeah,' Mulligan said. 'I got three kids.'

'You probably enjoy beating the shit out of the cons, that's probably what you really like.'

Gerard could see the guard bristle.

'I only use force when it's necessary.'

'Like with Kimble the other night?'

'He had a knife.'

'He didn't stab anybody.'

'Knives are against the rules.'

'You broke two of his ribs.'

'He wouldn't give me the knife. If I didn't take the knife away from him, he would've stabbed somebody for sure.'

'Maybe you, huh?'

'Yeah. Maybe me.'

So smug in this place, Gerard thought. Little low-pay tinhorn dictators is what these guards were.

Sometimes, as now, he positively couldn't abide taking any shit from them. They were so stupid they didn't even know that he was their superior in every way. Brains, looks, poise, cunning. In every way. Yet they treated him like an animal. This food in front of him. Any maid who'd ever served a meal like this in the Gerard house would have been fired.

Gerard looked down at his food then up at Mulligan. Uniforms always looked too tight on a big guy like this.

'This is slop.'

'What's slop?'

'This food. It's slop.'

'Are you crazy? You know how many guys in this place would love to have that food?'

Gerard lifted the tray then rose from the table.

'Hey, where the hell you think you're going?' Mulligan said.

'I'm going to put this food where it belongs,' Gerard said.

He walked the tray over to the corner.

Before Mulligan could figure out what he was going to do, before Mulligan could stop him, Gerard upended the tray and dumped it in the wastebasket.

'You stupid bastard,' Mulligan said.

Gerard walked over to the window just as lightning painted the world a momentary silver.

Somewhere out there David was putting the final preparations on everything.

A few more hours, Roy would be out of this place once and for all.

Just a few more hours now.

2

'Bacon and lettuce sandwich,' David Gerard told the waitress.

He knew this would be the last chance he'd have to eat until maybe tomorrow.

Still, he wasn't hungry for anything more than a sandwich and a Coke.

He sat in a busy sit-down restaurant and pored over the building plans he'd got from City Hall five weeks ago.

No problems at all. No questions. Simply told them he was a man taking night-school courses in architecture and that he was supposed to do a paper on a local building with more than thirty-five floors in it.

When they'd made copies, they'd even agreed to use 8 x 11-inch paper so they'd be easier to manipulate.

'Here you go, sir.' The waitress set down his Coke. 'I'll have your sandwich ready in a few minutes.'

'Thank you very much.'

She was cute.

Her eyes lingered slightly longer than they should have. He knew she was assessing him.

He returned the favor.

Not so great in the face department but extremely nice legs and breasts. Extremely nice.

'You aren't from around here, are you?'

'No,' he smiled. 'No, I'm not. Why?'

She laughed.

'Because the really cute ones never are.'

She left, and he went back to studying the plans of the building.

3

Eagle Electric divided the city into quadrants and tried to have the same crew work the same quadrant every day. The principals at Eagle felt that this was the simplest and best way to create a bond between the customer and the crew.

The northwest side, because it included all of downtown as

well as three new malls, had two crews.

Harrigan and Cates had been following the second crew for the past six work days.

The second crew, which consisted of two guys named Bill and Ned, stopped for donuts at around three-thirty every day. And always at the same place, DONUT CITY in a rundown strip mall off Westchester Avenue.

Bill and Ned were in there now, had been for the past ten minutes.

Harrigan and Cates sat in their rental car, watching the two Eagle men in the large front window. Bill was reading a newspaper. Ned was flirting with a waitress.

'I guess I've got time to use the phone.'

Cates made a face.

'Right.'

Harrigan had to control himself.

'You got a problem with that?'

'No.'

'Then what's the face for?'

Cates sighed.

Stared out the window.

'Didn't know I made a face.'

He knew better than to make Harrigan any angrier than he already was.

Harrigan glared at him a long moment then got out of the car.

He walked over to a phone booth.

The book was ripped out and the booth smelled of urine. He left the door open.

He dumped several dollars' worth of change into the phone and dialed the number.

'Hello.'

He recognized her voice immediately.

'This is Harrigan.'

'That's what I thought.'

She still hadn't forgiven him, not even after all these years.

'How's Linda?'

'Very well, considering.'

'Considering what?'

'What they had to do.'

He was afraid to ask.

'What did they have to do?'

'They took 'em both.'

'Breasts?'

'Yeah.'

'Shit.' Then: 'Shit.'

'The poor kid,' she said. 'She's still asleep. She doesn't know yet.'

'She's twenty-one god-damned years old.'

'Hey, you're not telling *me* anything, all right? I'm her mother, remember? I'm the one who raised her. Where were you all those years?'

'You've had plenty of husbands.'

'Is that supposed to mean something?'

'It just means you haven't exactly been high and dry.'

They were scared for Linda and taking it out on each other and when Harrigan realized this, he said: 'I'm sorry I never came back to see you.'

She sighed.

'She's such a good kid.'

'I'm putting a money order for five thousand dollars in the mail tomorrow.'

'She'd rather see you.'

'She *will* see me.'

'When?'

'Soon as I get to – situated.'

He'd almost said *Cuba*. He had to be careful when he got emotional like this. He'd end up blabbing everything the way Cates had.

'I got me a pretty good one this time, Harrigan.'

'Oh yeah?'

'He's a banker, if you can believe it. Me with a credit record like mine and I end up with a banker. I got the country club and the whole nine yards.'

'He treat Linda good?'

'Very, very well. He's been up here twice today. You know what she said the other night? "He's almost like having my real father." She never said that about the other three.'

He was starting to cry now.

'I just wish you could've seen her when she was a little girl, Harrigan. She was so god-damned sweet, she would've broken your heart.'

Harrigan hadn't cried in a long time.

The tears felt oddly good.

'You be sure and tell her about the five thousand dollars.'

'She'd rather have you here with her, Harrigan.'

'I'll call her very soon. I promise. Very soon.'

After he hung up, he leaned against the reeking interior of the booth and closed his eyes.

They'd taken both her breasts.

He shuddered.

Men having health problems, he could deal with, but women seemed so much more vulnerable than men. And breast cancer seemed to be everywhere you turned.

Oh, Linda.

Linda.

He started crying harder now but he knew he needed to stop.

A punk like Cates, seeing a man crying like this, he'd know right away he had a weak one here.

And when a punk like Cates spotted a weak one, it was only a matter of time until he made his move.

4

Detective Ribicoff turned it into a regular little feast right there in Jessica's office.

There were roast beef sandwiches, kosher pickles, potato chips, mustard, horseradish, ketchup and two small pieces of fudge chocolate pie.

There was coffee and Pepsi and even a bottle of Evian.

It was obvious that Ribicoff was trying to distract her from the terrible events of this afternoon.

Two co-workers savagely murdered.

And the implicit threat that Jessica might well be next.

'How's the sandwich?' he said.

Jessica, who had a mouthful of the sandwich at the moment, pointed to her mouth and nodded.

Great.

'You try one of the pickles?'

She nodded yes.

'My favorite deli,' he said.

'I really appreciate this.'

Now it was Ribicoff's turn to feed his face.

After he got done swallowing, he said, 'I just want to tell you how it's going to work.'

'Going to work?'

'Right. Another detective and I will be taking you down in the service elevator in back.'

'All right.'

'There'll be a car waiting for us.'

She nodded, took another bite.

'Then we drive over to the TV studio and go in via the rear entrance. There's a service elevator there, too.'

'You've really thought this through.'

'I don't want to take any chances. I intend to get that meal you promised me.'

She laughed.

'After you taste my cooking, you may regret having gone to all this trouble.'

Ribicoff sampled a potato chip. He seemed to enjoy it.

'Then we go up in the service elevator to the thirty-fourth floor where the TV studio is. We're on either side of you all the way.'

'Then in the studio—'

'In the studio,' Ribicoff said, 'you're safe. There'll be two armed police officers at the studio door, and one armed police officer in the studio itself.'

'Wow.'

'We're not taking any chances.'

'Apparently not.'

Then: 'By the way, I hope you don't have any plans for afterward.'

'I was going to meet Michael.'

'At a bar?'

'That's what we had in mind.'

'I'd rather you made it your apartment. We'll have police officers at your door for the next couple nights.'

'Well, I'll see Michael tonight at the studio. I can tell him about the change in plans.'

'Sorry,' Ribicoff said.

'I just appreciate all the protection. It's really scary thinking about David Gerard out there on the loose.'

Ribicoff nodded.

'But I have the feeling he won't be on the loose for long. He's taking a lot of chances.'

The anger and melancholy overwhelmed Jessica again.

'I just keep thinking about Dick and Tom...'

Ribicoff said, 'That's why we're going to nail both Gerards. One dies in the prison tonight; and the other one we get within twenty-four hours. I'm sure of it.'

'I just hope you're right.'

She glanced out the window at the wet black night.

Judgment night.

She wished it were over with.

One year ago . . .

She hadn't made love in a car since her college days. She'd forgotten how cramped and difficult it was, and all the acrobatics it required.

Still . . . she was with Bryce, who was just about the most gorgeous man she'd ever seen. So gorgeous in fact, she still couldn't figure out why he was taking her out. She was a plump thirty-five-year-old with a chubby if slightly endearing face, and a habit of biting her nails till blood ran. She was a receptionist in an ad agency. She'd met Bryce two weeks ago in one of the Loop bars where ad-types hung out.

Bryce . . .

His right hand moved inexorably up her skirt now, seeking the ultimate warmth between her legs.

It was sort of a nippy spring night . . . trees just starting to bud . . . the ground smelling wetly of mud that would soon be grass and flowers . . . the quarter moon casting a pale glow on Bryce's Pontiac Firebird. They were parked out in the boonies, a place frequented by high-school kids in warmer times.

Alone with Bryce . . .

That was when she started listening to the radio news that was playing softly in the background . . .

The words 'killer' and 'young woman' and 'rape' made the news story irresistible . . .

'Police are continuing their investigation, trying to determine if last night's rape and murder near the Loop had anything to do with a similar murder last week in Oak Park.'

Oak Park . . .

She'd never been to Bryce's place – but hadn't he once said that he lived in Oak Park?

'C'mon, babe,' Bryce said, obviously sensing that her attention was drifting away.

Then he found the silky warmth of her sex and she was stunned back into their lovemaking.

Bryce was an incredible lover.

He was also an experienced one.

Without quite realizing what he was doing, she found herself on top of him as she sat on the passenger side. He eased her wide hips downward, until she had mounted him.

This really did remind her of high school all over again . . .

For a time, she gave herself completely to the moment, riding him hard then slowing down to increase their pleasure.

Bryce could hold out for an incredibly long time. In fact, she could never recall being with anybody who could pace himself as well as Bryce.

The dark car began to rock in the moon-silvered night. The springs gave occasional comic moans, much like the moans of the participants in the front seat. A number of woodland animals came to the edge of the trees to watch the strange sight of the car rocking back and forth . . .

But her enjoyment was lessened when an unwanted thought began to play at the edge of her consciousness—

What do I really know about Bryce?

Nothing.

That was the real answer.

She knew nothing at all about him.

And he was sort of mysterious.

Never talked in any specifics about his life, or even where he worked.

Nor had he ever taken her to where he lived.

He simply appeared at her apartment at the appointed time and—

She suddenly became aware of how isolated they were at this very moment. Even as a little girl, her imagination had always gotten away from her. Many nights she couldn't sleep, lying awake in her bed, eyes frantically watching her dark closet for the creatures she just knew lurked in there...

That was how she felt now. Like a little girl trapped in a situation not even her parents could save her from.

Virtually anything could happen out here and nobody could hear her scream—

Bryce could be the killer the radio had just described.

'Babe?' Bryce said.

'Huh?'

'What's wrong?'

'Wrong?'

'You're just sitting there.'

'Oh.' Then: 'I think I want to stop now.'

'Stop? God, I haven't come yet, babe, and I don't think you have, either.'

'I wish you'd take me home, Bryce.'

'There — are you happy?'

'Happy?'

'My hard-on just shrunk.'

'Oh.'

'And I didn't even get to come.'

Bryce sounded like a petulant fifteen year old. He also sounded as if she owed him an orgasm or something.

She eased herself off him.

And that was when she noticed his face.

She wondered, in that terrible moment, if she'd ever really looked at him before.

She saw the icy cruelty there. The handsomeness was just a mask. The icy cruelty was what lay behind the mask. The icy cruelty was the reality of this man.

She was sure of it.

The way she used to be sure that night monsters lurked in her closet even though her dad never could seem to find them when he came in and turned on the lights in her bedroom.

By now, Bryce had slid over to the driver's seat.

He lighted a cigarette.

At the smell of smoke, she usually gave him her anti-smoking sermon.

But now she didn't care if he lived or died.

He scared her. She just wanted to be home, behind several locks, in her nice safe little apartment.

She didn't care if she never had a date the rest of her life. Who needed a man anyway when she had a humming thrumming sexual appliance that she'd comically named Fred?

'I don't have to tell you that I won't be seeing you anymore,' Bryce said, barely able to keep the rage from his voice.

'No, you don't have to tell me that, Bryce. All I want is for you to take me home right now.'

'You are really a bitch, you know that?'

'Please just take me home, Bryce. Now.'

'I take you out several times, I buy you some very nice dinners, and this is what I get?'

The angrier he became, the more longingly she looked out the car window.

She wanted to bolt.

Find her own way back to the city.

Bryce started the car. Snapped on the headlights.

'Where're we going?'

'I'm taking you home.'

'Oh.'

He backed the car away from the edge of the woods and then wheeled onto the small asphalt road that led to the arterial highway.

'I can't tell you how pissed off I am right now,' Bryce said.

'I'd appreciate it if you'd slow down.'

'And I'd appreciate it if you'd keep your mouth shut.'

She fell into silence. Didn't want to anger him anymore. His anger only enhanced the cruel aspect of his face.

Then: 'Where're we going?'

'I know a short cut.'

He had turned abruptly off one asphalt road and onto another. This wasn't at all the way to her house.

What had the radio newsman said just a bit ago: 'Police are continuing their investigation, trying to determine if last night's rape and murder had anything to do with a similar murder last week in Oak Park.'

Bryce lived in Oak Park.

And there really had been terribly slimy monsters in her girlhood closet all those years ago . . .

'Stop the car.'

'What?'

She shrieked. 'I said stop the car!'

He swung the Firebird over to the edge of the road.

All she could see on any side of her was flat cornfields, and far off in the distance, the silhouette of a scarecrow in the blanched light of the quarter moon . . .

She opened the door and got out.

'I know who you are. Don't think I don't, Bryce – or whatever your real name is!'

She started closing the door.

He said: 'I don't know what the hell you're talking about, lady!'

'You don't – you really don't? The rape and murder in Oak Park last week. Oak Park where you live. And then the rape and murder last night near the Loop.' She shook her head angrily. 'Were you going to rape me after you killed me, like the real pervert you are?'

He started laughing. 'Oh my God, you think I'm a killer? Are you serious?'

The laughter sounded oddly genuine to her. But as a crafty killer, he'd be able to fake anything, even laughter.

'Honest to God, I'm sorry you're scared. But I'm not the killer. Not at all.'

Even his speaking tone was sincere now. Warm and amused . . . but he'd be able to fake that, too.

'You just get out of here and leave me alone, you understand?'

'But how'll you get home?'

Now he was playing the tender friend.

'None of your business!' she said. And slammed the door.

She started walking down the empty country road that went up and down in bumps like a roller-coaster ride.

A couple of times he pulled up next to her and tried to talk her back in the car with that reasonable tone of his – but she knew better.

Soon as she got to a phone, she'd call the police and give them his name.

Here's your killer, Officer . . .

She wasn't sure when he finally gave up and went away for good.

RUNNER IN THE DARK

All she knew was that her feet were beginning to develop blisters and she was cold and hungry and she could feel a sore throat and a headcold coming on.

But at least I'm safe, *she thought.*

At least I'll make it home to my apartment tonight...

The convenience store was like an oasis in the prairie night.

Inside, she got a cup of coffee and a donut and then went up to the clerk and said, 'D'you suppose a cab would come out this far?'

He shook his head. 'Probably take you a long time. I mean, this being Friday night and all.'

That's when the man stepped up.

Slim in a khaki shirt and jeans. Handsome, too, and in a very comfortable kind of way.

'Where you headed?'

She told him.

'I'm going right by there.'

'Really?' *she said, unable to believe her luck.* 'Really?'

She was found six hours later by a Highway Patrol man. She'd been raped and murdered and thrown with great disdain in the ditch.

When Bryce read about it in the paper next morning, he immediately called the police and told them everything that had happened.

'My God,' he said, 'she thought I was the killer. Then she got out of my car – and look what happened.'

Chapter Three

1

The funny thing was, Ryan Ludlow really wanted to forgive his wife Sharon for what she'd done.

But somehow he couldn't.

Oh, he could *say* he forgave her. But deep down...

As chief of security for the Trealor building, Ludlow had a lot of anxieties. Take the one that Michael Shaw had stopped in to ask him about earlier today.

This crazy murderous bastard David Gerard was running all over the city killing people. Nobody was even sure what he looked like.

And Shaw, understandably, wanted to make sure that David Gerard didn't get into the building tonight. Because Jessica Dennis was going to be in Studio B.

Ludlow sympathized.

But it was just one more thing to worry about.

Six months ago, he'd decided it was just such crises as these that made him uninterested in sex.

The daily grind, the daily headaches.

Who wanted sex when stress brought on fatigue all the time?

But then, after a few months of not being able to do

anything with his wife, he had to admit that maybe he *hadn't* forgiven her after all.

Maybe that was the problem he was having with his sex drive where Sharon was concerned.

Not stress.

Not sex.

Sharon herself.

Ludlow had once read an article in a news magazine about office romances. The article estimated that more than sixty per cent of people admitted that they'd had some kind of office dalliance. More than thirty-five per cent said they'd had outright affairs. Work around somebody all day long, you were bound to feel some kind of attraction.

That's what had happened to Sharon, his thirty-six-year-old and very gorgeous wife.

She was working in this public relations firm and this new forty-year-old hot-shot VP came in and started cutting a swath through all the ladies... and eventually he got around to Sharon.

The night she told him, the night she'd finally explained why she'd been acting so strange for the past few months, Ludlow had made her tell him everything, including all the details about sex. What he'd really wanted to know was, was this hot-shot better in the sack than Ludlow himself? Even though Sharon had been extra careful not to hurt his feelings, Ludlow got the idea that the hot-shot was definitely great in the sack.

And that's why he couldn't perform with Sharon anymore.

Every time he started to touch her, he'd think of the hot-shot, how the hot-shot had delighted her, how the hot-shot had gone on for hours and hours, how the hot-shot had known just the right things to say afterward.

A guy couldn't perform when he was constantly comparing himself to somebody else.

The Case of the Disappearing Dick, he'd said sarcastically to his wife one night.

She hadn't been amused.

It was around then that Ludlow decided to give little Niki in the office next door a try. Seven weeks ago, now.

Ludlow knew the owner of a mid-town hotel. You could slip out the rear door of the Trealor building and walk in the rear door of the Regency within six minutes. The manager always arranged to have a room for them on the second floor so they could walk up the back steps.

The only downside with Niki was all the stuff about her counselor. Niki had been dumped by her husband of eighteen years last summer. 'Traded me in for a newer model,' as she'd put it. She really had this rage about men. She saw a counselor twice a week. She gave him a virtual word-for-word description every time they got together in the hotel room. One time, she'd said, 'The reason I like you, Ryan, is you're not like a man at all.' She could see she'd hurt his feelings. 'I guess that didn't come out right, huh?'

But Ludlow abided it all because she could get him up. Brother, could she get him up. Plus, she knew a lot more about bed than Sharon. In fact, a couple of things Niki knew, Ludlow had never even heard of before, which was pretty cool.

He always left the hotel room feeling like a man again.

Unlike leaving his house after twenty frustrating minutes of trying to get an erection.

Niki was good for him in every way.

Niki always left first.

David Gerard had followed them for the past three weeks and that was the way it always ran.

She left the Trealor building first, she left the hotel room first.

Nobody ever had the opportunity to see them together.

They usually arrived right at four, and left at a quarter to five, so they could get back to their respective offices and close things up for the day.

David Gerard checked his watch.

He stood at the far end of the hotel corridor.

Ludlow and the woman were only four doors away.

It was eighteen minutes to five.

Any second now, Niki would come out of the door of Room 226.

'I like that bra.'

'Yeah,' Niki said. 'Black.'

'I like what's *in* it, too.'

'You know what he actually said to me one day?'

Ludlow didn't have to ask who 'he' was.

'He said "maybe you should get a tit job." '

'A tit job?'

'Yeah, you know, get them surgically propped up.'

'Oh.'

'You really like 'em?'

'I love 'em.'

'Really?'

'Really.'

'This new wife of his? Tits like water balloons. Store-boughts. I hate those.'

'So do I.'

'Really?'

'Really.'

She came over and slid her arms around him.

He got an instant erection.

She was definitely good for him. Definitely.

'I sure don't know how your wife could screw around on somebody like you.'

He grinned and gave her a big wet kiss.

'I don't, either,' he said.

They laughed, and then she slid away from him.

'I better get going.'

'Yeah. Me, too.'

'Give me a couple of minutes' head start.'

'Right.'

She stood on her tip-toes and gave him a quick chaste kiss.

'Toodles,' she said. She always said toodles. The first couple times, it drove him nuts, toodles. Now he thought it was kind of cute.

He swatted her on the butt as she walked out the door.

She hadn't been gone more than a minute when the knock came on the door.

'Ryan?'

'Yes.'

'Mitch.'

Mitch was the manager of the hotel who let him use the room.

But funny. It didn't *sound* like Mitch somehow.

Ludlow, feeling pretty damned good about himself after the sex he'd just had, went over and pulled the door open.

There was a handsome blond man there.

The handsome blond man had a gun.

It was aimed right in Ludlow's face.

'Toodles,' the blond man said. 'She's a cutey.'

Then he walked into the room and closed the door behind him.

'You're going to help me get into Studio B in about half an hour,' the blond man said, 'or I'm going to blow your fucking head off. Understand?'

'You're David Gerard, aren't you?' Ludlow said.

'You just won the grand prize, asshole,' David Gerard said.

And then struck Ludlow so hard on the side of the head that he sank to his knees.

Then Gerard kicked him hard in the stomach.

Ludlow doubled over, fell headfirst to the floor.

'I just wanted you to know that I'm not a candy ass or anything like that.'

Then Gerard went over and poured himself a small drink from a bottle of Black and White scotch.

2

The Eagle Electric truck stopped at the TV station once every day, and usually late in the afternoon. When you had a big station as a client, you constantly needed to service it. This might mean dropping off equipment, or simply checking to make sure everything was working properly. The Eagle team worked as a backup to the station's own technical staff.

Harrigan and Cates had been following the Eagle truck ever since it had left DONUT CITY. The radio was alive with reports of the young cop being murdered. The woman across the street had given police and reporters accurate descriptions of Harrigan and Cates. Their disguises were slight but effective.

Cates was driving, and Harrigan had to admit that, if nothing else, Cates was adept at trailing people.

Traffic was a mess. Not only was it rush hour, the rain had started falling steadily again.

They saw three fender-benders, and any number of drivers leaning on horns, or pushing their middle fingers up in the air.

Cates was intrepid.

A few times Harrigan worried that they'd lost the truck but Cates didn't appear disturbed at all.

The truck reappeared.

'Park's coming up,' Harrigan said.

'Yeah.'

That was the plan. Force the truck into the small city park that sat on the edge of the river.

Seen through the raindrops on the windshield, the city had a watercolor feel, everything misty and very beautiful, especially the neon lights and the pretty young women hurrying to cars and buses.

To kill time one day, Harrigan had gone to a gallery showing of French Impressionists. He'd had no interest in art, but the gentle, melancholy feel of Monet and Renoir had captivated him, made him wish that he could walk the evening streets of last century's Paris.

'You ready?'

'Yeah,' Harrigan said.

Harrigan leaned down and opened the door no more than half a foot.

He got the pellet gun fixed in his hand, finger on the trigger, and then waited until the Eagle Electric truck turned the corner.

He fired off two quick shots.

In the clamor of rush hour, the sound of the pellet gun was lost entirely.

The Eagle Electric truck looked unfazed.

It continued driving down the street. It was moving at approximately 40 mph. In a few minutes, it would go right past the park.

Had he missed? Were the tires too thick to be damaged by the pellets?

'Damn,' Harrigan said.

Cates turned the corner.

The truck was three cars ahead.

'Something went wrong,' Harrigan said.

A slight smile touched Cates' lips.

Harrigan the Invincible was invincible no longer.

Then Harrigan said, 'Look.'

The Eagle Electric truck suddenly swung from the right lane into the opening of the park.

The truck was hobbled, traveling slowly on a badly flattened right rear tire.

The truck jerked and shimmied.

'Let's go,' Harrigan said.

The smile vanished from Cates' lips.

When they reached the park, Harrigan could see that the two men had pulled the truck up by the log-cabin style pavilion. One of them was down on his knees at the back of the truck with a flashlight. The beam looked lonely in the deserted gloom.

'Here's good enough,' Harrigan said.

Cates killed the lights and pulled over.

They were about half a block from the Eagle truck.

They got out, closing the doors quietly, and started walking up the drive to the truck.

Harrigan had his Walther in his hand. He'd fixed the silencer to it half an hour ago.

Every few moments, an image of Linda on the operating table would come to him. Both breasts removed. She was twenty-one years old.

'Evening,' Harrigan said when they reached the truck.

The chunky guy in the green Eagle coveralls looked up. 'Yeah, hi.'

'Flat?'

'Yeah. And that's what's weird.'

'What is?'

'These tires, they're not supposed to *go* flat.'

'Oh?'

'Yeah. They buy only the premium stuff.'

The second man jumped down from the driver's seat and walked back to where Harrigan and Cates stood talking to the man taking the tire off. The rear end was jacked up high. The second man carried a tire.

'Here's the spare,' he said.

He dropped it down on the rain-washed asphalt next to his working buddy.

Then he looked at Harrigan and said, 'Help you with something?'

'As a matter of fact, you can,' Harrigan said.

He brought up the Walther and pointed it directly at the man's chest.

'We want your coveralls,' Harrigan said. 'And we want you to give us your electronic passes for Channel 8.'

'Who the fuck are you clowns supposed to be?' the man said, not in the least intimidated.

That was when the Eagle man fixing the tire grabbed the jack and swung it at Harrigan's crotch, but caught him in the stomach instead.

Harrigan should have done a better job of covering them both.

The man who'd brought the tire took off running into the park, toward the river.

'Watch him,' Harrigan said to Cates, indicating the man next to the jack.

Harrigan ran as fast as he could.

Sometimes you could run past pain, even pain as bad as he was experiencing at the moment.

Had to find the jerk who'd gotten away.

Had to.

Harrigan had mentioned Channel 8 and the jerk would tell the police this. In no time, given the fact that Jessica Dennis was in the Channel 8 studios tonight, the police would tie the flat-tire incident to David Gerard.

His shoes squished as he ran. His breath came out in silver plumes. The fire in his groin was dying.

The man tripped.

In the silence, the city sounds around them fainter and fainter the deeper they went into the park, Harrigan heard a crash then a moan.

Tripped. Hurt himself.

Harrigan moved toward the sound of the moan.

Tip-toes.

Walther ready.

Next to a rain-soaked oak tree were three silver garbage cans. One of them rocked slightly.

The man was behind the cans.

Sneak up on him.

Tip-toes again.

Right up on top of him.

The man suddenly sprang up.

Harrigan squeezed off two shots but the man had already ducked behind the oak tree and was running away once again.

Harrigan went up the hill after him.

Harrigan got off two more shots. Both times the man was saved by falling down at exactly the right moment. The shots went over his head.

The man topped the hill and disappeared.

Harrigan reached the crest and looked down on the river below. Spring rains had swollen it; the usually docile waters ran fast and dangerous now.

The man was running down cement steps leading to the river's edge.

Harrigan went down the hill, and after him.

By the time he reached the bottom of the steps, the man was

no longer to be seen. The river roared and splashed, only a few feet away in the darkness.

Then he saw the drainage tunnel that hung out over the river.

There was no place else the man could have gone.

Harrigan worked himself along the concrete ledge that led to the drainage tunnel.

He reached up and grabbed the top edge of the tunnel and swung himself inside.

He listened intently.

And heard the whimpering sound.

He took his pocket flashlight out and shone it several yards down the tunnel.

The man lay back against the side of the tunnel. He wasn't moving. Only crying softly.

Harrigan played the light over the man's face until he came to the wound. The man had injured himself, and badly. The entire side of his head was bloody.

'My god-damned head,' the man said. 'I hit it against the edge of this drainage tunnel. My whole left side's paralyzed.'

He was scared; very scared. He was already imagining that he would be paralyzed for life.

He opened his eyes and looked at Harrigan.

'You going to kill me?'

Harrigan didn't say anything.

'I've got a family.'

Harrigan still didn't say anything.

The man started crying again.

'This is going to destroy them, if I die. Please don't kill me, all right?'

Harrigan calculated the odds.

By the time this guy managed to get out of the drainage tunnel, everything would be over with anyway.

There was no need to kill him.

Harrigan said, 'I need that uniform of yours.'

'You're really not going to kill me?'

The man sounded exultant.

Harrigan wished he felt that happy about something. It had been a long time since he'd felt happy about much of anything.

Harrigan thought of Linda again.

That was what scared him.

What if they took both her breasts, and the cancer came back?

He shuddered, and tried not to think about it. Tried *hard* not to think about it.

'I'm really not going to kill you.'

3

There was a female police officer waiting at the elevator when Jessica arrived.

The officer was holding the elevator doors open.

On one side of Jessica was Detective Ribicoff, on the other another detective named Hastings.

As they boarded the elevator car, they all nodded thanks to the female officer.

Once the car was moving downward, Jessica said, 'Not many people get this kind of protection, I'll bet.'

'Not many people have to contend with David Gerard,' Detective Ribicoff said.

Hastings, a black man with a handsome face and quick, intelligent eyes said: 'We'll ask you to wait on the elevator until we've double-checked the lobby.'

'All right,' Jessica said.

'Then after we've checked out the lobby, we'll move you out to the door. We'll ask you to wait there until we've checked out the walk in front of the car.'

Jessica nodded.

She tried to keep her mind on seeing Michael tonight. Given what she had to tell him, this would be the most important night of their lives together.

'How're you doing?' Detective Ribicoff said.

'Pretty good,' Jessica said.

'I'm sure this is making you even more tense, Jessica,' Detective Ribicoff said, 'but it's necessary.'

'I know.'

They reached the first floor.

The elevator doors parted.

Detective Hastings stepped off the elevator.

Two uniformed officers stood over by the front door. They both carried shotguns.

From the elevator, Jessica watched Detective Hastings check everything out.

He even opened up the door where the cleaning crew kept some of their equipment.

He came back to the elevator and said, 'Now if you'll just walk to the revolving door and wait there until I tell you to come outside.'

Detective Ribicoff took her gently by the arm and led her out into the lobby, and up to the door.

Inch by inch, Jessica thought.

This kind of protection would really get to her after a time. It only increased her anxiety.

She felt lonely, suddenly, as if she had no life but her official one as District Attorney. True, she wanted this career but she also wanted the home life she'd never had as a girl because of her father's alcoholism, the home life she'd dreamed of so long.

Through the revolving door, she could see Detective

Hastings moving around on the sidewalk, checking things out.

A police car sat at the curb.

The back door was open.

A police officer with a shotgun stood next to it.

Detective Hastings walked up to the door and signaled for Jessica and Detective Ribicoff to come out and get into the car.

They moved quickly out into the night, rain pelting them hard even though they were exposed for little more than a few feet of sidewalk.

Then she was in the back seat, and the police car was pulling quickly away from the curb.

'We want the back door of Channel 8,' Detective Ribicoff said to the uniformed man driving.

'Yes, sir.'

Ribicoff, sitting next to Jessica, leaned toward her and patted her hand.

'Good luck on the debate tonight.'

Jessica allowed herself a small smile.

'It won't be easy, arguing with a priest.'

'I went to Catholic school,' the uniformed driver said. 'It isn't the priests you have to worry about.'

He grinned into the rearview mirror.

'It's those darned nuns,' he said. 'They're the tough ones.'

Jessica laughed, and it felt great.

Chapter Four

1

On his drive over to the TV station, Father William Josek passed by the little pharmacy that brought back all the memories of his sin.

Even in his Roman collar and London Fog raincoat, Father Josek looked like a golf pro at a prestigious country club. He'd always had the handsome, almost rakish good looks of an upper-class sportsman.

For this reason, his family and his friends had expected him to go into the family business, which was steel, and to become the fourth Josek to dominate steel the way the Fords had once dominated automobiles.

But what none of them had counted on, himself included, was the summer of his sophomore year in college. He'd spent two months helping his uncle, a surgeon, at a hospital that mostly served the poor. Over the summer, he got to know an old Irish priest named Fitzsimmons. For all his gruffness – he loved his pipe and he loved his whiskey, did Fitzsimmons – the elderly priest was the tenderest, most patient, most inspiring man Josek had ever known.

The men of business dealt with money, power, ego.

The men of the cloth, at least in Father Fitzsimmons' case,

dealt with far more important things -- the human body and the human soul.

Father Fitzsimmons worked eighteen hours a day in the hospital giving hope to those who knew only despair, giving peace to those who knew only turbulence.

Astonished, Josek had seen the old priest actually deliver a baby on a night when there were too few doctors to go around. He'd also seen Father Fitzsimmons run into a burning hospital room – the fire set by a jealous ex-lover – and drag a black woman out to safety. And then there'd been the legendary night when Father Fitzsimmons took on the toughest pimp in the neighbourhood, and not only gave him a black eye but a broken nose in the bargain. God worked in mysterious ways, but never more mysteriously than through Father Fitzsimmons.

By the end of the summer, Josek knew what he wanted to be.

His parents had laughed when he told them; and then when they understood that this was no fleeting notion, they became angry.

Why would anybody as handsome, rich and socially poised as he want to waste his life on the priesthood? Certainly, the Joseks were good Catholics but the priesthood was for – other people. Not the Josek family.

He went to the seminary, despite them, and studied there for six months. During that time, they didn't contact him once.

Finally, he contacted them. He told them of his vocation, of how deep and true and wonderful it was to him, and how they should feel honored that God had chosen their son to help do His bidding here on earth.

He said all this in a letter.

When his father finished reading it, he pointed to the TV screen where anti-war protestors were burning flags and bras alike, and said to his wife: 'This is a terrible thing to say, darling, but I wish our son was a dope-smoking hippie.' She smiled and said, a bit wistfully: 'Me, too.'

Josek asked to work in the poorest parish they could find. While there were many of the older priests who saw Josek as a possible Bishop or even Cardinal someday, they knew that he had doomed himself to obscurity by his choice of a poor parish. Most would-be Bishops and Cardinals had powerful and wealthy secular benefactors. You didn't find such benefactors in poor parishes.

Josek was pastor of St Catherine's for eight years before he met the woman. He saved kids from jails, he saved foundering marriages, he put food on the tables of dozens of families, and he endured two savage beatings from gangs that felt he'd been meddling in their affairs. When his parents died, he took his inheritance and gave it all to the local hospital that helped the poor. He was not a perfect man, by any means. He prayed for the patience and forbearance he'd seen in Father Fitzsimmons, but it was not to be his. He had a bad temper, he lost patience, upon occasion he even lost hope. But overall he was the best friend the predominantly black parish had ever had.

The beautiful young mulatto Rachael came to him after her common-law husband had beaten her severely. She wanted advice, counseling. That's how it had begun. He saw her three times a week for five weeks and by then he was almost painfully in love with her. She was all he thought about. He sensed that she felt the same way. He was thirty-eight and she was twenty-two. One day, when she was in tears, he took her in his arms. And could not help himself. He kissed her. He knew then all the joys of the flesh he had surrendered when he'd taken the Roman collar. But he did not want to be one of those priests who betrayed his vows by sleeping with women or, far worse, molesting vulnerable children. He arranged with a family friend to give Rachael a job in a faraway city where her husband could never find her. And where she would likewise be beyond the reach of Josek. When he told her what he'd done, she sat primly in her chair in the ancient dusty rectory, and wept. 'I love you,' she said once, lifting her eyes to meet his. 'And I'll always love you.' Two nights later, in the middle of the night so her husband could not find her, Josek drove her to the train depot. She left at once. His life was never the same. There was the joy of the spirit, to be sure, and yet there was also the joy of the flesh. He was forever after a hermit of sorts, taking his drab little meals alone, lying late into the night on his solitary bed, an image of a beautiful dusky face playing before his eyes like an apparition.

There had been a pharmacy three blocks from the church where they'd gone on several summer nights. They'd had malts at the old-fashioned Coke fountain, and laughed softly at each other's jokes.

Now, as he turned into the parking garage adjacent to the TV station, Josek thought of Rachael again.

Even fourteen years later, desire for her quickened his pulse, dizzied his mind. He wanted to hold her again, feel that exquisite and heartbreaking flesh pressed tenderly against his own flesh.

He pulled in and parked, sighing.

The years had gone so quickly.

In the rearview mirror, a stranger – balding now, and wrinkled about the eyes and mouth – stared back at him. He wondered what Rachael looked like now, and if she still thought of him sometimes.

Father William Josek got out of his rattletrap Datsun and walked over to the elevator that would take him to the thirty-fourth floor of the TV station.

RUNNER IN THE DARK

For the first time, he felt a little anxious about the debate tonight. Jessica Dennis was bright, articulate and passionate about the subject of the death penalty.

It was time for him to put Rachael out of his mind and concentrate on the discussion that lay ahead.

Then he had a jarring thought: what if Rachael lived somewhere within the viewing area?

What would she make of the balding middle-aged man he'd become?

He smiled to himself.

Maybe it was time he looked into a toupee.

The elevator arrived and took him up to the thirty-fourth floor.

2

At fourteen minutes after five, the Eagle Electric truck entered the Channel 8 parking garage.

The truck drove up fourteen floors and then pulled into an empty parking space.

Harrigan and Cates jumped out of the truck and then walked around back. They opened the doors and lifted out the metal suitcases with the EAGLE logo on the sides.

Harrigan set one of the suitcases flat and opened it up.

He checked quickly through the weapons and the ammunition. Everything was in place, and ready to go.

He closed up the first suitcase, and picked up the other one, repeating the process of laying it flat inside the truck, and then opening it up for inspection.

Everything was there. Two handguns, two automatic rifles.

Before closing the suitcase, Harrigan took the Walther and shoved it down inside the wide pocket of his coverall. He snapped shut the suitcase and handed it to Cates. He picked up the first suitcase himself, and then locked the truck.

They walked over to the elevator.

Cates pressed the UP button.

'You fellas must be having a long day.'

'Yeah,' Cates said.

'Thank God, my day is done. It was a pisser, believe me. A real pisser.'

'Yeah,' Cates said.

The elevator passenger was a yakker.

'Then you know what I did?'

'Forgot your briefcase?' Cates said.

'Hey, did I tell you that already?' the guy said.

His chunkiness was sleekly hidden inside expensive custom-tailoring. The blue topcoat was especially well cut.

'No,' Cates said. 'but you said you forgot something.'

'Well, you're a good guesser, my friend. That's *exactly* what I forgot. My bleepin' briefcase.' Then he smiled. ' "Bleepin'." My wife doesn't like me to use the "F" word. She's afraid the girls will pick it up.' He smiled. 'So I say "bleepin'." The wife thinks it's kind of cute.'

'Yeah,' Cates said.

He looked at Harrigan.

Harrigan was afraid Cates was going to say something sharp to the guy and then the guy would get suspicious. Harrigan had to admit, the guy was driving him crazy, too. This was like the elevator ride from hell.

'The gals at the office appreciate it, too,' the guy said.

'Appreciate?' Cates said.

'Yeah. Not using the "F" word.'

'Oh.'

'I figure, if you really have respect for women, you won't

use the "F" word around them. That's just my personal opinion, of course, but that's what it all comes down to anyway, right? Personal opinion.'

Finally, they reached thirty-two, the guy's floor.

'Well, here we are,' the guy said. 'You fellas have a nice night.'

With that, he strode from the elevator.

When the door was closed, Cates said, 'That fucker doesn't know how close he came to getting popped.'

That would be just like Cates, Harrigan thought. Popping somebody just because he was running his mouth.

The thirty-fourth floor was laid out with the newsroom taking up a third of the space, and the rest of the floor divided between four equal-size TV studios.

The first studio was the standing news set. Nothing was ever moved or changed around in here. You had to be prepared to go on the air instantly if there was some kind of crisis or emergency. So the lights were set, the news desk was fixed in place, the Chroma wall behind was left uncovered and ready for use, and the camera positions were marked off on the cold concrete floor with big red Xs of tape.

When Harrigan and Cates reached the thirty-fourth floor, they used their electronic passes to get inside the glass outer doors.

Because most of the non-news staff had gone home for the day, Harrigan and Cates had little trouble sneaking past the newsroom.

The reporters were all running around doing last-minute edits of videotape, rewriting copy, or putting on makeup for their brief on-camera appearances. Michael Shaw had been on the air since 5:00 and would remain on the air for another thirty-four minutes.

Harrigan and Cates walked down a narrow, dark corridor.

The armed guard appeared when they reached a black door marked STUDIO B in silver. He stood in front of the door.

He was not a standard-issue security guard. Most of them were young, out of shape, willing to swap poor pay and benefits for the excitement of wearing a uniform and carrying a walkie-talkie.

This man was a retired cop. He had the uniform and the nightstick. He also had the hard suspicious gaze of the long-time lawman. And he had the big imposing body of a guy who could kick ass when he had to.

Harrigan noted that the man's right hand had dropped to his holstered Magnum. He had already sensed something wrong.

'Evening,' he said.

'Evening.'

'Where're the boys tonight?' he said.

'They got into a little fender-bender on the expressway,' Harrigan said, 'so they asked us to cover for them.'

'How'd you get in?'

'We used their pass,' Cates said.

Stupid bastard.

Harrigan had been going to say that one of the news people had seen them at the door and buzzed them in.

The guard said, 'If they were in an accident, how did you get their card?'

Exactly, Harrigan thought. That's why it had been so stupid to say they'd used an electronic pass.

Cates glanced at Harrigan, his eyes filled with panic. Then he looked back at the guard and said, 'Well, we drove over to make sure they were all right.'

'Shit,' Harrigan said to Cates.

The guard was going for his gun.

RUNNER IN THE DARK

All Harrigan could do was take advantage of the empty hallway.

He grabbed the man's gun wrist, and at the same time clamped his other hand over the man's mouth.

Then he rammed the man hard against the door.

Cates came in fast, striking the guard hard on the side of the head with the butt of his handgun.

The guard went limp in Harrigan's arms.

Harrigan nodded to the Studio B door.

Cates opened it. Harrigan dragged the guard inside.

'Find the lights,' Harrigan said in the darkness. 'We have to look like we know what we're doing in here.'

Harrigan dragged the guard back against the nearest wall. Even in the darkness, he had no trouble tying up the man, and gagging him.

3

'To a second term,' Dylan Ames said, raising his wine glass and toasting Governor Standish and his wife Karen.

Early on in his relationship with the Governor, Dylan Ames had seen that Karen was the one with the brain, the drive and the balls for politics.

The best you could say for Governor Standish was that his great-grandfather and father had both been Governors of this state before him. Oh, and one other thing: Standish looked good in an expensive blue suit. With his gray hair, his noble features, and his bland mannerisms, he was the perfect TV politician.

'And thanks to you,' Karen Standish said, 'we'll *have* a second term.'

'I just can't thank you enough,' Governor Standish said in

that voice he used at all the podunk Kiwanis clubs when he was thanking them for giving him a plaque.

They were having a private dinner in the small but elegant dining room just off the main dining room in the Governor's mansion. Despite the carping of the press, Karen Standish had appointed the Governor's mansion most regally, including the $200,000 chandelier imported from Austria.

They finished their toast, and then Dylan Ames glanced at his watch. Ames was a rangy redhead given to tortoise-shell glasses, gray suits and endless tales about his days at Dartmouth. 'It won't be long now.'

'The debate?' Karen said.

Dylan Ames nodded.

'The debate. And Jessica Dennis is going to have that poor priest for dinner.'

Standish didn't really believe in capital punishment. Twenty-five years ago, during his father's first term in the Governor's mansion, a black man had been executed for a murder he said he didn't commit.

A year after the man's death, a private detective came up with the real murderer.

Standish's father was destroyed by this. He spent the rest of his life arguing against capital punishment. He took full responsibility for the innocent man's death. He preached the anti-capital punishment gospel – that most people who are executed are poor, black, and lastly, uneducated.

Despite Karen's protests, her husband ran as an anti-capital punishment conservative. He followed the party line in every way but that. And he won the election, despite a bitter primary battle with the Christian right. It was a squeaker, true, slightly less than one per cent being his margin of victory, but to the governor's mansion he went.

Midway through his term, however, violent crime increased

dramatically. In some parts of the state, vigilante groups were said to be forming.

Governor Standish's popularity plunged. He wouldn't change his mind about capital punishment. He'd been challenged especially hard by an extremely right-wing state senator. How could you have a Republican Governor who didn't favor capital punishment? the senator had asked.

When the party openly advocated challenging Standish in the next primary, Karen brought in Dylan Ames.

At first, Standish wouldn't even speak to the man. He saw Ames as a cynical barbarian and an enemy of true democracy.

But eventually, Karen and Dylan wore him down. He bought a five minute block of state-wide TV time one night to inform the voters that he'd changed his mind. He now advocated capital punishment in some cases.

He didn't really believe this, of course. Indeed, if anything, he believed more than ever that capital punishment didn't deter violent crime in any way.

But as his polls plummeted, he'd learned something terrible about himself. He'd always prided himself on his selflessness. He came from a political family and saw his venture into politics as an expression of noble purpose. The upper classes *should* give of themselves.

Then, when his popularity in the polls reached twenty-two per cent, he saw himself for what he was: a politician who loved the status of office, and who would do virtually anything to keep that office. And now his hold on the governor's office was threatened with a recall movement if he attempted to stay Roy Gerard's execution.

But Standish didn't like to be reminded of his cynical shift on the matter of executions.

'Well, the debate starts in a few minutes,' Dylan Ames said, trying to lessen the tension that was suddenly in the air.

'Why don't we go in the den and get the old TV set warmed up?'

Governor Standish smiled. He really did have a photogenic face. He looked like every actor ever used in a milk commercial. He stood up and smiled at Dylan.

'Let's go watch Jessica Dennis kick some priestly butt tonight,' Governor Standish said, trying in vain to sound like one of the boys. But he'd never *been* one of the boys, and never would be.

4

They would be in place now.

Or in a very few minutes.

Roy Gerard stood at the window staring out at the rain-lashed darkness.

Soon.

Very soon.

Freedom.

He literally ached at the prospect of it.

Tears shone in his eyes.

Freedom.

Even in Cuba, the good life could be his. God knew there would be sufficient money. David had told him that there was more than nine million dollars in cash and negotiables.

The ache came again, a longing both physical and psychological, a longing to walk the streets, to sleep with women, to spend a day golden with sunlight on an ocean of deep and abiding blue.

David and the others would be in place now.

And soon he would be free.

Soon.

5

'Slow down, Mr Ludlow, or I'll shoot you right here.'

Huddled deep in his topcoat, Ryan Ludlow kept looking for some way to escape David Gerard.

Ludlow and Gerard walked through the rain. They'd left the hotel ten minutes ago and were now nearing the Trealor building.

Ludlow had to give Gerard credit for making his plans thoroughly and carefully.

Gerard had obviously followed him for at least a few weeks. He'd figured out Ludlow's patterns and vulnerabilities. Then he'd seen the easiest way to use Ludlow to get into Channel 8. Walk into Ludlow's hotel room after the assignation was over with.

Ludlow looked around frantically for any opportunity to bolt from Gerard but none presented itself.

The streets were dark and empty.

By now, the downtown workers had fled to the expressways and were well on their way home to the suburbs.

Ludlow slowed down for a red light but Gerard nudged him.

'Just keep walking,' he said.

Ludlow could hardly believe this was David Gerard. But the man not only told him his name but boasted about the plastic surgery he'd had done in Europe.

They continued walking side by side, the gun in Gerard's trenchcoat pocket ready to explode at any moment.

In his left hand, Gerard carried a small metal suitcase.

Ludlow noted the careful, almost delicate way that Gerard held it.

They reached the corner of the Trealor building.

This time, because of the traffic, they couldn't cross against the red light.

Ludlow was soaked by now. He could feel his throat starting to scratch.

Darkness. Rain. Whipping wind.

He wanted to be home in his basement TV room, a beer in one hand and the Sports Channel on the tube. There would likely be a couple of prize fights tonight.

'Let's go,' Gerard said when the light changed.

Ludlow sighed, and whispered something like a prayer.

This was the real start of it.

Now.

Whatever Gerard had in mind for tonight.

A cold, clammy, invisible hand gripped Ludlow's bowels. Why couldn't he find anybody to help him?

'Get your pass out so we can go past the guard with no trouble,' Gerard said.

Once again, Ludlow felt the impulse to simply flee.

Maybe Gerard wouldn't fire in the downtown area this way. Or, if he did fire, maybe he'd miss.

Ludlow was in reasonably good shape.

He could run and—

But no, he knew he wouldn't.

Running from somebody armed like Gerard took a kind of crazy courage Ludlow simply didn't have.

6

Right after the newscast was over, Shaw got up from behind the desk, thanked the crew for their help, and then hurried out of Studio A.

Three minutes later, he peeked in the office of Ryan Ludlow.

The office was empty.

Shaw hoped this meant that Ludlow was personally

checking out all the critical entrances tonight.

Finished here, Shaw hurried back to Studio B. He knew that Jessica would be arriving soon. The debate was only twenty minutes away.

7

Detective Ribicoff stepped off the elevator and looked around the lobby.

He saw nothing untoward.

Jessica watched him with great fondness. He was so good at what he did, so careful and methodical. She really appreciated it.

He walked around the lobby, giving it a quick survey and reporting their status to someone over his walkie-talkie. Then he came back and said: 'Looks all right, Jessica. There's a sign that says STUDIOS. We'll just go down that hall.'

Jessica got off the elevator car and followed Detective Ribicoff through the lobby. The walls were decorated with framed photos of local news stars as well as key network stars. The empty desks lent a lonely touch to the lobby.

'Well, well, well, look who's here,' Detective Ribicoff said as he followed the STUDIOS sign around the corner. 'A familiar face.'

'How are you?' Michael Shaw's voice said. He'd known Ribicoff for many years. They liked each other a great deal. 'You wouldn't happen to have a beautiful young woman with you, would you?'

That's when Jessica came around the corner, smiling.

She couldn't help herself. She walked over to him and hugged him. She was eager to talk to him tonight, eager to try and settle everything and get on with a life together.

Shaw returned the hug, and topped it off with a quick but fond little kiss on the lips.

'That's just what I needed for the debate tonight,' Jessica smiled. 'Energy.'

'You don't need anything,' Detective Ribicoff said. 'You'll do just fine.'

'She sure will,' Shaw said.

'We'd better get going,' Jessica said. 'Cornell wanted us there a little early.'

'I'm going back to my office and watch from there,' Shaw said.

'Wish me luck.'

He gave her another quick kiss.

'I'm looking forward to tonight,' he said.

She smiled. 'So am I.'

Detective Ribicoff said, 'Well, lovebirds, I'd say this is where we'd better get to work.'

They all laughed as Ribicoff led Jessica to Studio B.

Shaw was walking through the lobby, on the way to his office in the newsroom, when the elevator doors opened and Ryan Ludlow appeared. There was a blond man with him.

'Hi, Ryan,' Shaw said. 'I was just over at your office. I wanted to see how security was going tonight.'

'Going just fine,' Ludlow said.

Shaw had the sense that something was wrong with Ludlow. Usually, he spoke in a hearty voice. He sounded tight, almost strained now, as if the words were difficult to get out.

His normally animated face – one of those wide Irish faces that reflected feeling like a mirror – looked closed and tense.

'I'm Win Besler, by the way,' the blond man said.

He put out a hard, strong hand and shook with Shaw. He smelled of expensive cologne.

'I used to work with Ryan on the force.' He smiled. 'Used to try and keep the big guy here out of trouble.'

'You bring him in to help tonight?' Shaw asked Ludlow.

'Yeah,' Ludlow said. 'That's right. Brought him in to help tonight.'

Ludlow seemed increasingly uncomfortable. Shaw watched his face carefully but didn't see anything obvious. The Irishman just seemed – inhibited, somehow.

'Well, we'd better get to the studio, Ryan. We told them a quarter of.'

'Oh, right,' Ludlow said. 'A quarter of.'

Shaw took a final look at him.

'You feeling all right, Ryan?'

'Just fine.'

'You sure?'

Win Besler grinned.

'He took me out for a spaghetti dinner. I think we both overate.'

Win Besler nodded.

'Nice to meet you, Mr Shaw.'

'Nice meeting you.'

Shaw went to his office trying to figure out what was going on with Ryan Ludlow.

Something sure was.

Chapter Five

1

Jessica was impressed with how quickly the cool dark room became a functioning TV studio.

Three people with headsets invaded the room and began turning on key overhead lights, all focused on a small set near a wide flat near the back of the studio. There was a logo on the flat: NEWS TODAY. In front of the flat was a good round mahogany table with three matching magazine chairs. This was where William Cornell and his two guests always sat.

Jessica watched as monitors, snake-like lengths of cable, and more lights were put in place. The people setting up the studio talked constantly to the director's booth over their headsets.

An older woman in an artist's smock came over and started daubing makeup on Jessica's face.

'You've got a wonderful complexion,' the woman said.

'Thank you.'

As the woman was finishing up, a man in a dark suit and Roman collar approached them and put out his hand.

'Jessica, I'm Father Josek.'

The priest was a nice-looking man in his early fifties. His

dark eyes were grave. She felt comfortable with him immediately. There was a wisdom in his gaze.

'I'm very glad to meet you, Father.'

She was going to say more but a voice near the front of the studio boomed, 'There they are – my two sumo wrestlers for the evening!'

William Cornell was making his entrance, complete with three-piece suit, hairsprayed head, and clipboard.

'The big thing to remember, you two,' Cornell said, talking to both of them as if they were very lowly employees, 'is that we want drama and passion. That's why people watch my show. And that's how I got to be the most important political reporter in this state.'

And the most modest, Jessica thought sarcastically.

'You understand that, Father?'

'Well, I'm sure you don't want to hear this, Mr Cornell, but I can actually see both sides of this issue. My belief in God precludes me from taking a human life, but the desire for vengeance is very understandable.'

'Oh, great,' Cornell said. 'An open-minded guest. You're here to argue *against* the death penalty, Father. Jab at this woman every chance you get.'

Father Josek looked at Jessica and smiled.

'Maybe Mr Cornell here will loan us a couple of dueling pistols, Jessica.'

'Or swords. I took a semester of fencing in college.'

But Cornell, who was all nervous energy before the start of a show, had no interest in their little jokes.

He was already walking away from them, barking at one of the technicians who had apparently done something to displease the great man.

Father Josek and Jessica chatted for the next few minutes. She liked the priest more and more.

RUNNER IN THE DARK

It was during this time that she noticed the two men in the far north corner. They both wore green coveralls with EAGLE ELECTRIC stitched on the back. They had been working at a small bench ever since she'd come in the studio. They didn't seem to be doing anything in particular, either. They'd also kept their backs to everybody, not turning around even once. She wondered what they were doing.

But then her attention was distracted when Detective Ribicoff came over.

Jessica introduced him to Father Josek.

'I don't know how you could disagree with anybody as pretty as she is,' Detective Ribicoff said.

The priest laughed.

'It won't be easy, believe me.'

'Actually, Father,' Detective Ribicoff said, 'I've heard a lot of good things about you and your parish. You've done a great job over there.'

Father Josek looked embarrassed.

'Thank you.'

Then William Cornell – 'the most important political reporter in this state' – started kicking everybody out of the studio who didn't belong there.

This included Detective Ribicoff.

'Good luck to both of you,' Ribicoff said to Jessica and the priest. 'Though I have to admit, Father, I'll be pulling for her side.'

The priest smiled and the men shook hands again.

'Now's when I give you my little pre-game pep talk,' Cornell said, starting to bend over as if he was going into a huddle.

As Jessica leaned over to listen to him, she glanced at the two men in the green overalls again.

EAGLE ELECTRIC.

231

They still hadn't turned around. They still didn't seem to be doing anything at that small table over there.

Maybe she should have said something to Detective Ribicoff...

Michael Shaw couldn't help it.

He just kept thinking of Ryan Ludlow's face there in the hallway.

Something was wrong.

He'd never seen Ludlow act like that before.

Sitting in his office, Shaw leaned over and picked up the receiver and punched in Ludlow's number.

Maybe Ryan was alone now and could tell him what was going on...

One more guard to get past.

As David Gerard and Ryan Ludlow approached the security man standing in front of STUDIO B, Gerard slipped his gun out of his coat pocket and brought it up into plain sight.

The guard saw Gerard's gun but way too late.

'Take your gun out of your holster and set it nice and gentle down on the floor,' Gerard said.

'Should I do it, Mr Ludlow?' the guard asked his boss.

'There isn't any choice,' Ludlow said.

The guard did as instructed.

'Now I'm going to walk into that studio, and you two are going to stand right where you are. You understand?'

He gave Ludlow a violent shove.

Ludlow and the security guard now stood next to each other on the far side of the STUDIO B door.

'Just stay right there, and don't move,' Gerard said.

He walked over to the door and opened it up. He kept his eyes on Ludlow and the security man.

He was just stepping over the threshold when he sensed somebody walking toward him from inside the studio—.

The image registered very simply on Sam Ribicoff's mind: man in doorway with gun.

All of Ribicoff's training took over.

He crouched, jerking his police weapon from its shoulder rigging.

Ludlow took out his own weapon and started to fire at Gerard's back. But it was too late.

Gerard was already inside the studio and firing his own gun.

Just as Ludlow moved to the door, it slammed shut.

All this happened in less than two seconds.

But it was one second too long because by the time Ribicoff's finger reached the trigger, the other man was already—

—Firing.

Two quick shots and the man's chest exploded.

Cop. He had to be a cop, with a weapon like that.

He lay in the center of the floor now, blood already forming a puddle around his torso.

His legs had started twitching.

Death throes, Gerard knew.

They were ugly as hell to watch.

Jessica watched it all in disbelief.

Detective Ribicoff drawing his gun.

The man in the doorway turning toward the policeman, gun in hand. And then the shots.

The two terrible shots.

Jessica heard herself scream.

She ran to where Detective Ribicoff lay in the middle of the studio floor. She held his head gently between her hands, as if he was an infant who required the most tender of care.

Then the blond man was standing over her.

'All right, bitch,' he said, pointing the gun right at her upturned face. 'Get back to your seat or I'll kill you right here.'

She noticed two things in quick succession: the blond man carried a metal suitcase.

And the two men in the EAGLE ELECTRIC coveralls were finally turning around.

They had automatic pistols in their hands, the favorite of terrorists around the world.

2

Kray took off from the small airport just after six that night. The rain had abated somewhat, but he fought south-southwest winds at about thirty knots.

Kray had done some of his yoga exercises before taking off. He'd learned yoga from a Korean chick he'd spent a spring with. At one time, he'd done a lot of drugs but after learning yoga, drugs no longer appealed to him. Yoga was a faster and better way to relax.

There were going to be two very spooky moments tonight and he needed to be prepared emotionally for them.

The first one was coming up very soon.

The state prison was less than thirty miles away. He would be there in practically no time.

He had rehearsed his landing many times – in his mind. But nothing could prepare him for the tension he'd feel just sitting there on the yard. He would be surrounded by guards with guns. Guards who would be eager to kill him.

He swung wide to the west now, headed straight for the tall gray walls of the prison.

David Gerard was paying him a quarter of a million dollars for tonight.

Kray knew that he was going to earn every penny of it.

3

Detective Ribicoff lay unmoving by the studio door. His blood flooded the floor now.

David Gerard, who had introduced himself to Jessica, had cleared the studio of everybody except his own two men and Father Josek, William Cornell, Jessica and one cameraman whose pink shirt was already soaked with sweat.

Gerard had put all the chairs in a row in front of the mahogany table. This was where the priest, the host and Jessica sat now.

'I want that camera turned around so I can talk to it,' David Gerard said.

The camera operator looked over at William Cornell.

Cornell nodded solemnly.

The camera operator turned the camera around and found Gerard in the lens.

'How long before we're on the air?' Gerard said.

'Thirty-five seconds,' said the cameraman.

'You tell them in the director's booth that if they don't broadcast this I'm going to kill you. You understand?'

The cameraman nodded slowly.

He spoke quietly into the microphone of his headset.

From inside his coat pocket, Gerard took a TV set about the size of a paperback.

He turned it on and put the channel on 8.

The six-inch screen read:

TECHNICAL DIFFICULTIES
PLEASE STAND BY

Gerard walked over to the cameraman and put the weapon up against the man's left temple.

'I want live coverage of this. I don't want any slide. You hear me?'

There was a long pause. Easy to imagine them in the booth, scrambling around, trying to figure out what to do next.

'God dammit,' the cameraman said into the microphone. 'You gotta do this, man. He'll kill me. He really will.'

Gerard grinned.

'Damned right, I will.'

He checked the tiny screen again.

And there it was.

The studio.

'Pan around,' Gerard said. 'Show the folks at home what's going on here.'

Gerard looked over at the body of Detective Ribicoff.

The man's legs were still twitching. The acrid smell of feces intermingled with the scent of blood now, and David Gerard's sensitive nostrils twitched fastidiously.

'We're on the air,' the cameraman said.

The blond man addressed the camera as if he had spent his entire life acting.

'My name is David Gerard. I realize that I don't *look* like David Gerard, and for that I'm very grateful to two plastic surgeons in England.'

He nodded to Harrigan and Cates.

'These men are here to help me tonight. There isn't much

time – and to show you that we're all very serious about what we're doing, I'd ask the cameraman to widen out a little so we can see our friend on the floor over here.'

In the monitor, the camera showed Detective Ribicoff's body.

'Just so there's no mistake about how serious we are...' David repeated.

The camera lingered on the body on the floor.

'*That's* how serious we are,' he finished.

He looked back at the camera.

'We're in this studio tonight for one reason. We want to swap hostages. I want my brother released from prison in exchange for these three folks sitting here now. Show the people what they look like,' he said to the cameraman.

His calm was chilling.

He sounded like a host on a game show.

A very slick host.

Jessica stared vacantly at David Gerard. She hadn't recovered from the shock of watching Sam Ribicoff get shot.

'Let's have the camera back here,' David said.

Then smiled.

'Nice-looking, isn't she? Well, I'm going to have to mar those looks just a little bit when I strap a bomb to one of those shapely legs of hers.'

He reached inside his jacket pocket and took the silver canister from the metal suitcase he'd opened earlier.

'This may look small but there's enough material in here to blow up the entire floor of this building we're in. Imagine what it'll do to Jessica if it's set off. And I can set it off very easily.'

From the other pocket he took a black plastic oblong with a red button in the center. The entire device was no more than five inches long and two inches wide.

'This red button will detonate the bomb from up to three hundred yards away. And, yes, I know that I and my men will die. But we're prepared for that. We knew that that was the risk when we went into this.'

He put the trigger device back in his pocket, picked up his gun and walked calmly over to Jessica.

The camera followed him.

Jessica wondered how many million viewers were already watching. She could imagine how rapt they were – one person had already been horribly shot.

And in all likelihood, a few others would die in this studio before the night was over.

Yes, millions would be watching with grisly fascination – and millions more would soon be watching, too.

Jessica couldn't blame them.

She'd tune in, too. Who could resist?

David Gerard had a wide hard hand and it came out of nowhere and caught Jessica on the left corner of her jaw. She was jarred so hard that blackness filled her eyes momentarily, and she could taste blood where her teeth had chomped down on her tongue.

'I just want to make sure you don't give me any trouble when I strap this bomb to your leg,' David said, smiling down at her.

The camera recorded every single moment of Gerard bending over and strapping the bomb to her leg. There were three small buckles fixing the canister to her.

Then he stood up and said, 'At exactly eight o'clock tonight – which is one hour and forty-six minutes from now – a helicopter is going to land at the prison and pick up my brother. If it *doesn't* pick up my brother, everybody in this studio is going to die. I just want to make sure that you all understand that.'

Then he looked directly into the camera and grinned. His resemblance to Jack Nicholson became particularly noticeable when he grinned.

'Good,' he said. 'Now we'll start doing things *my* way.'

He turned then and cracked his left leg against one of the monitors. 'Shit!' he cried, bending to touch his left leg. He glared at Jessica. 'I broke the damned thing a year ago and it didn't heal right.'

He grimaced and limped away.

Shaw had been sitting in his office, waiting for the debate to start, when he heard the gunshots. He glanced quickly at the TV monitor and saw the picture go dark and the standard TECHNICAL DIFFICULTIES slide go on.

He'd run down the hall to Studio B but Ryan Ludlow was on his feet, his head bleeding, telling people to stay back.

'But Jessica's in there,' Shaw said.

'He's taken them hostage, Michael. We've all got to stay calm.'

Blood was pouring out beneath the hand he held to the top of his head. Ludlow had explained to Shaw what had happened, Gerard forcing him at gunpoint to take him inside the TV station.

Outside the studio, the night had already become shrill with siren-topped emergency vehicles racing to the thirty-nine-story building that housed Channel 8.

'There isn't any other way in there?' Shaw said.

'Not that I know of,' Ludlow said.

Shaw forced himself to calm down. Ludlow was correct. Now was the time for sober thought.

'You'd better have somebody look at your head, Ryan,' Shaw said.

'Thanks, Michael. Once the police get here, we can put a

plan together. Right now we just have to stay cool.'

Shaw went back to the newsroom, so he could watch on the monitors there. Every few seconds, he would almost explode, then force himself to back off.

Shaw watched as the camera once again panned the hostages David Gerard had sat in chairs and grouped together in a straight line in front of the set – Cornell, the priest, Jessica.

Their eyes had the slightly glazed look of shock victims. They were still trying to sort through everything that had happened in the last few minutes.

David Gerard might be used to this kind of death; his hostages weren't.

'There's somebody to see you, Michael,' one of the videotape editors came up to him and said. 'Out in the hall.'

Shaw thanked him, and started to walk out the door, but couldn't pull his eyes from the TV screen—

If he just kept watching her, maybe nothing bad would happen to her . . .

David Gerard was bending over now and taping the small silver canister to Jessica's right calf.

Shaw had no doubt that it was the powerful bomb David Gerard claimed it was.

David was clearly not a man given to idle threats.

Shaw watched as Jessica's entire body shrank back from Gerard's touch, as if she wanted to climb up the chair backward and escape.

Shaw was getting caught up in it all again. He was terrified that something would happen to Jessica if he turned away.

As long as he kept watching her, she'd be all right—

Irrational, he knew.

But then this whole evening was irrational, unthinkable. Even, in some ways, dreamlike . . .

The hall.

RUNNER IN THE DARK

Somebody.

Waiting.

He forced himself to divert his eyes from the TV screen, to make his legs move in the direction of the door that opened onto the hallway.

He recognized her instantly, of course: Samantha from Jessica's office. The woman Jessica always said 'really does most of my work for me.'

She was slumped against the wall, her eyes downcast, her body lost in the folds of her dark blue raincoat.

When she heard Shaw, she looked up. Tears filled her eyes.

'I can't believe this,' she said.

'No,' he said, 'neither can I.'

And then she was in his arms, and he was holding her as tightly as she held him.

Her body felt reassuring, comforting.

Finally, after they let go of each other, she said, 'I came over to give her a little moral support. I thought I'd just sit quietly in the studio and watch the debate. Surprise her, you know.'

'That was nice of you.'

'But now—'

Tears took her eyes and voice again.

Shaw let her cry. She obviously needed to.

Then: 'There's something I need to tell you, Michael.' She paused. 'About Jessica.'

Alarm coursed through his entire body. Was he about to learn some dark secret that would make this night even worse?

For several long moments, Shaw was a being of fear, of dread, and dire apprehension.

'What is it?'

She said it simply: 'She wanted to tell you herself today but somehow the right moment never came along. So she was going to tell you later tonight.'

'Is she sick?' Shaw said, terrified of the answer he might receive.

Then Samantha startled him by smiling through her tears. 'Oh, no. She's not sick. Aside from a little morning sickness, anyway.'

She reached out and touched his hand.

'She's three months pregnant, Michael.'

Part Four

Chapter One

1

Roy Gerard tried hard not to smile.

The Warden had dispatched two armed guards to stay with him in the visitors' room.

Stationing the guards in the hall wasn't good enough anymore.

The Warden was clearly rattled by the events of the past fifteen minutes, almost all of it broadcast over Channel 8 and picked up by their national network and CNN.

Apparently, he was afraid that Roy Gerard was going to turn into a bat and fly through the barred windows.

Roy sat in one of the lumpy armchairs and watched the TV set.

The guards watched, too, spellbound.

Roy fought against the smile that played at either end of his mouth.

So perfect, this whole thing.

Killing the detective had been great.

Exactly what the Governor and the Warden needed to see to convince them that there was no use fighting, that David would kill every single one of the hostages unless he got his way.

For the first time in the entire year they'd been planning all this, Roy Gerard knew absolutely that this plan was going to work out.

He was going to be leaving this prison.

Tonight.

'Somethin' funny?' one of the guards said.

'What?' Roy's mind had been drifting.

'I asked if somethin' was funny. You were smilin'.' Like too many prison guards, this one was slow of mind but quick of temper.

'I didn't mean to smile.'

'He just killed some poor cop and you're smilin',' the guard insisted.

He started across the room to Roy but the other guard put a hand on his arm.

'Calm down,' the second guard said. 'He's smilin' 'cos he thinks he's gonna get out of here tonight. But he's wrong. He ain't ever gettin' out of here except tomorrow morning when they carry him out in a pine box.'

The first guard shrugged off the halting hand.

'You hear that, Gerard? That's the only way you're gettin' out of this place. In a pine box.'

Roy couldn't resist pissing the guard off just one more time. It was like teasing a mean dog who was fenced in and couldn't get at you.

Roy smirked.

He said, 'I guess we'll see about that, won't we?'

He made the smirk as obnoxious as possible.

2

Governor Bob Standish said, 'He'll kill all of them, won't he? If he doesn't get his way, I mean.'

He spoke to both his wife and his consultant, Dylan Ames.

After dinner, they'd gone into the den to watch the debate about capital punishment.

Then David Gerard suddenly appeared on the screen.

Dylan Ames was up and pacing the handsomely appointed room. 'It doesn't matter what *he* does, Governor. All that matters is what *you* do.'

He stopped pacing.

'This is the biggest opportunity you've ever been handed.'

Standish looked at his wife. He obviously wasn't quite sure what Dylan Ames was talking about.

'How is it a big opportunity?' Standish said to Ames.

'Because it's going to show the far right of our party just what an ass-kicking tough guy you really are.'

Political consultants loved melodrama.

Half of what they said sounded like the copy in their TV spots – lurid, angry, intimidating.

'You don't give in to David Gerard,' Ames said.

'What if he keeps killing people?'

'You still don't give in.'

'What if he says he's going to detonate that bomb he strapped on to Jessica Dennis' leg?'

'You don't back down. *You don't back down.* That's the message, Governor. Think about the TV spots.'

Ames started painting pictures aloud with words. He also started pacing again.

'The only sound is of this bomb ticking. Can you hear it? Then we see this really grotesque picture of David Gerard. And Jessica Dennis with the bomb strapped to her leg. Can you see it?'

'I can see it, Dylan,' the Governor's wife said.

' "Only one man stood tall against the barbarians at the gates of democracy." ' Ames said, pacing faster now, his voice ever more dramatic. ' "And that was Governor Bob Standish." '

And then the ticking sound stops and we see Bob with the mountains in the background, and he's dressed up kind of western, and he looks right at the camera and says, "Americans like us, we don't back down just because a few bad guys want to destroy our country." Something like that, anyway.'

'God, it's wonderful,' the Governor's wife said.

But Standish only shook his head.

'A lot of people could die tonight, Dylan. Right now I couldn't give a damn about my re-election campaign. How. would you feel if it was your daughter in that studio tonight?'

Dylan Ames said, 'It's my job to think ahead, Governor. That's what you pay me for.'

But Standish was still disgusted by the cynicism of Ames' proposal.

'Sometimes I wonder why I pay you at all,' Standish said.

Wife and consultant exchanged quick glances. This was the side of good old Bob Standish they both hated. When he got independent like this.

A knock on the door.

'Yes?' Standish said.

The maid peeked in and said, 'Your brother is on the phone, sir.'

'Thanks, Dolores.'

'Yessir.'

Standish glanced at his wife.

'I'm going to take it in my office. Let me know if anything special happens with the hostages.'

'Wait a minute,' she said. 'I'm coming with you.'

3

The police responded to the situation in the studio by putting in place eighteen members of their hostage/terrorist unit. This meant nine male and female detectives who had been trained in hostage negotiation and nine men and women called containment officers. The first group was trained to use persuasion and patience; the second group was trained to use, when and if necessary, deadly force.

Along with their Commanding Officer – Commander William Beaudine, a much-decorated black lawman who was being talked about as a possible mayoral candidate – the hostage unit fanned out up and down the hall. The negotiators worked in teams of three, usually – one group who gathered information about the hostage-taker; one group who relayed the information to other officers; and the primary negotiator, the man or woman who stayed in constant contact with the hostage-taker in an effort to keep him calm. Because David Gerard was a known quantity, not much of a background check had to be done on him.

There were two other officers present, both members of the Bomb Squad, both trained extensively at the Redstone Arsenal in Huntsville, Alabama by the FBI. In their time, they had worked with everything from huge bombs meant to destroy buildings, to hand grenades meant to destroy a single room, to letter bombs meant to kill the person opening the letter.

Shaw watched as the police filled up the corridor leading to the studio.

Commander Beaudine was an old friend of Shaw's. They'd both worked the worst areas in town when they'd been rookies, Shaw at journalism, Beaudine at being a cop.

When Shaw walked over to him there at the head of the corridor, Beaudine gave Shaw's arm a squeeze and said, 'We're going to get her out of there alive, Michael. We're going to get all of them out of there alive.'

'I'm not sure your negotiators are going to do any good.'

Beaudine, a solidly built man of six foot, said, 'They surprise me all the time, Michael. They may be able to reason with him.'

He nodded at the elevators.

'Somebody's bringing me the architectural plans for this floor. I'll know more when I go over them.'

'I want to be involved in any way I can. Directly, if I can be.'

Beaudine, who was in his full uniform, indicated the negotiators in the corridor.

'For right now, we'll stick with them, Michael. The big thing you need in a situation like this is patience.'

A small war was what it looked like to Shaw at this point, all the good guys massing outside the studio door with weapons, their equipment, their skills and their hopes that things turned out well.

The bad guys were inside, working through the plans they'd obviously been making for a long time.

The chief hostage negotiator, a short man with a gray crewcut and dark eyes that crackled with intelligence, was already on the phone and trying to establish contact inside with David Gerard.

The elevator doors opened and a young man who looked out of breath walked directly to Commander Beaudine.

'You asked for plans to this floor, Commander.'

The young man, dressed in a sweater, shirt and tie, handed over a roll of architectural whiteprints.

'Thanks,' Commander Beaudine said. Then to Shaw: 'Can we use your office to look these over?'

Shaw was grateful he was being included.

He turned and led the way back to the office.

★ ★ ★

Meanwhile, more than thirty uniformed police officers went floor to floor, office to office, clearing the building.

4

Harrigan had to force himself to concentrate. He kept thinking about his daughter Linda.

He kept wondering if she was going to be all right.

He shuddered inwardly every time he thought of her losing her breasts.

The poor kid.

Harrigan returned his mind to the studio.

By now, David Gerard had worked himself into his Jack Nicholson mood. He was doing his 'Heeeeere's Johnny!' routine.

He kept walking back and forth, back and forth, in front of the hostages.

Every few steps, he'd suddenly lunge at one of them, seeing if he could make them show fear.

Gerard had to keep doing it a few times but then he suddenly got to William Cornell, the columnist.

Without warning, Gerard turned on Cornell.

He put the gun up to Cornell's mouth and said, 'Open wide, fat man. We're going to give you a little dental checkup here.'

Cornell's wide face crawled with crystal bubbles of sweat.

He wouldn't open his mouth.

Gerard said, 'I'm going to kill you, fat man. Do you understand that?'

Cornell's eyes widened. He gulped.

His lips parted.

Gerard pushed the gun inside.

★ ★ ★

The prison searchlights cut through the black night enshrouding the prison. The lights criss-crossed each other in the silver slanting rain, picking out the rainclouds obscuring the moon. Occasionally, silhouetted guards could be seen in the tower, their automatic rifles held at the ready.

A half-dozen state police planes and helicopters were in the air space surrounding the prison. Because of the gloom, none could be seen but their engines could all be heard.

They were all on the lookout for the helicopter that David Gerard had said would be landing.

Down on the ground, near the entrance to the prison, the two groups of protestors kept up their vigil.

When word came of David Gerard commandeering the TV studio, the pro-death penalty protestors gleefully informed their foes what had just happened.

Their foes tried to pretend that it didn't matter, that this was a matter of principle, not simply the matter of one man.

But you could see in their tired faces that this was just about the worst news they could possibly get.

They marched on as they had marched on so many other nights for causes as varied as civil rights, saving whales, doing away with nuclear energy, and sparing forests from clear cutting.

Though they were frequently depicted as fools, they were not foolish at all, not in their hearts anyway, nor in their minds, where they envisioned a revolution that would make of humanity all the things that Buddha and Jesus Christ of Nazareth and Gandhi and Martin Luther King, Jr had longed for it to be.

But David Gerard sure wasn't making their mission any easier.

He sure wasn't.

They marched on through the rain and mud, past the hoots and scorn of those who thought them foolish.

5

'You're lucky, fat man,' David Gerard said to William Cornell. 'You're lucky I didn't waste you right on the spot.'

Slowly, he withdrew the gun barrel from Cornell's mouth.

Then he looked right at the camera: 'I hope you're watching, Governor Standish. And I hope you're just about ready to pick up that phone and release my brother.'

Then he walked quickly to the far end of the line, to where Jessica sat.

'How we doing with that bomb, sweetheart?'

He brought the detonator out from his jacket pocket. Put his thumb dangerously close to the red button in the center of the detonator.

'Boom, sweetheart. Boom boom boom.'

Then he looked at the camera directly again. 'See those two friends of mine over there?' He pointed his gun at Harrigan and Cates. 'Well, I'm going to let them decide who dies first. They can vote on it. I mean, this is a democracy, isn't it, folks?'

Jessica tried not to notice the stain in the lap of William Cornell. While she'd never cared for the blustery, arrogant political reporter, she didn't enjoy seeing him reduced to wetting his pants.

She wasn't the only one who noticed, either.

When David Gerard saw it, he said, 'Bring the camera over here.'

Cornell seemed to sense what was coming. He tried to cover

the big wet spot on his trousers with his coat.

'Stand up, Cornell.'

Cornell glanced at the other hostages. Shame had replaced terror in his eyes. He looked meek as a small boy.

Jessica felt terrible for him.

'Why don't you leave him alone?' Jessica said to Gerard.

But Gerard paid no attention.

'Stand up, Cornell,' he said again. 'I want to share this moment with the folks at home. You know what a cocky bastard this guy is on his TV show, folks? Well, you know what he just did?'

'Leave him alone!' Jessica said.

And started out of her chair, despite the bomb attached to her calf.

Father Josek grabbed her, pulled her back down.

'That's smart thinking, Father. Because the next time that bitch bothers me, she's going to be in a lot of pain. You talk to her, Father. Make sure she understands that, all right?'

Jessica tried to get up again but the priest kept a tight grip on her waist. And he followed that by putting a hand on her shoulder, too.

Gerard turned back to Cornell.

'You want to tell all the folks at home what you just did?' Gerard said.

Cornell kept his head down.

He looked as though he was trying to will all this to simply go away.

'You hear me, Cornell? You want to tell all the folks at home what you just did to yourself?'

Cornell's head remained down.

Gerard smirked into the camera.

'Guess he's shy. I'll have to give him a little help.'

From his trouser pocket, he took something long and black.

A switchblade knife.

He snicked it open.

'Cornell? You hear me?'

But he didn't wait.

He glanced at the camera again then brought the knife across the side of Cornell's neck in a vicious arc.

The political reporter boiled up out of his seat, screaming in pain, clamping a hand to his already bloody neck.

Gerard pointed to the big wet spot around the crotch of Cornell's trousers.

'Look at that, will you, folks? That's how tense things are up here tonight.'

Cornell was more concerned with his pride than his wound.

He took a handkerchief out of his pocket and clamped it over the cut, which was really only a minor one, and sat back down so nobody could see the crotch of his trousers.

Gerard continued laughing and smiling, apparently having a lot of fun.

'You know what, Cornell? This is what folks are going to remember you for – wetting your pants. Isn't that right, folks?'

Then, almost shouting into the camera: 'I'll bet you're starting to get tense, aren't you, folks? You're starting to wonder if any of these three people are going to get out of here alive, aren't you?'

He smiled at the camera.

'Well, I guess we'll just have to find out now, won't we?'

The state planes picked up Mitch Kray when he was still seven miles from the prison. They hung back, not giving him any real trouble, but they definitely planned to stay right along beside him all night.

Kray did some yoga breathing exercises. And he thought of

all the things the Gerard money was going to buy him. Eventually, after his time had run out in Cuba, he'd go to Europe and live out his life there. While he was not a racist exactly, he didn't want to spend his life among the darker-skinned people of South America. Europe, specifically Austria and Germany, would make him much more comfortable.

Eventually, he saw the prison outlined against the night. The rain continued and a heavy fog was setting in.

The state planes continued to track him.

His mouth was dry. He was scared. He just had to keep thinking of the lifelong freedom the Gerard money would buy him.

He would set down in the prison yard, waiting for Roy Gerard to be brought out to him, and suddenly the helicopter would be surrounded.

Scary as shit, even for an old mercenary hand like Kray.

He just had to keep thinking about the money that waited at the dark end of this night . . .

He guided his helicopter toward the prison.

Chapter Two

1

'Is everybody watching the clock?' David Gerard said. 'The way I'm counting, we've got eleven minutes to go before we execute somebody.'

Then he looked at the clock on the wall: 'A little less than ten minutes now.'

The hostages sat in their chairs looking at him.

They had no doubt he was willing to kill them.

All of them, if necessary.

Jessica had never seen a man come apart as quickly and thoroughly as William Cornell was doing at the moment.

He'd not only wet his pants, he'd also started twitching violently, so violently that his entire body and chair moved when one of the spasms passed through him. His clothes were soaked with sweat, and he made tiny wailing noises that Jessica suspected were involuntary. He wasn't going to last much longer.

Father Josek, on the other hand, looked focused and steady.

Josek's face frequently registered the contempt he clearly felt for Gerard. The way Josek kept glancing around the room, it was also clear that he was looking for some way of escape.

'I want to hear from the Governor,' David Gerard said. 'I

want him to call me and tell me that he's going to do exactly what I tell him to do. And I want to hear from him right away. There's no place you can hide, Governor Standish, you spineless bastard. For once you've got to stand up and make a hard decision. I want to hear from you right away, you understand me?'

Obviously knowing a good theatrical prop when he saw one, Gerard moved over by William Cornell.

The political commentator looked up at his captor with a pleading, pathetic expression.

'This poor bastard's about had it, and the fun's only starting,' Gerard said. 'He's not gonna last the night, that's for sure.'

He pulled back, raised his gun, and pointed it directly at Cornell's head.

'I hate picking on the easy target all the time, folks, but he's just *asking* for it, don't you think? Look at him.'

Jessica had to avert her head.

She couldn't watch Cornell anymore.

She didn't blame him.

She might easily have reacted the same way herself.

But something helped her keep herself together.

She couldn't . . . *wouldn't* give in to her worst fears the way poor Cornell had.

'Now tell the Governor you want him to call me,' Gerard told Cornell.

'Please call.'

'You think that's going to make him call? You'll have to *beg* him to call. That's the only way he's going to pick up that phone.'

'Please call.'

'That's not begging, you fat piece of shit.'

'PLEASE CALL!' Cornell wailed.

And to reinforce his tone of pleading, Gerard put the tip of the gun right next to Cornell's head.

Tears started streaming down Cornell's fat face.

'Please call, Governor. I've got a family at home. They need me, they really do.'

'Isn't that sweet?' Gerard said. 'His family needs him. Aw.' Then he scowled. 'Nobody needs you, you piece of feces. You think you're some big powerful man but you know what? People laugh at you behind your back. And right now – all those friends you think you've got – they're sitting at home in the comfort of their living rooms, and they're hoping you're going to die. Yep: that's their most fervent wish. They've had to kiss your ass for years. And now, fat boy, it's pay-back time.'

Then he took his gun and cracked Cornell a good one on the side of his head.

This time, the tears flowed real nice and free.

2

Commander Beaudine was having a difficult time meeting Michael Shaw's gaze.

Beaudine had seen his old friend go through many bleak times before – nearly losing his job on occasion; breaking up with Jessica because she wouldn't or couldn't make a commitment to marriage – but he could never recall Michael looking this angry and frantic.

They were in Shaw's office in the newsroom, the whiteprints of the building in front of them . . .

Shaw had cleared his desk by pushing everything off the surface. The things that hit the floor, he let lie there. At a time like this, Shaw obviously didn't give a damn about pencils and pens and stray pieces of paper. Only a few pink phone slips remained on the edge of the desk, perched there precariously.

This was the Shaw of the drinking days, a violence about the man that was spooky to see. Beaudine didn't have any trouble seeing Shaw as a hero over in Nam. Heroism often meant coupling rage to skills – and Shaw had both of them. Beaudine had seen Shaw scale brick walls just to see if he could do it. As a boy, Shaw had suffered from rheumatic fever. He wasn't allowed to play much, and then only carefully. He got a reputation of being a sissy. He'd spent the early days of his manhood in Nam, proving to the world – and more importantly, to himself – that he was anything *but* a sissy.

Then his friends were killed in Nam . . .

Beaudine knew a lot of Viet Nam veterans who were still suffering from the war, and would suffer all their lives. His own brother was one of them.

Michael Shaw was one of them.

'So what're you saying?' Shaw demanded to Ryan Ludlow who had appeared two minutes ago.

'I'm saying that there's only one possible way into the studio.'

'You mean that door down there?' Shaw said.

'Correct.'

Beaudine could see the rage building in Shaw. He was afraid of what would happen if Michael didn't get to *do* something very soon.

Useless action was better than no action at all, at least with a man like Shaw.

He was no good at sitting around, especially when the woman he loved was in terrible jeopardy.

And carrying a baby . . .

If Beaudine and Shaw could just figure out some way to get Jessica out of that studio alive . . .

'What's this?' Shaw said.

'What's what?'

'That little mark.'

'*What* little mark?' Ludlow said.

'There.'

Ludlow leaned down, holding his steel-rimmed glasses tight on the bridge of his nose.

'Oh.'

' "Oh," what?'

'A window.'

'A window?' Shaw said, sounding as if he'd just made a discovery that would improve the lot of all humankind. 'A window's exactly what we need.' He looked closer at the whiteprints laid out on his desk.

'I forgot about this one. There are three flats that run behind the standing set in Studio B,' Ryan said. 'And the window's behind them.'

'A window,' Shaw said. 'That's great. That means there's a way in.'

'Not when it's as narrow as this one. And on the thirty-fourth floor,' Ryan said.

Shaw looked at Beaudine.

'A helicopter? I could suspend from a helicopter and get in that window.'

Beaudine sighed. 'Michael, even if we could *get* in the window, I wouldn't send you. You're too involved in this. And a helicopter would make too much noise, anyway. We might panic Gerard into killing people.'

The frenzy was back on Shaw's face.

He pushed very close to Beaudine, and said, 'Then what the hell do you suggest?'

Beaudine was genuinely sorry he didn't have a quick and easy answer for his buddy.

'What I suggest, Michael,' he said, 'is that we all stay calm.'
Ryan nodded somber agreement.

3

Loosening the top strap was an accident.

Jessica had merely been trying to scratch her leg, which was itchy from the three buckles that helped strap the small bomb to her leg. Her thumb hooked into the top buckle and pulled an inch or so of it free.

She knew instantly what she could do. Men like Gerard, sociopaths who enjoyed killing others, were frequently cowards themselves.

If she could secretly unstrap the bomb from her leg and then threaten to detonate it if he didn't turn all the hostages free . . .

She glanced at him, then at his two cohorts.

None of them was looking at her.

For the last few minutes, Gerard had been picking on Father Josek.

He'd dragged the priest up from the chair, and over by the camera. She didn't know why but she was afraid for the slender cleric. His mere existence seemed to irritate Gerard.

'I want you to look right into that camera, padre, and say a prayer for me. For my eternal soul.' Then he slammed the priest angrily into the camera. 'Understand, asshole? Pray for my soul.'

The priest tried to keep his poise but it wasn't easy. He'd hit his mouth on the camera lens. A glistening line of blood trickled down his chin.

'You hear me, padre? I want you to pray for my soul,' Gerard said.

Then: 'Hey, you know what's wrong here, padre? You should be down on your knees.'

And with that, he seized the priest by the hair and flung him to the floor.

Watching Gerard standing over the priest, seeing the way he exulted at the priest's pain and humiliation, she realized that the Gerard brothers were beyond any sort of mental or spiritual help. All society could do was isolate the Gerard brothers from everybody else. And that isolation, by now, could take only one form: extermination. The Gerard brothers had proved that they did not deserve to cohabit the same planet as their fellow human beings.

With David Gerard momentarily distracted, with his other henchmen watching him, she took the opportunity to ease the top strap free.

A sharp pain stabbed through her stomach.

The baby—

She had to get out of here to make sure the baby was safe—

The pain subsided.

Had to focus on this moment . . .

By now, her plan was taking real shape.

If she could just get the other buckles undone before he noticed what she was doing . . .

'Oh your knees, padre.'

Father Josek slowly lifted himself from the floor to a kneeling position. His face was pale and drawn.

'Now say a prayer for my eternal soul, padre.'

Father Josek took a deep breath. His face was smeared with blood and sweat.

'Believe it or not,' the priest said to Gerard, 'I have prayed for your soul. At that first trial . . . when I heard all the things your father had done to you—'

'He was a real sweetheart, my old man, wasn't he, padre?'

'I'm sorry for everything that's happened to you. But that still didn't give you any reason to kill all these people—'

Gerard chopped the butt of his gun down through the air and caught the priest directly on the jaw.

Father Josek was flung on his back, sprawling on the cold floor of the studio.

'Don't give me any speeches, padre. You haven't lived my life so you haven't earned the right to say anything about me at all. You and that bullshit God you're supposed to believe in. All that sanctimonious crap you hand out—'

Jessica wanted to get out of the chair and fling herself in front of Gerard, but she had to use this moment, when Gerard and his men were still distracted, to loosen another strap.

Keeping her eyes fixed on Gerard, as if she were mesmerized by what he was doing, Jessica quickly loosened the bottom buckle.

She needed the center one to stay in place so the bomb wouldn't slip off her leg and fall to the floor.

She worked as quickly but carefully as possible.

She'd seen what a bomb of this type could do. A group of skinheads had blown themselves up in a garage one night. The destruction had been total. Identifying the bodies, which were in small pieces and chunks, had taken more than a week.

Gerard had gone back to addressing the camera as the priest slowly picked himself up from the floor and wobbled back to his chair next to Jessica.

'For those of you keeping score, we've got three minutes before we hold our very first lottery drawing of the night. Let's take a look at our lineup for tonight. That's right, Mr Cameraman, pan that attractive group of people over there.'

He smiled.

'Just a few more minutes now, unless I hear from the Governor, and one of these handsome people will be executed.'

He leered into the camera.

'Your move, Governor Standish.'

All Jessica could do was sit there, waiting for her chance to free the last buckle holding the bomb to her leg.

David Gerard might not want Father Josek's prayers but Jessica sure did.

Sometimes, when he was a little boy and life simply got too overwhelming, Standish would go up to the attic and hide out there.

He always took comic books, Tootsie Rolls, and his long-time friend and confidant, Sir Lancelot the teddy bear.

Once he stayed up there so long, he went to sleep. His parents were frantic, calling the police and helping organize a manhunt.

Only to find him, a few hours later, cuddled up in the attic.

Governor Standish wished he had an attic to go to now.

He paced. He sweated. He cursed. He prayed.

If he acquiesced to David Gerard's demands, the lives of the hostages would most likely be spared.

But if he allowed the Gerard brothers to go free, how many people would they kill in their attempt to get out of the country?

He paced some more. He cursed. He prayed.

If only he had an attic to hide out in right now.

If only.

4

Harrigan picked up on it again, peripherally.

Every so often, Jessica Dennis would lean forward in her chair and cough.

The regularity of the coughing was what bothered him.

Harrigan was supposed to be guarding the door, turned halfway front so he could see if anybody tried to storm the studio.

Cates stood on the other side of the door doing the same thing.

Cates, apparently, wasn't picking up on Jessica Dennis.

But Harrigan was.

And there – just now.

She'd done it again.

Leaned forward in her chair and coughed.

This time, he turned toward her.

Checked out her leg.

From here, the bomb still seemed to be buckled in place.

But Harrigan wanted to make sure.

In a minute or two, he'd go over there and check the bomb close up.

5

Shaw needed to smash something.

Sometimes it came down to that.

You had so much anger, so much frustration that there was nothing you could do but attack a door or a wall or – as he'd done a few times in his drinking days – somebody who was about twice your size and would let you know that you'd really been in a fight.

He traced his fingers across the building's whiteprints once again, and stopped at the window that was his only entrance into the studio.

Right now, he was still in the newsroom with Commander Beaudine and Ryan.

He wanted to be in with Jessica – even if it meant laying down his life.

'What if a helicopter would suspend me?' Shaw said.

Beaudine shook his head.

'Like I said, Gerard would still hear you coming, Michael, unless the helicopter was suspending you from about fifteen stories. And anyway, I wouldn't let you go in there. I'd send one of my trained men.'

'The hell you would. He's got Jessica, which means that this is between me and him.'

'You're serious?'

'Hell, yes, I'm serious.'

'But my men—'

'Your men can come in later,' Shaw said. 'I need to see if he's willing to swap me for Jessica. That is, if I can't kill him first.'

'And how would you go about killing him?'

Shaw pointed to the whiteprint again and nodded to Ryan.

'If I can get through the window—'

'If you can get through the window, and that's one hell of a big *if* . . .'

'If I can get through the window without him hearing me, then maybe I can sneak up to the edge of the flat and get a shot at him.'

'So now you're a marksman?'

'I was a damned good marksman in Nam.'

'Nam was a long time ago, my friend.'

'I still go to the range once in a while. I'm a good shot, I really am.'

Beaudine shook his head.

'Well, good shot or not, Michael, there's no way you're going to use a helicopter without him knowing what's going on. As soon as he thinks somebody's trying to get in, he'll have that window covered.'

'How about you?' Shaw said to Ryan.

The man moved back a step and a half. Being this close to pure fury was unnerving.

'I don't see what we can do, Michael. Gerard obviously studied the building. He knows what he's doing.'

Shaw looked at both men.

'Well, that's just fucking great, isn't it? You're telling me that there's nothing we can do to save those people? Absolutely nothing?'

Shaw picked up the whiteprints and crumpled them in his big hands.

Two pink phone slips, still sitting on the edge of the desk, fluttered to his feet.

The gun was a Smith & Wesson Model 19. Warden Russ Atkinson had used it back in the days when he'd been a prison guard. He kept it cleaned and oiled in the top right-hand drawer of his desk. He had never had occasion, as Warden, to use it.

Now, sitting at his desk, he pushed .357 Magnum hollow-point bullets into the cylinder. Six of them.

When he was finished loading the gun, he walked over to the window and looked out at the helicopter that had just landed on the yard.

He knew the way David Gerard's mind worked.

Do something so breathtakingly brazen that people would just go along with it.

Hold some people hostage in a TV studio and trade them for a prisoner who was about to be executed.

There were two things the Gerard brothers hadn't counted on, however.

One: no way could Governor Standish cave in to a swap like this. The far right wing of his party, which already considered him suspiciously liberal on crime, would bolt and put up its own nominee if Standish ever gave in to such demands.

Two: they hadn't counted on the wiles and stealth of one Russell Thomas Atkinson. In just a few minutes, he was going to take a stroll out to the yard and, man, was he ever going to give that helicopter pilot a surprise.

Atkinson walked back to his desk, picked up his Smith & Wesson, took his rain slicker from the coat-tree, and strolled out of his office.

Yes, indeed. He was going to give that pilot one hell of a surprise.

He was just closing his door, when the phone rang.

Chapter Three

1

Jessica leaned down and was about to ease open the final remaining buckle that helped fasten the bomb to her leg—

—when she saw the gunman watching her.

The last few minutes, in fact, he'd been watching her a *lot*.

Was he aware of what Jessica was really doing? Or was he simply suspicious in general?

She sat back in her chair, heart pounding, chill sweat slicking her body, the infant in her body seeming to shift suddenly, as if it was reacting to Jessica's stress and anxiety.

Now that the man had started watching her, would she ever have a chance to get at that last buckle?

2

Shaw bent over and picked up the two pink phone slips that had fluttered to his feet.

Just before doing so, he'd seen the glances exchanged between Commander Beaudine and Ryan Ludlow.

They were clearly worried about him.

Maybe they even saw him as a nuisance. His temper

couldn't be helping the situation.

'Michael, I'd like to make a suggestion,' Beaudine said.

Shaw held up his hand. 'You don't need to tell me. You want me to go over and sit in the corner like a good little boy.'

Ryan said, 'C'mon, Michael. I'll buy you a cup of coffee.'

If Shaw heard the man's offer, he didn't let on.

Beaudine said, 'Michael, this is a command post here. I've got a lot of things to worry about.'

Shaw sighed, nodded.

'I'm sorry for my temper. I really am.'

'Good. Then please just go get yourself a cup of coffee and give yourself a little rest. Ryan even said he'd buy you a cup. There's a machine right down the hall.'

Shaw watched the bank of monitors out in the newsroom. Because only one camera was operating in the studio, a single image filled all the screens: David Gerard pointing to the clock on the wall.

Just a few minutes now, Gerard would have an excuse to kill somebody else.

No wonder he was smiling . . .

The camera panned the faces of the hostages. William Cornell still looked like an overfed baby in the throes of some unimaginable depression, his jaw resting on his chest, a silver line of spittle running from the side of his mouth all the way down to his chin.

Father Josek's face, on the other hand, showed every second of horror that the hostages were feeling. He was sweating and trembling from his confrontation with Gerard, and every few moments he'd wince from the pain in his side where his captor had kicked him earlier. Anger flashed in his eyes whenever he glanced at Gerard.

Then there was Jessica.

As Shaw saw her sitting there in her chair, all he could think about was that here were the two people he loved most in the entire vast unknowable universe: his lover and his child.

Because she was the daughter of an alcoholic, and because she'd learned so early how to survive in hostile and emotionally crushing conditions, she demonstrated a calmness now you didn't find in the other hostages.

Her hands were in her lap, her feet flat on the floor.

She watched Gerard with no expression whatsoever.

She also watched the gunman who stood nearest her, his automatic pistol cradled in his arms.

Only when she looked at this man did Shaw see a certain anxiety in her eyes. He wondered why she'd fear him but not Gerard . . .

Then the camera panned back to Gerard.

'Not very much longer, Governor. Are you listening? Not very much longer.'

Ryan came up to Shaw and said, 'C'mon, I'll buy you that cup of coffee.'

3

'Here's the hotline, folks,' David Gerard said, pointing to the black desk telephone that sat on an empty chair. 'All your Governor has to do is pick it up and tell me that we've got a deal — and nobody's going to get hurt.'

The camera pushed in for a tighter shot.

'This could get pretty ugly before the night's over folks, so if you've got kiddies around, I'd put them to bed. I don't have any kiddies myself but I sure wouldn't want them to see anything like this.'

The cold chilling smile.

'Of course, this doesn't *need* to turn ugly.'

Checked the clock.

'Eighteen seconds left. All Governor Standish has to do is pick up the phone and call me.'

Pointed to the phone.

'He knows the number.'

Another reference to the clock.

'Eleven seconds now.'

The smile.

'Some of you are probably making private bets at home, aren't you? If I were you, I'd bet he *will* call because he doesn't really want all this blood on his hands, now, does he? I sure wouldn't.'

The clock again.

'Nine seconds, folks.'

A look at the phone again.

'I've got to admit, this looks pretty grim, folks.'

Straight on into the camera.

'Are you watching this, Governor Standish? Are you watching this?'

4

Governor Standish picked up the receiver and began punching in the numbers he'd been given.

He heard the phone ringing in the studio.

Five rings.

Six rings.

He watched the screen.

David Gerard was grinning, nodding at the phone.

'He made *me* wait, now I'll make *him* wait.'

Eight rings.

Nine rings.

'I'll bet he's really pissed off,' Gerard smirked.

And then suddenly picked up the telephone.

'Is this the Governor?'

'Yes, it is.'

'Before we say anything else, I want you to know that I think you're doing one great job, Governor. I really do.' And: 'And I had this call patched in so everybody at home can hear what you say.'

'I want you to let those people go.'

'You do, huh?'

'Yes, I do.'

'Well, I want you to let my *brother* go. That's the whole idea behind this, Governor. It's called a s-w-a-p – swap.'

'I can't do that, and you know it.'

'Who would you vote for, Governor?'

'I beg your pardon?'

To the cameraman: 'Pan the hostages there. Good. Right. Let's get a good look at each of them.' Beat. 'Are you watching, Governor? I'm sure you are.' Beat. 'Getting a good look at them? Now which one do *you* think we should kill first? Personally, I'd like to ice the padre. Oh, yeah. He's such a smug little guy. Definitely be a thrill to kill him.' Beat. 'But how about *you*, Governor? Which one do you want to kill?'

Pause.

'Gerard?'

Gerard winked into the camera.

'Yes, Governor?'

'I want you to let them go.'

'Correct me if I'm wrong, Governor, but I believe you already said that, and I *believe* that I already said no-can-do. Not unless you let my brother go, too.'

'I won't trade for hostages.'

Gerard addressed the camera again.

'Well, folks. You heard it here first. The Governor won't trade for hostages. I guess you know what that means, don't you?'

'I'll tell you what I *will* do, Gerard. I'll delay the execution for twenty-four hours. And then we can talk about any extenuating circumstances that might lead to a new trial.'

Gerard smiled at the camera then drew invisible circles around his temple, indicating that he thought the Governor was crazy.

'That's your best offer?'

'That's my best offer,' Governor Standish said.

Gerard smirked at the receiver then held it over the phone and let it drop.

Then he looked into the camera.

'It's time to vote on who we kill first.'

The smile.

'I told you folks this was going to be an exciting night, and I'm not letting you down, am I?'

5

The hallway was crowded. They were close enough to master control so that Shaw could still see the monitors on the other side of the glass.

Shaw needed some quiet time to think. He'd allowed himself to give in to panic, and that hadn't helped anybody, especially Beaudine, who was in charge of this entire operation.

'You mind if I ask you a question?' Ryan said.

'Of course not.'

'You're a recovering alcoholic, right?'

'Uh-huh,' Shaw said.

'I've got a brother-in-law I wish you'd talk to. He's got a problem, I think.'

'Have him give me a call sometime.'

'That's the problem.'

'What is?'

'He *wouldn't* give you a call. He's in – what do you call it?'

'Denial?'

'Yeah. Denial.'

Shaw played with the two pink phone slips that had fallen to the floor as he'd been leaving the newsroom. Hadn't even noticed that he'd brought them along. Hadn't even looked to see who'd called him.

'I think he slaps her around sometimes.'

'Your sister?'

'Uh-huh.'

'She tell you that?' Shaw said.

'No. But she had a faded black eye the last time I saw her.'

'You ask her about it?'

'Yeah. But she kind of protects him. I hear that's pretty common with the spouses of alcoholics.'

' "Co-dependence" is what they call it.'

'Yeah. Co-dependence. That's Martha.'

Shaw noted the name on the top pink slip: Bob Adler, an old friend of his from his first reporting job in Milwaukee. Hadn't heard from Bob in years. Bob lived in Denver now. Under most circumstances, seeing Bob's name on a phone slip would have buoyed him. Bob was a great guy. Shaw hoped everything was all right with him.

'He may be doing drugs, too.'

'Your brother-in-law?'

'Right.'

'What makes you think so?'

'His nose.' Ryan tapped his right nostril. 'Red a lot of the time.'

'Cocaine?'

'Probably.'

'That's a pretty bad combination, coke and booze.'

Shaw kept glancing at the bank of monitors on the other side of the glass.

'He's a high-roller. Investment banker. MBA from Harvard Business School and the whole nine yards. And he's pissing it all away.'

'I'm sorry.'

Shaw read the name on the second pink slip: Milt Simon, the old AA friend he'd run into at the synagogue meeting this afternoon.

'You wouldn't call *him*, I suppose?' Ryan said.

'Doesn't work that way, I'm afraid.'

'He has to call, huh?'

'Right,' Shaw said.

'He has to *want* to call.'

'Exactly.'

'He's a proud sonofabitch, that's for sure.'

'Maybe your sister could talk to him.'

'I guess I could try it.' Then: 'I'm sorry I'm talking so much. You know, with Jessica up in the studio and all.'

'It's all right. You did Beaudine a favor getting me out of there.' Shaw rubbed a hand across his face. He was a man of contrasts right now – great anger, then sudden great exhaustion; great foreboding then sudden great optimism. And now there was another feeling, too . . . a feeling of some matter he wasn't quite addressing . . .

'I should talk,' Ryan said.

'Huh?'

Ryan grinned. 'Here I am bitching about my brother-in-law

and you know what I want to do right now? Have a beer.'

'Yeah, but there's a difference.'

'Oh?'

'You don't have a drinking problem.'

'I hope not. Sometimes I worry I overdo it.'

'You sure haven't overdone it at the parties I've seen you at.'

'Really?'

'A very moderate drinker.'

'That's good to know. I mean, you're kind of an expert.'

'Yeah, there's one thing drunks are good at,' Shaw said, 'and that's spotting other drunks.'

'You think if you met my brother-in-law, you could spot him right away like that?'

'Maybe.'

'Maybe I could have you out to the house sometime, when he's there, I mean. Or would you mind?'

'I'll help you any way I can.'

'That's damned nice of you.'

And then Shaw looked at Milt Simon's name on the pink slip and saw the solution to the dilemma.

Right now, he had to contain himself. If Beaudine realized what Shaw was about to do, he would stop him for sure.

'Well, I guess I'll get back to the studio,' Shaw said as casually as possible.

'I thought you were relaxing a little bit here.'

Shaw made a face.

'No way I can relax here. All I do is worry about Jessica.'

'Well, I can sure understand that.' He hoisted his cup. 'Maybe I'll just sit here and finish this.'

Shaw nodded.

'Thanks for babysitting me. At least I'm calmer now.'

But he was anything but calm once he left the hallway.

He raced to an empty office, looked up Milt Simon's name in the phone book, and dialed his number.

Shaw had the solution.

He was sure of it.

Milt Simon could help him.

The line was busy.

Chapter Four

1

David Gerard wasn't letting up.

His showbiz approach to hostage-taking continued.

He walked behind each hostage and called out their numbers.

'I wish we could let each and every one of you at home vote but unfortunately, there's not enough time for that. We'll just have to vote among ourselves, won't we?'

His two gunmen simply watched, no expressions on their faces.

'Will it be contestant number one?'

Move.

'Contestant number two?'

Move.

When he reached Jessica, he paused and said, 'Unfortunately, contestant number three has to be saved till later.' The smile. 'She's got the bomb, after all. And she was the chief prosecutor when my brother was convicted.'

Without any warning, he grabbed her hair, twisted it hard and tight in his fist.

She rose at least a foot off her seat, a silent scream shaping her mouth, fear and disgust in her eyes.

'I don't want you to feel left out, little lady,' Gerard said.

'You know what I mean? I want you to know that you're on my mind all the time.'

He pushed her back down in her chair.

He started walking again.

'Contestant number one, contestant number two.' He looked at his two gunmen. 'Which is it going to be, guys?'

He reached William Cornell.

He put his hand on the top of Cornell's head.

Cornell looked as if he'd burst into tears.

Given his weight, and all the stress reflected in his face, he seemed dangerously close to having a heart attack.

'Number one?'

The gunman with the long blond hair nodded.

'Or number two?'

The other gunman nodded for number two.

They continued to watch impassively.

Gerard looked over at Cornell.

'You want the priest to go first, don't you? Instead of you, I mean?'

Then he did just what he'd done to Jessica, seized the priest by the hair, lifting him up out of his seat.

Gerard smiled.

'I wonder if God is watching now, padre?'

Gerard made a clucking sound.

Yanked the cleric's hair even harder.

'He sure doesn't do a very good job of taking care of His own, does He? Maybe it's time you got a different God. You ever think about that, padre?'

He pushed the priest back down in the chair.

Looked into the camera. Smirked.

'You know what we got here, folks? We've got us a tie. Contestants one and two each received one vote. I wonder how the hell we can settle that?'

RUNNER IN THE DARK

Cornell began shuddering then, some kind of involuntary spasm of the nervous system.

It was ugly to see, ugly in the way Ribicoff had looked earlier as he lay on the floor twitching and dying.

'You know what?' Gerard said to the camera. 'I think there's only one way we *can* settle this.'

Reached deep into his right trouser pocket.

Fumbled about for a moment.

Brought forth something round and shiny.

And then wedged it between thumb and forefinger and held it up to the camera.

'Fifty-cent piece.'

Turned it over.

Tails.

Turned it back.

Heads.

'You folks at home trust me, don't you? I mean, you can see for yourself that this is just a regular good ole American coin. And by the way, I should take a moment here to tell you that I'm *proud* to be an American. Just as you are at home. Now, in a few seconds, I'm going to flip this coin . . .'

The studio seemed to get very, very quiet suddenly.

'Heads, it's number one, our old friend Mr William Cornell here. Tails, it's the padre.'

Held the coin up to the camera again for all to see.

Showed heads.

Showed tails.

Milking the moment the way a good stage magician would.

'Are we ready at home?'

He sneered into the camera and got ready to flip.

The coin went up high, trembling through the air, rolling over and over . . . and then came down on the back of Gerard's right hand.

Gerard peered down at it.

Then mugged for the camera.

'Oh, my God,' he said.

And then winked.

'One of these two men sitting behind me just got some very bad news, didn't he?'

2

With great fear and misery, he watched the coin go up in the air, and then come back down, flipping and turning, turning and flipping . . .

He knew which it would be.

William Cornell had a terrible thought: this was the day a lot of people had waited to see.

During his twenty-year reign as a political kingmaker, Cornell had made enough enemies to fill a couple of Rose Bowl stadiums.

He had smitten politicians by publicly repeating gossip about them; by quoting things they had *not* said; and by using innuendo to keep them from public favor.

The 'last bulwark against the screaming hordes,' one conservative magazine had pronounced him – and by 'screaming hordes' they'd meant blacks, feminist women, union members, teachers who wouldn't teach Creationism, gays, liberals of even moderate persuasion, and single working mothers.

Now those people would be watching from the safety of their homes.

Oh, they'd pretend that this was simply terrible – 'Look at him, poor bastard. As much as I hated him I didn't wish that on him, for God's sake . . .' but in fact they *had* wished that on him.

And were now taking pure pleasure from his predicament, and imminent death.

He was crying but didn't care.

Snot was running out of his nose, into his mouth.

And his shirt and tie were a snot-stained mess.

But he didn't care about that, either.

What was the point of pride when you were going to be dead in a few moments?

He didn't even hear what David Gerard said when he glanced down at the coin resting on the back of his hand. Luck had deserted Cornell utterly tonight, and he knew that he would be the first of the hostages chosen and killed . . .

He looked angrily at the priest.

He was the one David Gerard should kill.

Probably buggered little boys in his spare time—

But no.

The priest was nobody.

And William Jennings Cornell was *somebody*.

So he would be a lot more fun to kill.

A *lot* more fun.

Then he was wetting his pants again, and he didn't care about that, either.

First couple of times, he'd done everything he could to stop the flow.

But now, why bother?

Why fucking bother at all?

3

When David Gerard grabbed the priest's hair, both the gunmen started to watch him.

Jessica felt she had at least a few seconds to try and undo the final buckle, and put the bomb in her hand.

She kept her eyes fixed on the gunman closest to her.

She slowly moved her hand toward the bomb.

Slowly...

This time, she didn't cough. She'd realized that the cough had started warning the gunman of her intentions.

She just slowly, slowly brought her hand down to the final buckle and—

Damn!

Not only did the gunman turn and look at her, he even started walking over to her.

He was going to find the buckles undone!

4

'I guess I'm not sure where I should start,' Milt said as soon as Shaw contacted him.

Milt Simon was trying to be as helpful as possible.

He'd spent thirty years in the window-washing business, thirty years doing the skyscrapers that only a handful of businesses in the entire country knew how to do.

Way back when, all you had was platforms that you attached to hooks up on the roof.

You had safety belts, too, but the truth was, if the platform rope ever broke, you were pretty well screwed.

Milt had an uncle who'd fallen eighty-six stories to his death. He'd had an employee who hung twenty minutes from his safety belt and *then* plunged fifty-one floors to the street.

When Milt had first started in this business, his wife used to have nightmares all the time, leading her to plead that he take a job in insurance sales the way his very successful brother had. But no... Milt actually *dug* being up at the very top of skyscrapers. He'd never felt freer. Or more confident about himself.

Then, ten years ago, he had a teeny tiny heart attack and Sara wouldn't even let him *talk* about going back up there. He became a desk-bound bossman.

Now he was trying to help his friend Shaw.

'Your company does our building, right?'

'Right,' Milt said.

'Tell me about it.'

'I know you're in a hurry, Michael, so I'll make it as simple as possible.'

'Thanks.'

'There's a little garage on top of the building. There are tracks leading from the garage all the way from the roof to the sixth floor or so. There's a little car that rides those tracks. That's what you ride in to do the windows. It's a lot safer than it used to be in the old days, believe me. You can move the car around to the track you want pretty easily.'

'Does it make a lot of noise?'

'The basket? That's what we call them, baskets.'

'Right. The basket.'

'No. Not much noise at all.'

'Great.'

'It'd take me an hour to get in there but I'd be happy to—'

'I appreciate it, Milt, but I don't *have* an hour.'

'I've been watching. It's really sickening, seeing something like that.'

'Can Ludlow help me find the right track?'

'Sure. Ludlow or one of his men.'

'Now I need you to tell me about the window.'

'It's not going to be easy, Michael. From the inside, no problem. But opening it from the outside—'

'I'm going to write down what you tell me.'

'I'll do what I can.'

'I appreciate it.'

Milt did what he could.

He hadn't been kidding, either.

Getting that window open from the outside wasn't going to be easy at all.

5

The phone started ringing just as soon as Warden Russ Atkinson walked out the door.

He hurried back into his office, grabbing the call on only the fourth ring.

All calls tonight were likely to be critical.

'Warden,' he said.

'This is Governor Standish.'

'Good evening, sir.'

'I assume you're aware of what's going on with David Gerard.'

'Yes, sir, I am. Unfortunately.'

'I may have you turn Roy Gerard over to the helicopter pilot.'

'Oh Lord, sir, are you sure that's what you want to do?'

'I'm only saying this as a contingency, Warden. I'll wait and see what happens with David Gerard. But if he starts killing people—'

Russ Atkinson sighed. Governor Standish, true to his reputation, was a wimp.

'Yessir,' Atkinson said.

Now he knew that his plan was the right thing to do.

If the Governor of the state wouldn't stand up for law and order, then Warden Russ Atkinson would have to. He gripped the Smith & Wesson in his raincoat pocket.

'I may need to contact you again very soon.'

'Don't worry, sir,' Atkinson said, feeling the small phone in his other raincoat pocket. 'I have my flip phone. You know the number.'

'Thank you, Warden. Let's just say a prayer that I don't have to call you back.'

'Yes, sir.'

You'll be calling me back all right, Russ Atkinson thought, *to congratulate me on stopping these bloody bastards.*

They hung up.

Russ Atkinson left his office.

He was excited.

6

The gunman was no more than three feet from Jessica when William Cornell bolted from his chair and started to run for the door.

For a man his size, Cornell moved with surprising agility and speed.

The gunman turned away from Jessica and ran to grab Cornell. He reached him just as Cornell was about to trip over the body of Sam Ribicoff.

Poor Sam, Jessica thought, a terrible sorrow overcoming her.

Then she was grateful for the distraction Cornell had given her.

Maybe the gunman would forget all about checking Jessica out now.

She hoped so.

The gunman shoved Cornell back towards his chair.

Pain shot through Jessica's stomach again.

The baby.

Had to save the baby.

She waited for her chance to undo the last buckle.

7

Michael Shaw took the fire stairs two at a time.

He had to reach the roof of the building before any cops were stationed there.

Two police copters flew overhead but before they could figure out what he was doing, he could already be doing it.

He just hoped there were no officers on the roof.

That would kill the whole plan.

Beaudine would raise holy hell if he found out what Shaw was up to.

Shaw raced up the fire stairs.

8

'It's show time, folks!' David Gerard said.

He was, as usual, speaking directly to the camera, walking up and down in front of the hostages.

He hefted his weapon.

Then turned abruptly on William Cornell, pointing the gun directly at him.

'You know, this isn't very nice, is it, Mr Cornell? All those years you were a good NRA member, and now look.' He smiled. 'You should never give guns to people as crazy as I am.'

Gerard faced the camera again and mugged sorrow. He

RUNNER IN THE DARK

lifted his gun so that it was in the camera frame with him.

'Ask not who the automatic weapon is pointed at, Mr Cornell; it is pointed at thee.'

Once again, he abruptly turned on Cornell.

The smirk was gone.

Gerard had suddenly turned serious.

'You fat pontifical piece of shit, this is going to be a real pleasure, believe me.'

At just this moment, as Jessica was bending to unclasp the remaining buckle, she looked up and saw that the gunman, back in place, was watching her again.

She sat back up straight in the chair, pretending to scratch her leg as she did so.

She had to get the bomb in her hand: it was the only hope the hostages had.

'Stand up, Cornell,' Gerard said.

'Please,' Cornell said. 'Please don't do this.'

'I said to stand up.'

'Please,' Cornell said. 'I have a family. The priest – he doesn't have a family. It isn't fair to shoot me when the priest is here.'

Gerard crossed to Cornell in two steps.

Brought the butt of his gun down against Cornell's jaw.

Cornell fell comically from his chair, an awkwardly fat man taking an Oliver Hardy tumble.

The only thing that wasn't funny was the way he was crying. Like an infant that couldn't catch its breath.

Jessica's hand automatically slipped back to the strap.

Had to work fast now.

Had to work the bomb free and get it in her hand and—

But then she felt eyes on her again: the gunman.

And then sat up straight once again.

'Please, please don't do this,' Cornell said.

'I'm going to count to three.'

'Please, I can't—'

'One.'

Cornell was a huge wounded animal that had neither the energy nor the skill to get to his feet at the moment.

'Two.'

'Oh God, please—'

He made the effort.

And somehow, though it was grotesque to watch, he accomplished it, managed to sit up on his bottom and clutch the back of the chair, and pull himself, with great obvious struggle, to his feet.

Face red. Panting. Drooling. Still sobbing.

'Three,' Gerard said.

Then: 'You're a lucky man, Cornell.'

To the camera: 'God, does he need to go on a diet, or what?'

Sniggering, of course.

Back to Cornell: 'I want you to take your suit jacket and your shirt off for us.'

'What?'

'You heard me, sweetie. Your suit jacket and your shirt. Kind've a striptease for the folks at home.'

'But I can't—'

What he was saying was that he was at least 120 pounds overweight, and that being so, he could never possibly agree to – could never even consider taking them off . . .

'Sweetheart?'

'Yes?'

'I'm going to blow your fucking head off right now if you don't remove that sportcoat and that shirt.'

'But I'm so—'

'Fat! You're so fat! That's the whole point, sweetheart. I

want the folks at home to see just how *fat* you really are.'

To the camera, mouthing: 'Is this guy really dumb, or what?'

Back to Cornell: 'You going to do what I say?'

'All right.'

'Louder.'

'ALL RIGHT.'

Jessica was glad she had the bomb to distract her. She didn't want to see Cornell humiliated any more. Gerard's pleasure in all this was obscene.

Jessica was ready to work the bomb strap again.

But the gunman seemed to read her mind.

The moment her hand started to drop, he turned to look at her.

She put both her hands in her lap.

The strip was already beginning.

Sweaty, disoriented, Cornell, whimpering, *bleating* now, took off his suit jacket and let it fall to the floor.

Gerard said, 'I don't know about you folks at home but *I'm* sure getting turned on here.'

He laughed appreciatively at his own joke.

'Now the tie and shirt, sweetie.'

He winked at the camera.

'This is the sexy part, folks.'

Cornell had trouble unknotting his tie.

It was as if he'd been presented with an overwhelming mechanical problem he needed to solve.

His fingers got twisted up in the knot.

He tugged and pulled but the knot wouldn't come undone.

Finally, he tore it.

Not easy, tearing a tie like that, but the strength of his fear enabled him to.

'Man,' Gerard said. 'I hope you folks at home are properly impressed. Fat boy here is one strong dude.'

Cornell had some of the same trouble with the buttons on his shirt. He was so scared, his pudgy fingers wouldn't operate properly; so scared, the very concept of *unbuttoning* his shirt overwhelmed him.

'I don't know about you folks, but I'm getting pretty bored.'

Cupped a hand to his ear, as if the TV set were talking back to him.

'You're bored, too? I kind've figured you would be.' Another wink. 'I guess Fat Boy needs a little help.'

He walked over to Cornell.

'You're a mess, you know that? If your mother's watching, I'll bet she's ashamed of what you look like right now. Big important man like you.'

Over his shoulder to the camera: 'You folks ready for the big unveiling here? And I do mean *big*. Get your barf bags out because this is really going to be *sickening*.'

He reached over and grasped Cornell's collar, and then ripped the entire front of the shirt away. The other parts slid off with no help.

And there he stood, a grossly overweight man, chittering and blubbering and pleading, a powerful public figure who would never be powerful again, not the way the public had seen him tonight. Not only naked from the waist up but naked in emotional and spiritual ways, too.

'Wow, is this the body beautiful or what, folks?'

And then Cornell lost it again.

Started crying, started begging.

'Please, please, I've got a family. Please don't do this. Please.'

'I'm sorry, Mr Cornell. That coin toss was fair and square. I mean, unless you're implying that I *cheated* or something.'

He stepped up to Cornell and nuzzled his cheek with the barrel of the gun.

'*Are* you implying that I cheated?'

Cornell blubbered no.

'Whew, folks, I don't know about you but I'm relieved. I mean, that would have been a very serious accusation. Implying that it wasn't a fair coin toss.'

Back to Cornell: 'You *sure* you weren't implying that I cheated?'

Again, Cornell blubbered no.

But this time Gerard drove his fist deep into Cornell's stomach.

Given the state of Cornell's nerves, the response was predictable. He leaned to his left, and threw up.

Gerard: 'Poor baby. He must've eaten something tonight that didn't agree with him.'

He pointed his gun at the wall clock.

'Seven minutes since the Governor called here. Now in my foolish generosity, I was giving him those extra seven minutes so he might change his mind. But you know what? He's just going to let these people die. Every single one of them. And he's going to make me use the bomb I strapped to that very lovely lady over there. How you doin', babe? I notice you scratching your leg every once in a while. Is that strap starting to itch a little? You have my sincere apologies, babe. You really do.'

Back to Cornell: 'Maybe you shouldn't have said all those terrible things about the Governor, Mr Cornell. He's probably thinking, "Here's a real simple way to get rid of Cornell, and I don't even have to do anything." '

He raised his gun and fired then.

That fast, that unexpected.

The bullet ripped into the floor next to Cornell's left foot. The noise of the gunshot echoed off the walls.

Cornell jerked about wildly, crying, 'No!'

To the camera: 'I just thought I'd fire a little warning shot first. You know, Preview of Coming Attractions?'

He raised his gun to fire again.

Father Josek was up and lunging at Gerard before anybody could stop him.

The priest's body slammed into Gerard just as his gun was about to be fired.

Gerard squeezed off two shots but they both went wild again, this time up into the ceiling.

The priest was a tenacious little guy.

Not even when Gerard kneed him in the groin, not even when Gerard tried to fling him across the room, did the priest let go of his iron grip on Gerard's weapon.

'If you want to kill somebody, kill me,' Father Josek said as the two men struggled for possession of the gun. 'Cornell's right. I don't have a family.'

The second kick in the groin, one rendered with greater skill and force, finally broke the cleric's grip on the gun.

He fell over on his back, clutching his groin.

The rest happened quickly.

Gerard got a firm grip on his weapon once more and then walked over to where the priest lay on the floor.

'You want to die first, you sanctimonious piece of shit? Well, guess what? I'm going to *let* you die first.'

He then shot the priest.

Shot him ten, eleven, twelve, thirteen, fourteen times.

Chapter Five

1

Governor Standish looked at the phone and thought about Russ Atkinson. He knew that he was ending his political career tonight. Forever more, he would be seen as 'weak.' He didn't care. He didn't want any more blood on his hands.

'You want me to go with you, sir?' the guard asked Warden Atkinson.
'No, thanks. I'll be all right.'
'You don't know what you're walking into, sir.'
Atkinson smiled coolly. 'Whatever it is, I'll be able to handle it.'
He was standing next to the electronically operated gate that would let him into the yard where, during daylight hours, men exercised and walked around.
The guard nodded, pushed a button, and the rumbling gate began to roll back. Atkinson had turned this into one of the most secure prisons in the entire federal system.
The rain was now no more than a mist, a glowing nimbus around the lights that beamed down on the helicopter at the far end of the yard.
He had to give the pilot his balls.

Sitting there all alone, surrounded by so many men with guns, had to be terrifying.

Atkinson touched the Smith & Wesson in his raincoat pocket.

Of course, what *he* was about to do also took balls. In fact, he was sure that was how the press would play it up. Not 'balls,' of course, but courage.

COURAGEOUS WARDEN ENDS
HOSTAGE DRAMA

He was about to create another headline for himself when his flip phone rang.

His first reaction was disappointment.

David Gerard had surrendered and the whole situation was over. Or David Gerard had been killed by a police sniper.

The courageous Warden wouldn't get to be courageous, after all.

He answered the phone.

'This is Governor Standish.'

'Yes, sir.'

'Did you see what happened?'

'I haven't seen a TV set for a few minutes.'

'Gerard just killed the priest. I've never seen anything like it.'

The Governor's stunned voice perfectly conveyed his shock. 'I'll tell you something. I'm now a firm believer in capital punishment. I've never seen this kind of animalism before.'

'Yes, sir. Unfortunately, it goes on all the time.'

'This is a funny connection.'

'I'm on the cellphone.'

'Oh?'

Obviously, the Governor expected him to explain himself.

'Some prison business in Cell Block K, sir. Just a little trouble between inmates.'

'Nothing serious, I hope?'

'Nothing serious at all, sir. But that's why we're using the cellular phone.'

The Governor was silent a moment.

'Warden, I want you to release Roy Gerard to the man in the helicopter.'

'But, sir—'

'I've already put three state planes in the air. They'll trail them anywhere they go. If they cross the state line at any point, we can get federal help.'

'But giving in to them, sir—'

'Gerard will kill everybody in the studio – I'm convinced of that now. And I can't let it happen.'

Weak, Atkinson thought. As weak as his critics said he was.

But one good thing would come of it.

Now Atkinson would put his plan into action for sure.

DEATH-DEFYING WARDEN RISKS
LIFE TO END HOSTAGE CRISIS

'All right, sir. I'll release him.'

'I realize you're not happy about this.'

'I'll certainly abide by your decision, sir.'

'I appreciate that.'

'I'll check back with you in a while, sir.'

'Thank you, Warden. I hope to hell nobody else gets killed tonight. At least none of the good guys.'

'I'm with you there, sir. None of the good guys.'

They broke their connection.

2

'I've got to tell you folks – and I certainly don't mean any disrespect to the dead – but our friend the priest here is really starting to smell pretty bad.'

With that, David Gerard walked over to the slain cleric and gave him a hard swift kick in the ribs.

To the camera: 'Boy, it makes you wonder what this guy had for dinner tonight, doesn't it?'

To Cornell: 'Don't worry, we haven't forgotten about you.' Gaping at the studio clock. 'We'll be executing you in just a few minutes here.'

To the camera: 'Unless, of course, good ole Governor Standish comes to his senses and gives me a call.'

He walked over and placed his hand on the telephone.

'So many lives could be saved just by the Governor giving me a call on this line right here.

'Are you listening, Governor?

'Do you want to see even *more* people die?

'Won't you pick up that phone and give us a call, Governor?'

Then he saw Jessica and walked down the line of hostages to her.

'You sure are pretty.'

She just watched him.

'Give us a close-up, Mr Cameraman. Let's get a better look at that sweet sweet face of hers.'

By this time, Jessica was starting to show the strain of the past few hours. Her makeup was pale under the hot lights and her clothes were getting wrinkled with wear and perspiration.

'I'll bet you sang in a church choir, didn't you?' Gerard asked her.

She just stared at him. Said nothing.

To the camera: 'These people just don't get it, do they? Here I try to be real nice and make polite conversation and what do I get? She just glares at me, like she doesn't like me or something.'

He slapped her viciously and then seized her throat, strangling her with such force that he raised her up out of her chair.

'Are you going to answer me when I talk to you from now on?'

To the camera (still strangling her): 'I probably should be more careful, shouldn't I? She's got a bomb strapped to her leg.'

He slowly eased her back down into her chair.

And then slapped her even harder this time.

'You going to answer me from now on?'

Fighting tears, confused, drained, scared, she did the only thing she could do – nodded her agreement.

Yes, she would answer him from now on.

No resisting.

She promised.

To the camera: 'Maybe she's a nice person, after all. Maybe I was wrong about her.'

Then: 'But if she's really a nice person, then she'll let me unbutton her blouse, give us a better look at those nice juicy breasts of hers. No silicone here, folks. No, sir. You can see that they're real. They have such a nice shape.'

He reached down.

Touched one of her breasts.

She winced.

But she knew better than to object.

To the camera: 'Sex and violence. I promised you folks that you were going to get quite a show, and I sure haven't let you down, have I? We've had a lot of violence tonight. Now it's time for a little sex.'

He undid the first button.

'One down.'

The smirk.

To the camera: 'Are you as nervous about this as I am?'

He undid the second button.

She froze.

Tried to *will* herself out of existence.

Maybe if she closed her eyes – maybe this was just some kind of extended nightmare – maybe this wasn't real at all . . .

With the second button now undone, you could see the shape of her breasts above the white lacy bra she wore.

To the camera: 'Ummm-hmmm. Very, very nice.'

Then: 'Now comes the *real* test, folks. That's the third button. When I undo that—'

She steeled herself.

Didn't want to get slapped again.

The last time, his slap had temporarily blinded her, filled her mouth with the hot iron taste of blood.

Not again.

Had to get out of here alive for the sake of the baby—

She glanced down at the bomb. If only she could get to the last buckle—

Gerard to the camera: 'Dast I? You know, that's a word I've always wanted to use. "Dast." Pretty cool word, don't you think? Dast I try the third button? Dast I?'

He tried the third button.

And she couldn't take it.

Had *tried* to take it but just couldn't.

Even now, she had some pride left.

Even now, she couldn't take his obscene hands feeling her body.

She grasped his wrist.

Stopped him.

To the camera: 'See? I knew she was going to get mad this time. One button was okay; even two. But three—'

And then he tore her hand away and once more brought down his open palm at an angle.

He chopped into her nose this time, and instantly she could feel a cold swirling darkness take her. Maybe he'd broken her nose.

'You pig!' he screamed at her. 'You pig!'

He was ready to do it again, to really let her have another angry chop, when it happened.

Just like that.

Right behind him.

On the wheeled stand on which the TV monitor rested.

The telephone.

Ringing.

3

Killing the priest meant there was no way back for sure, Harrigan knew.

First, the cop. Then, the priest.

Every lawman in the country would be hunting them.

He thought about Linda in the hospital, her poor breasts gone, watching TV and seeing her father—

Harrigan sighed.

He just wanted to get out of here, and away to Cuba. If they took hostages with them, they'd be able to make it all the way to Havana and nobody could stop them.

Poor Linda.

Couldn't get his mind off her.

Then the phone in the studio started ringing and Harrigan sensed who it would be.

The Governor.

Maybe things were finally going to start breaking their way.

Maybe.

4

When he reached the roof, the first thing Shaw did was check for police officers.

None. Not right now. But soon.

Circling overhead were two police helicopters, however.

He had to hurry.

He ran across the roof to what resembled a small garage. This was what his friend Milt Simon had described to him. Milt had also told him what he would find inside the building.

When he was about halfway to the garage, one of the police copters swooped low and trained a searchlight on him.

A voice over a speaker set-up said: 'Stop and identify yourself to the officer who will be on the roof in just a few minutes.'

But Shaw knew that the last thing he could afford to do was stop.

He kept running.

Nearly forty stories in the air, on a cold and misty night, the world was a strange and dangerous place.

He kept slipping as he ran. But he got right back up and started running again.

Now two different copters had searchlights on him.

The speaker was barking something but Shaw didn't have time to listen.

Out of breath, cold with hot sweat, his hands bloody from one of his falls, he got the garage door opened and burst inside.

RUNNER IN THE DARK

Shaw smelled motor oil and cleaning solvent. He flipped on a light.

The basket, which was the cage the cleaning men stood in while they worked on skyscraper windows, sat in the corner. Next to it were various buckets, squeegees, containers of cleaning solvents.

Shaw needed two things quickly: the basket, which he had, and what Milt Simon had called 'a glazer's suction cup.' He'd said it resembled a toilet plunger.

Shaw looked around frantically, didn't see it.

Without the glazer's suction cup there was no way he could cut into the window, and let himself inside.

The copters dropped even lower, huge and angry insects.

The cop using the speaker system shouted heated demands.

There – in the corner.

He'd mistaken the handle for some kind of broom or mop.

The glazer's suction cup.

It looked almost identical to a toilet plunger.

He grabbed it and the basket and carried them back out to the roof.

Just as Shaw got the wheels of the basket fixed to the tracks, three cops appeared at the far end of the roof. Their guns were drawn. They were running toward Shaw.

The basket, which resembled the size and shape of a Tilt-A-Whirl car at a carnival, was operated by four simple controls on the right side of the craft. Milt Simon had given him very clear directions.

Old buildings still used ropes and platforms to suspend window cleaners.

Newer buildings, like the Trealor, had tracks built along the sides of the buildings, tracks that fitted the baskets perfectly. It was like driving a car up and down the sides of the building.

Just as the three policemen reached the edge of the building, Shaw hit the DESCEND button.

The basket dropped quickly, and just far enough to be out of reach to the policemen.

Shaw was on his way.

5

... the beauty of the plan, at least as Warden Atkinson sees it, is its simplicity.

The helicopter pilot sees him coming, sees that he has his arms raised high.

Atkinson approaches the helicopter and says he wants to talk to the pilot.

The pilot agrees.

Then Atkinson throws himself to the ground, rolls over, and takes out his weapon.

By now, the pilot is completely confused, and probably panic-stricken.

Atkinson takes advantage of the moment by getting the drop on the guy.

That's Part One of The Plan.

Part Two is — now that Atkinson has the pilot under control, he makes the pilot take him aboard.

When they reach the TV station where David Gerard gets aboard, Gerard sees a figure in the back seat of the chopper and assumes it's his brother.

Then Atkinson gets his gun on Gerard, and Gerard surrenders, and then all the reporters start mobbing the Warden ...

The ground was soft, almost gooey in places, as Atkinson walked across the yard to the helicopter.

The lights trained on the chopper were obscured by swirling

RUNNER IN THE DARK

mists. Everywhere he looked, Atkinson saw the silhouettes of armed guards. The air was damp. He could feel it in his lungs. The ground fog, shimmering and shifting, cut him off at the knees.

The guards would love to open fire on the helicopter.

But Atkinson's plan was better. This way, by night's end, both Gerard brothers would be in captivity.

Both brought down by a warden too modest to ever call himself a hero.

As he got closer, Atkinson could smell the oil and grease and wet plastic of the whirlybird.

'Stop right there.'

Voice from inside the copter.

Thirtyish man in leather flying jacket and baseball cap. Intelligent-looking. Too smart to be involved in something like this, that was for sure.

'I'm Warden Atkinson.'

'Wow. I'm really impressed.'

'I want to talk to you.'

'About what?'

'About Roy Gerard.'

'You can talk from there.'

'I'd prefer to get closer.'

'You want to date me or talk to me?'

'I have my hands up. I don't know what you're worried about.'

'You're the one who should be worried. I can waste your ass any time I feel like it. Count off ten paces. That's as close as you get.'

Ten paces took him much closer to the machine.

He could see some of the instruments, the collective pitch lever, the control column, the rubber pedals. He'd taken a few lessons from a warden in Ohio who was a pilot.

'We're bringing Gerard out,' Atkinson said. 'I'll be walking him out here.'

The pilot looked happy suddenly.

'Great. Let's get going, then.'

Now. He had to throw himself to the ground now—

'I'm going to walk back and get him,' Atkinson said.

Now. Right now.

'I just wanted to let you know what was going on.'

Throw himself to the ground. Roll to the right. Get his gun out as he was rolling.

'I'll be right back,' Atkinson said.

It must have been his eyes, he must have looked funny just then, because the pilot said, 'Aw, shit,' and before Atkinson could make even a single move, the pilot said, 'C'mere.'

'You said not to come any closer.'

'Yeah. But now I said c'mere.'

The pilot produced a sawn-off shotgun and pointed it directly at Atkinson's chest.

Atkinson walked right up to the cockpit.

'Give me your gun,' the pilot said.

'I don't have a gun.'

'My ass you don't have a gun. Now give it here.'

The pilot raised the shotgun and pressed the barrel of it against Atkinson's forehead.

'The Lone Ranger,' the pilot said.

'What?'

'You heard me. You were going to pull some kind of heroic bullshit, weren't you?'

The pilot smiled.

Put his hand out.

'Give me the gun, Warden.'

Atkinson shook his head miserably.

★ ★ ★

HERO WARDEN'S LAST-MINUTE
FOILING OF DESPERATE FUGITIVES

It wasn't to be.

Shit.

Atkinson handed him his Smith & Wesson.

6

David Gerard took great pleasure in slamming the receiver down. Some jerk-off from the hostage negotiation team had called. No way was Gerard going to talk to him...

Jessica was just about ready.

In the chaos of the past few minutes, she'd been able to undo the final buckle holding the bomb in place.

She felt she could now ease it free and then take control of the situation in the studio.

She felt the living child in her womb.

She had to pull this off—

Had to—

Her breathing was ragged. Her slender hands twitched. She could never recall being quite this frightened before. Holding all the power of the bomb in her hands—

What if she dropped it?

What if it was so fragile that it simply exploded when she tried to lift it from its holster?

But she had to do it because she knew that David Gerard planned to kill her. He held her and her fellow attorneys responsible for his brother being incarcerated.

Her trembling fingers hovered above the bomb.

The right moment, she thought.

Exactly the right moment to lift it up and then call out to Gerard and show him what she'd done.

He'd give in.

Despite his icy smile, and seemingly fearless manner, he didn't want to die. If he did, he wouldn't have made so many elaborate preparations, or brought two additional armed men.

No, he didn't want to die.

And when he saw the bomb in her hand, he would certainly surrender.

All she needed now was the right moment.

But she was aware of eyes on her.

The gunman was looking at her again.

Harrigan thought: *what the hell is she doing?*
Whatever it is, I can't catch her at it.

He turned toward her completely, and started walking over to her again.

This time, he was going to check out the straps holding the bomb in place.

This time, he was going to figure out what was going on with her, what those guilty glances were all about.

7

As Michael Shaw began his descent in the window-cleaning basket, he realized suddenly how isolated he was this high up, and marveled at the men and women who used these small square baskets on a daily basis.

If nothing else, he had a spectacular view of the city – if, that is, he was willing to turn around as the basket slowly descended the side of the building.

There was a watercolor quality to the downtown area when it rained like this, all the electric reds and blues and yellows fuzzy with mist. Even the emergency personnel in the street below had an almost peaceful quality now, as if they were watching some kind of athlete perform a daredevil feat.

His coat had soaked clear through, his hair was plastered to his face.

His impression was that he had come a long way. Then he leaned back and looked up and saw that he hadn't descended even a full story yet.

Two cops were up there shouting at him to come back but their voices were mostly lost in the clatter of the police helicopters.

Suddenly, Commander Beaudine appeared up there, shouting in pantomime, and shaking his fist at Shaw.

But Shaw just kept descending.

The wind was the worst thing.

It was strong and cold and whipped the cage around every few moments. The cage rattled and shuddered and it would have frightened him if so much weren't at stake.

The woman he loved. And their child.

The new window-washing equipment might do great things for safety but it didn't do much for speed.

He shoved his hand inside his jacket and touched the butt of his weapon. He looked down at the floor to make sure that the glazer's suction cup was still there.

The glazer cup was a hollow metal tube seven inches long that attached to a large round suction cup. Windows in new skyscrapers were sealed. They did not open. In order to sneak in the window behind the standing set, Shaw, per Milt Simon's careful instructions, needed to take the putty knife that had been in the garage and cut away the vinyl gasket that sealed the window. Then he needed to wiggle the window so he could get his knife into the vinyl gasket sealing the window on the other side. That vinyl needed to be cut away, too. Then you took the glazer's suction cup and literally pulled the pane of glass free of its frame. You just kept pumping air into the tube until you force-freed the glass from the grooves.

He remembered Milt's words about this being a very dangerous descent on a night like this. He'd assumed Milt had merely been trying to talk him out of it. Now he knew that Milt had been telling him the truth.

Another paroxysm shook the cage, causing Shaw to cling hard to the sides of it. A cry of rage and fear caught in his throat.

Once again, the floor felt as if it would buckle beneath him.

Despite his best judgement, he looked straight down at the street, the whirling red emergency lights staining everything an electric red color, the stick-figures all looking up at the crazy man in the window-washing basket.

Memories of Viet Nam returned, jumbled moments of dread and terror. Trying to save his two friends . . .

The dread and terror were back as he held on to his only hope of salvation – thirty-eight floors above the hard and unyielding pavement below.

Then the wind dropped momentarily, and he had another problem.

The cage wasn't moving.

He gently shook it, trying to get it to descend again.

But no luck.

Was he going to be stuck here until a helicopter could rescue him – until David Gerard finally did what he wanted to do . . . killed Jessica and the child she was carrying?

The cage *had* to move again.

And then—

The cage moved again, but more slowly than before.

He still had three floors to go.

Three floors that felt like a mile apart.

8

The number of armed guards doubled when Atkinson led Roy Gerard from the prison to the helicopter.

All Atkinson could think of was the headlines-that-might-have-been.

The headlines that described the kind of courageous act that could turn a warden into a governor or a senator. Or maybe even a TV host like the guy on *America's Most Wanted*.

Atkinson felt his cheeks redden under the steady, cynical stare of the pilot.

'My hero,' the pilot said. Then chuckled.

Roy Gerard looked from the pilot to Atkinson, not understanding the joke.

'He tried a little grandstanding earlier tonight,' the pilot explained. 'He was going to go meet your brother pretending he was you.'

Gerard looked at Atkinson and said, 'He's a clown.'

'Yeah,' the pilot said. 'That's just what I was thinking.'

Roy Gerard jumped up into the cockpit and quickly slammed the door.

The pilot turned on the powerful engine.

Atkinson was forced back from the machine immediately.

The pilot warmed up the engine briefly then took off.

Leaving Atkinson to stand there and think of what might have been.

FEARLESS WARDEN RECEIVES
PRESIDENTIAL MEDAL

Sonofabitch.

Sometimes the cards just didn't fall your way at all.

9

The process sounded a lot easier in the abstract than it was in practice.

Shaw had the basket set flat against the proper window. No sweat there.

But the process of using the knife to loosen the vinyl was much slower and more tedious than he'd been prepared for.

He kept thinking—

An inch of glass is all that separates me from Jessica.

A single inch of glass.

He kept working his putty knife into the vinyl.

Desperately.

10

One more pass at the buckle.

Then the bomb would be in her hand.

Jessica's fingertips felt the shape of it.

Her heart-rate increased at the mere touch of it.

Free.

Soon now.

Soon.

'Twenty-six minutes have gone by, folks, since the Governor released my brother,' David Gerard told the camera. 'And you know what? I'd better see that brother of mine real soon now or I'm going to be one pissed-off sonofagun, believe me.'

He walked over to William Cornell, who had managed to drape his clothes over himself. He looked miserable.

'How you doing, my friend?'

But when you looked at Cornell's eyes, you realized that he had tuned out. It was the only way he could deal with this – by no longer dealing with it at all.

None of Gerard's words had registered.

Harrigan was no more than seven or eight feet from Jessica.

This time, he would find out what was going on.

This time, he'd stop her.

'This puppy just isn't paying any attention,' Gerard winked at the camera.

'Yoo-hoo in there! Yoo-hoo!'

Gerard waved his hand in front of Cornell's face.

No reaction whatsoever.

To the camera: 'I must be one real boring sonofabitch, to put a guy to sleep like this.'

His hand disappeared into his pocket and brought out a switchblade knife.

'You recognize this, my friend?'

He snicked the knife open a mere half-inch from Cornell's face.

As soon as he heard the knife snick open, Harrigan stopped.

He had no idea what David Gerard would do next.

Nor did he know what Cornell would do.

Guy in his state might do anything at this point.

Even fling himself at Gerard.

Harrigan had to cover Gerard for the next few minutes. Then he'd finish with Jessica Dennis.

★ ★ ★

Cornell still sat unmoving, unblinking.

'You recognize this?'

He put the point of the knife against Cornell's neck.

Pushed in.

To the camera: 'Wow. This guy is really out of it.'

'Leave him alone,' Jessica said.

Gerard paused, looked over at Jessica.

'Did you say something?'

'I said to leave him alone.'

'Oh? And why should I do that?'

'Because he's suffered enough.'

Gerard straightened, seemed to lose interest in Cornell.

To the camera: 'You think she's coming on to me, folks? You think that's what this is all about? That she really just wants my body but is too shy to say so?'

Jessica knew there was no point in threatening him but she couldn't think what else to do. He was obviously looking for some reason to kill Cornell, and would invent one if he had to.

Gerard put the knife to Cornell's throat.

'That bitch over there thinks I'm just an ole meanie, doesn't she?'

Cornell still did not move, did not blink.

He was in a kind of mental state that was horrifying to see.

Jessica wanted to rush over to him and take him in her arms and hold him the way she would a small child.

She remembered what Michael always told her about Viet Nam, how you never knew who would survive, physically or mentally, the constant spectacle of violent death.

There was a small-boy quality about Cornell now that was heartbreaking to observe.

'You better start talking to me,' Gerard said, 'or I really will be a meanie.'

To the camera: 'Are you wondering how sharp this knife is?

You know, I'm kind of curious myself.'

To Cornell: 'How about you? Are you curious, too?'

To the camera: 'Let's just see how sharp this knife really is, shall we?'

Icy smirk.

'This is going to be fun, isn't it?'

'No!' Jessica screamed, sensing that Gerard was now ready to slash Cornell's throat.

She did the only thing she could do.

'I want you to give yourself up, Gerard. Right now.'

When he turned to look at her, his face showing both surprise and irritation, he didn't notice her right hand at first.

Harrigan saw what she was doing but too late.

She'd managed to unbuckle the bomb.

The small silver canister was now in her hand.

'You want me to give myself up, bitch? Is that what you said?'

Gerard's eyes saw it, then.

The bomb.

In her hand.

This time his face showed fear.

'Well, well,' he said, trying to sound as cool as ever, 'I'll be damned.'

Chapter Six

1

Just as the helicopter carrying Roy Gerard reached the city limits, Michael Shaw was finishing up on the window.

The wind had lessened, as had the rain. It no longer came in icy sheets. Now it was little more than a fine cold mist.

Shaw knelt inside the basket, using the putty knife Milt had left in the garage. The vinyl gasket, which was the rubber-like sealant around the window, came off stubbornly, but it did come off.

His knees were sore and his fingers numb from the cold. He'd tried gloves but they slowed down his progress with the putty knife.

He kept waiting for the sound of gunfire.

Hard to say who was the more psychotic of the two, David or Roy Gerard.

All he could think of was Jessica, and their child.

God, if only he'd known before.

He worked harder, faster.

Had to get in there.

Had to.

There was one side of the vinyl gasket yet to strip.

He estimated it would take ten minutes.

Shaw knew that if David Gerard managed to get Jessica aboard that helicopter, he would never see her alive again.

2

Jessica held the small bomb with a kind of obstinate pride.

She looked at the nearby gunman, then at David Gerard.

'Do you want to die? I don't know what I'm doing with this bomb and so it could go off at any time. You want to take that chance?'

She glared at Gerard.

She held the bomb up higher so he could get a look at it.

'Why don't you just give me that?' Gerard said, starting to walk toward her.

'Stay there. Right there. And don't move.'

'You don't know what the hell you're doing.'

'No, and that's what makes me dangerous, isn't it? Do you like being scared, Gerard, the way you've scared everybody here tonight?'

Gerard sighed, glanced around at his men, then back to her.

'I want you to very gently hand it over to me.'

'No way.'

'You don't want to kill everybody, do you?'

'Right now I'm willing to do that as long as you're included.'

Gerard started sounding like a hostage negotiator, soft voice, soothing words.

'You're tired. You're not thinking clearly, Jessica. You don't want to put everybody's life at risk. You really don't.'

He had started to move again.

'Stay there.'

'Jessica, please, please listen to reason.'

He was still moving.

'Stay there, I said.'

The sharpness of her voice stopped him.

She saw Cornell watching her. For the first time in hours, a curious hope showed on his round, sweat-slick face.

'Jessica, please,' Gerard said.

Two more steps.

Then he stopped.

'Do you know how fragile that thing is?'

'Put down your guns, then, and tell your friends to do the same.'

One more step.

She watched him, warily.

'What if you dropped it by accident?'

One more step.

'Right there. And don't move,' she said.

'What if you jarred it and it went off? Can you imagine how many people you'd kill? Good, family people. Your kind of people, Jessica. Can you imagine?'

One more step.

'Jessica. Use your head.'

She had a feeling of being surrounded, even though nobody was on either side of her, of being surrounded and of not knowing what to do.

She couldn't throw the bomb.

All she could do was bluff with it.

She couldn't—

'Jessica, we just can't keep having scenes like this—'

And then he was on her, flinging himself at the four feet that separated them.

She screamed and tried to turn away, tried to tuck the bomb into her like a football, but he was too fast and cunning.

He got her wrist with the bomb and started to twist it viciously.

She cursed him, and slapped him on the side of the face, but he was immovable.

He just kept twisting, twisting.

'It could go off any time,' she said. 'Any time.'

She kicked him hard in the left shin.

She could see pain tighten his face, feel his hot curse on her cheek.

But he didn't give in – not even when she kicked him a second time.

'Let me have it,' he said between grinding teeth.

Commander Beaudine, along with millions of other viewers, felt his entire body tighten as he watched Jessica struggle with Gerard.

He stood in the newsroom, transfixed by what he saw on the monitors.

'Kick him in the nuts, Jessica,' Beaudine said, 'kick him in the nuts.'

Just then a young female reporter passed by him and gave Beaudine a startled look.

Then she stuck her thumb up in the air. And then, like everybody else, she became transfixed by the images on the screen.

'Right where it hurts, Jessica,' she said. 'Right where it hurts.'

Gerard gave her a wrist a final turn, one so violent, her whole body was jerked hard against him.

He slid the bomb from her grasp.

Then he pushed her back toward her chair.

She crashed into two chairs, actually, which was fortunate because together they broke her fall.

Instantly, she felt sharp pains in her stomach. She had the terrible feeling that she might miscarry now.

RUNNER IN THE DARK

Gerard said to the camera: 'Boy, that was a close call, wasn't it? This thing could've blown up the whole building and everybody in it. I mean, what if somebody suddenly went crazy and took this bomb and hurled it against the floor—'

He raised the bomb over his head, said to Jessica, 'Sayonara, babe,' and then threw it hard against the floor.

It bounced once and sat there.

To the camera: 'You think she's figured it out yet, folks, that sneaky ole me gave her a fake bomb just to make her sweat a little? Now that wasn't very nice, was it?'

Still smiling, he walked over to his suitcase, opened it up, and took out a silver canister identical to the one he'd thrown on the floor.

Then he removed a small black plastic square from his jacket. In the center was a red button. This was a detonator.

'We've got fifteen minutes to get out of this studio – then I push this little button and blow everybody up.'

He closed the suitcase, set the bomb on top of it.

He walked down in front of Jessica.

'How's our little Princess Jessica doing? Huh?'

At the moment, she didn't look much more aware of her surroundings than Cornell had earlier.

A fake bomb.

All the fear—

For nothing.

He grabbed her hair and snapped her neck back.

'I asked you a question, bitch.'

But she didn't answer him.

So he slapped her – so hard, he made her mouth bleed.

To the camera: 'And I used to think she was such a nice girl, didn't you?'

Strode back down toward the monitor.

Looked up at the studio clock.

'I'd better see my brother pretty damn quick, that's all I've got to say.'

He pointed to the bomb on top of the valise and then said to the camera: 'Can you blame a guy for getting impatient?'

3

The helicopter carrying Roy Gerard and Kray was in sight of the building now. Police helicopters hovered in the air space around it and the roof itself was filled with police officials.

Kray had been in radio contact with police officials for the past twenty minutes.

'Our agreement was that the roof would be cleared,' he said.

'We'll start now,' the police spokesman said.

'We'll be landing in a couple of minutes.'

He cut contact.

The closer they got to touching down, the more agitated Roy Gerard became. All he could think about was the waiting jet and the quick trip to Cuba.

That's when he saw the man on the side of the building in the window-cleaning basket.

'What the hell's he doing?' Gerard said.

Kray didn't see the man at first.

'Get in closer,' Gerard said.

Shaw still had about three or four minutes of work left when the helicopter appeared and swept down on him. It carried no official insignia, so he knew it wasn't a police machine. He was too late now. Getting inside the window no longer mattered.

The helicopter made one pass, during which it trained a

spotlight on him, and then angled away from the building.

This had to be the helicopter carrying Gerard.

'Go back,' Gerard said.

'Back where?'

'To that guy on the window.'

'Why?'

'Because we don't know what the hell he's up to.'

'Let's just pick up your brother and get the hell out of here,' Kray said. For the first time tonight, his face and voice were beginning to betray the turmoil and fear he felt.

'Anything goes wrong, asshole, I kill you first, understand me?'

Roy Gerard jammed his gun hard into Kray's side.

David Gerard had just finished telling the camera that he was going to blow up this entire building if his brother didn't get here within fifteen minutes ... when Commander Beaudine told him over the studio speaker that his brother's helicopter was just now setting down and that the roof had been cleared of all police personnel.

Gerard put his hands together as if in prayer and said in his best hammy voice: 'Oh Lord, You have smited the infidels ... and there's going to be a little something extra in that pay-check of Yours next week.'

To the camera: 'Folks, I guess this is it. The big pay-off. The grand climax. Your favorite TV star is about to go on to greater glory. But don't worry. I won't forget you. You'll always be right here.'

He thumped his heart.

Then he quickly went and picked up the automatic pistol he'd set out earlier.

He looked over at Jessica and smiled.

'You still pissed off at me, babe? That wasn't very nice, was it, fooling you with that fake bomb.'

He went over and grabbed her by the arm and said to Beaudine, 'Open up. I want two cops in here to give me an escort to the roof.'

Harrigan went over and opened up the studio door.

He hoped he got to talk to Linda sometime tonight. He really had the urge.

Twenty-one years old and a damned dirty shame like that happens to you.

Jessica knew she had only a few moments left to escape. Once David Gerard got her on the helicopter, he would kill her.

Shaw saw the helicopter with Roy Gerard aboard land on the roof.

He had to get back up there, somehow stop the copter from taking off again.

He started moving the basket back up the tracks.

Hurry.

He had to hurry.

The climb took even longer than the descent. Shaw had his gun ready.

He alternated cursing with praying.

'There he is,' Roy Gerard said as they hovered over the roof.

'So the police were trying to send a guy up in a window-washing unit.'

Gerard smiled. Nothing to worry about. A basket like that was too slow to pose much of a threat.

Kray started to set the big craft down on the roof.

★ ★ ★

RUNNER IN THE DARK

The basket stuck on its tracks again.

The headwinds had picked up, as had the rain.

In frustration and rage, Shaw shook the basket and kicked at its side.

It suddenly began moving upward once more.

The basket was just like all the appliances you found in the home.

All you needed for maximum performance was to kick the shit out of them once in a while.

4

David Gerard was dragging Jessica toward the studio door when he suddenly stopped, looked at Cates, and then opened fire.

'He was a loser, man,' Gerard said to nobody in particular.

'What the hell're you doing?' Harrigan said, looking angry enough to fire on Gerard.

He ran up, his gun ready.

'There wasn't room for him in the helicopter, anyway,' Gerard said.

'So you fucking *killed* him?'

'Yeah, but I'm going to kill you for a different reason. Because you and Kray planned to kill me and Roy and take all our money. That's not very nice, Harrigan. Not nice at all.'

Harrigan pulled his spare gun. He'd emptied his primary weapon.

Now he pulled the trigger.

Nothing happened.

He looked down at his automatic pistol in amazement and disbelief.

Click click click.

'I took care of it for you, sweetheart. I didn't want you to hurt yourself with guns so I made sure yours wouldn't fire.'

Then Gerard opened up on Harrigan, who did a nice grisly little dance before he hit the floor, and started leaking blood all over the place.

Harrigan's last thought was of his daughter Linda...

5

Shaw heard the gunfire inside and paused for a moment.

David Gerard had been very near a total breakdown. Maybe he'd gone over the edge.

Maybe he'd just decided to kill *all* the hostages and get it over with.

Jessica...

Faster.

Faster.

Had to go faster.

He started rattling the basket again.

Faster, faster.

'You two men lead us to the elevator and then to the door that takes us on to the roof. You got it?'

The two uniformed police officers nodded. They didn't try to hide their contempt for David Gerard but they had no choice but to go along with him.

He had his gun trained on Jessica's back.

She still hadn't figured out a way of escaping.

Kray had no trouble setting the machine down on the rooftop.

The night was windy and rainy but he was an extremely able pilot.

The only trouble he was having was with Roy Gerard.

Roy was extremely agitated.

He sat in the seat with his automatic pistol raised, swearing at demons Kray couldn't see.

'Motherfuckers, you motherfuckers.'

Roy Gerard was one spooky sonofabitch all right.

Wind wailed, rain rioted.

The hall had been cleared.

The two police officers led the way to the elevator, got the doors opened, and then stood aside.

As she passed by them going into the car, Jessica noted that one of the officers smelled of cigarettes, the other of Brut.

They both gave her sympathetic glances.

David Gerard put the gun to her head and waited while the two policemen got in the car, and then started the elevator on its ascent.

He was going to see his brother in just a few minutes now.

The moment Gerard left the studio, the Bomb Squad moved in: two men in American Body Armor, which gave them the same look as lumbering astronauts on the moon. They had to work quickly. They had no idea how Gerard had set the timer. Grimly, they approached the studio.

Shaw stopped the basket. It was almost even with the roof. He wanted to get a good look at everything before he decided what to do next.

He pawed rain from his face, checked the clip in his weapon, and then eased his head up over the edge of the roof.

That was when Shaw realized he wasn't as helpless as he thought.

What if he was able to take care of the helicopter pilot and Roy Gerard before Jessica and the others reached the roof?

There was no more time for thinking.

He crawled up out of the basket and on to the roof, the heavy rain continuing to lash and soak him.

He lay for a second, gasping with effort, then raised his head.

The pilot was working on the tail with his wrench, completely preoccupied with his frantic work.

Crouching low, Shaw began running along the far side of the roof. He couldn't afford to have Roy Gerard see him from the inside of the helicopter. Shaw stood no chance against two armed men.

Shaw kept moving in a wide direction away from the helicopter. There was a small chimney on the eastern edge of the roof. From there, he would be able to fire on the helicopter pilot.

Just so long as Roy Gerard didn't see him . . .

Shaw slipped once as he darted for the protection of the brick chimney. Pain stung his knee where he'd landed, but he brought himself back up and continued running through the slashing rain.

He made it to the chimney.

He took a long moment to lie flat against the bricks and catch his breath. He was convulsed by the hard and treacherous work of working the basket then being forced to cross the roof.

David Gerard would be rendezvousing on the roof soon.

No time for pampering himself.

He swung out around the chimney, took aim, and fired off three rounds at the helicopter pilot.

He'd aimed for the legs and the bullets took immediate toll.

The man dropped his wrench, bent over to clutch at one of

RUNNER IN THE DARK

his limbs. All the while, he searched the roof to see where the bullets came from.

Then the man had his own gun and was squeezing off shots in the direction of the chimney.

One of the bullets took a large piece of brick off the edge of the structure. Shaw was forced to huddle back behind it.

Then, curiously, the gunfire stilled from the direction of the helicopter.

Why would the man simply quit firing?

He quickly found out when he peeked around the chimney again.

The pilot had been joined by Roy Gerard. Guns drawn, they were both making their way toward him, the pilot staggering.

Several of the police helicopters in the sky took note of the two men approaching the chimney on the roof below. Picking off one or both of them would be no trouble. But they'd been told to hold their fire, the fear being that if Roy Gerard was injured or killed, David Gerard would certainly kill Jessica on the spot.

Even though he'd injured the helicopter pilot, Shaw had no doubt that the pilot and Roy Gerard could and would kill him.

He looked back across the roof for somewhere to hide. But there was nowhere.

Another shot tore off an edge of the brick chimney.

They were getting closer by the moment.

Roy Gerard started walking wide of the chimney.

He was going to approach from one direction, Kray from the other.

They would trap him.

★ ★ ★

Shaw saw what they were doing and realized he had only one chance of escape.

He had to get back to the basket, which was suspended below the parapet about twenty yards to his right.

From the basket, he'd have at least some semblance of protection. He'd stand a chance of surviving, anyway.

Just then, Roy Gerard fired off another shot.

Shaw did the only thing he could – fired back several shots of his own so that Gerard was forced to pitch himself flat on the roof to avoid the gunfire.

Then Shaw broke and started running toward the basket.

He slipped twice before he reached it, two shots from Gerard coming close to hitting him.

When he reached the ledge of the building, he grabbed on with one hand and virtually flung himself into the rickety basket below.

His head had barely cleared the ledge before three more shots sang past above him.

Not until he was crouched down in the basket, not until he was giving himself another moment to get his breath again, did he realize that he'd been wounded.

Shoulder.

Terrible pain suddenly.

Hot spreading blood.

He looked down at his coat and saw, in fact, that the blood was spreading all over the left side of the coat. Nothing he could do about it now other than hope that the blood-loss was slow enough that he wouldn't pass out.

He had to remain conscious, and strong, for a good while longer.

More bullets smashed into the metal of the basket.

They were close now, probably within a few yards.

Not until this very moment, when the blood-loss was

starting to make him feel vulnerable, did he comprehend that he could also be trapped here in this basket.

If they kept enough gunfire concentrated on him, there'd be no way he could stand up to get a clear shot.

Jessica and David Gerard would reach the roof, and the helicopter, and take off.

And it would be too late for Shaw to do anything about it.

He had to return fire now. Had to.

He inched up toward the ledge of the building.

Three shots from above.

He ducked back down quickly.

Pain from his shoulder made him double over. Getting a lot worse suddenly...

He looked up at the police helicopters hovering above, their searchlights crossing and criss-crossing the roof, occasionally picking him out huddled here in his basket—

He had to stand up.

Had to return fire.

Had to—

He saw him before he heard him, Roy Gerard peering over the ledge of the building above the basket, getting ready to shoot. He'd snuck all the way over here, any noise he made being covered by the rain and the sound of the helicopters above.

Gerard was smiling. And pointing his gun directly down at Shaw.

Shaw did the only thing he could. He hurled himself to the other side of the cage, squeezing off two shots in the process, both of which struck Gerard in the chest.

Gerard screamed and fell forward, off the building, landing on top of the basket.

He clung with four fingers to the edge of the basket, trying to raise his gun to squeeze off another shot.

'You sonofabitch!' he said. 'You sonofabitch!'

Shaw raised his weapon, put it against Gerard's forehead on the other side of the basket, and pulled the trigger a single time.

Screaming, Gerard's grip loosened on the cage, and he pitched dozens of dark floors down . . . to his death.

Shaw was just starting to turn around when he saw the pilot leaning over the edge of the building now. The man was wildly firing off rounds but none of them caught Shaw.

Shaw whirled, ducked, and squeezed off a shot of his own.

The pilot's face exploded.

But instead of pitching forward, he fell backward, and disappeared from Shaw's sight.

Now he had to get back to the roof again.

Shoulder bleeding more than ever, the pain strong enough to cause small blackouts, Shaw heaved himself up over the ledge just as Jessica and Gerard walked out onto the roof.

Gerard saw him at once. He paused, halfway to the helicopter.

What the hell was going on here?

Clutching the woman even tighter, Gerard glanced across the roof like a frantic, caged animal.

The helicopter was empty.

A man who looked very much like Kray was lying dead, next to where Michael Shaw stood.

What the hell was going on here?

There on the rain-slashed roof, the helicopter rotors running ceaselessly and uselessly, Shaw began his slow advance on David Gerard, the shoulder of his trenchcoat growing ever bloodier, his right hand wrapped firmly around his weapon.

This whole night was coming down to Shaw and Gerard and that was the way it should be, after all the ways Gerard had terrorized Jessica.

Shaw's temptation was to somehow divert Gerard's attention momentarily, and then, when he got a clear shot, to open fire.

But how was Shaw ever going to divert his attention?

'Don't go any further!' Gerard shouted.

Shaw stopped.

Gerard raised his gun and put it directly to Jessica's temple.

'If I don't get out of here alive, neither does she,' Gerard said. Then: 'Where's my brother?'

'I wouldn't know.'

'You bastard!' Gerard screamed. 'You killed him, didn't you?'

Then he slashed his pistol down across the side of Jessica's face.

She started to scream and fall but he grabbed her, clamped his hand across her mouth again.

'You tell them I want a police helicopter to come down here and pick us up,' Gerard said. 'You tell them that right now, you understand?'

Jessica knew that she was probably not going to get out of this alive. At this point in hostage situations, the survival odds were grim.

But he'd be killing two people, she thought, and dwelt for a moment on the other life she was carrying within her.

After the bomb incident, the *fake* bomb as it had turned out, she'd felt depleted of rational thought. She knew only fear.

But now, as she watched Michael approaching them through the slanting silver rain, she experienced her first moment of hope in a long time.

Then she saw the blood all over his shoulder and wondered what had happened. Had they shot him? Probably. What else could account for all that blood?

There had to be some way she could help him, she thought.

If she could just obtain for him a moment or two where he could get a closer shot at Gerard—

And that was when she remembered something that had happened in the studio . . .

Maybe there was a way she could help Michael, after all.

Police helicopter, Michael Shaw thought.

Once they got up in the air, there was no way a madman like Gerard would let himself be taken into custody. He'd kill everybody aboard, including himself, if need be.

But what choice did Shaw have?

'I'm going over and using the two-way in your helicopter and then I'll be back,' he shouted to Gerard.

Gerard just watched him, silently.

Jessica kept thinking about her idea. If it worked, she might indeed give Michael that moment of opportunity he needed.

But if it didn't work . . .

Maybe it would be better to not even try it.

She stood watching as Michael went over to the helicopter and used the two-way.

There was no way to know for sure what he was saying, but she knew that Michael would take no chances with her life.

He came back.

'They said they'll land a police helicopter in three minutes,' he called to Gerard. 'It'll take you where you want to go. But I want you to take me instead of Jessica.'

Gerard smiled. 'You're not pretty enough, Shaw.' Then: 'They better make it in three minutes.'

Gerard tightened his grip on Jessica, and did so in such a

way that Shaw could see her writhe in pain beneath his brute strength.

'Now I want you to drop your gun.'

'What the hell are you talking about?' Shaw said.

'Just what I said. I want you to drop your gun on the roof. And right now.'

Jessica knew that her last hope was vanishing.

If Michael didn't have a gun—

She didn't have any choice.

She had to try her plan after all.

'I'm giving you thirty seconds,' Gerard bawled to Shaw.

And Michael saw that he didn't have much choice.

At this point, Gerard was going to get anything he asked for.

Anything.

Shaw was just starting to bend down to set his weapon on the roof when it happened.

Because the rain was still coming down in sheets, it was difficult to see exactly what happened—

But Jessica raised her right foot and kicked backwards and Gerard let out a scream of pain—

And he saw it then, even through the rain, just a few moments when Jessica was able to swing herself away from Gerard's grip and—

Give Shaw an opportunity to fire.

And fire he did.

Three, four, five, six, seven rounds in a few moments.

And then Gerard was dancing.

That was the only way to describe it.

Dancing.

His arms flailing.

His legs tossing about like a puppet's.

Even his head lolling at strange inhuman angles.
And all the while, Shaw kept firing.
And moving closer with every single bullet.
Until at last he stood over Gerard's bloody body there on the rain-washed roof—
Until at last Jessica, sobbing and laughing at the same time, was in his arms and kissing him.

Chapter Seven

Several hours later, Jessica was being wheeled out of an examination room in a downtown hospital.

The young doctor on duty had insisted that he put her in a wheelchair and that he take her back to the room where Shaw lay, bandaged and sedated, but happy.

'Just because the baby's fine,' the young doctor said, 'doesn't mean that you aren't tired and suffering a mild case of shock.'

'I can't wait to tell Michael about the baby.'

'Well,' the young doctor said, 'now's your chance.' He wheeled her across to the bed and left the couple together.

He nodded his goodnight, and left.

Shaw drowsily reached out and took her hand.

'You know what I'm thinking?'

'No,' she said, in a similarly sleepy voice.

'That we both need the same thing. A nice breakfast and then a long, long sleep.'

She looked at him and lifted his hand fondly to her face.

'Oh Michael,' she said. 'It's going to be all right for us, isn't it?'

'Yeah,' he said, smiling.

He put his gentle hand on her stomach.

'Yeah,' he said again. 'It's going to be just fine for all three of us.'

She kissed him, then, right there in the hospital, where not that much longer from now she would give them their first child.

ABOUT THE AUTHOR

ED GORMAN has been called "one of suspense fiction's best storytellers" by *Ellery Queen*, and "one of the most original voices in today's crime fiction" by the *San Diego Union*. Gorman's work has appeared in magazines as various as *Redbook*, *Ellery Queen*, *The Magazine of Fantasy and Science Fiction*, and *Poetry Today*. His work has won numerous prizes, including the Shamus, the Spur, and the International Fiction Writer's awards. He's been nominated for the Edgar, the Anthony, the Golden Dagger, and the Bram Stoker awards. Former *Los Angeles Times* critic Charles Champlin noted that "Ed Gorman is a powerful storyteller." Gorman's work has been taken by the Literary Guild, The Mystery Guild, Doubleday Book Club, and the Science Fiction Book Club. He lives in Cedar Rapids with his wife, novelist Carole Gorman, and their three cats. For more information on Ed and his projects, you can visit The Ed Gorman Homepage at:
www.geocities.com/Athens/Acropolis/3192/edbio.html.

COMING MARCH 2005

BLOOD MOON
A ROBERT PAYNE PSYCHOLOGICAL THRILLER
by Ed Gorman
ISBN: 0-7434-9845-3

New Hope, Iowa. The kind of small town that restores a hardened FBI agent's faith in America. But when mysteriously seductive Nora Conners gives Robert Payne $25,000 to find the maniac who brutally killed her young daughter, he uncovers this close-knit community's most sordid secrets.

Why does televangelist Cal Roberts have such shady followers? And why is abused wife Eve McNally afraid to talk about her own missing daughter? Soon Payne's investigation is arousing the suspicion of New Hope's beautiful police chief, Jane Avery. But when Nora herself turns up at an abandoned farm with her throat slashed, Payne realizes the killer is on to him, and that he and Jane are facing a more evil criminal mind than they ever imagined.